W9-BNN-012

BEYOND THE NIGHT

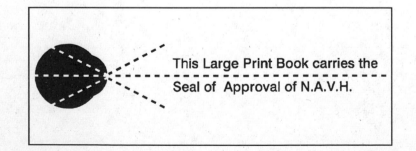

This Large Print Book carries the
Seal of Approval of N.A.V.H.

BEYOND THE NIGHT

MARLO SCHALESKY

THORNDIKE PRESS

A part of Gale, Cengage Learning

GALE
CENGAGE Learning

Detroit • New York • San Francisco • New Haven, Conn • Waterville, Maine • London

GALE
CENGAGE Learning™

LIBRARY OF CONGRESS CATALOGING-IN-PUBLICATION DATA

Schalesky, Marlo M., 1967–
  Beyond the night / by Marlo Schalesky.
    p. cm. — (Thorndike Press large print Christian fiction)
  ISBN-13: 978-1-4104-2265-1 (alk. paper)
  ISBN-10: 1-4104-2265-8 (alk. paper)
    1. Terminally ill—Fiction. 2. Coma—Patients—Fiction. 3. Spouses—Fiction. 4. Blindness—Fiction 5. Large type books. I. Title.
  PS3569.C4728B49 2010
  813'.54—dc22   2009045153

Published in 2010 by arrangement with Multnomah Books, an imprint of Crown Publishing Group, a division of Random House, Inc.

Printed in the United States of America
1 2 3 4 5 6 7 14 13 12 11 10

To Bryan:
I loved you then
I love you now
And I'll love you beyond the night

I am the light of the world.
The one following me will never walk in
the darkness, but will have
the light of life.

JOHN 8:12

PROLOGUE

They tell me it never happened. They say it couldn't have. Some call it a dream. Others say I'm a romantic. But I know what they're thinking: I'm crazy. Touched by grief. Making up stories to ease my pain.

But I have no grief. Not anymore. And my pain is only a single note in the symphony of my peace, for I know what's true. I was there that day. I watched her hand reach toward him. I heard his voice in the darkness. I saw their love. Paul and Maddie. So call me crazy if you must. But I know the power of love. I've glimpsed its mystery. I've witnessed its light.

If you doubt, come with me. Step through the shadows of time to when it began. A cold night. Dark. And beyond the night . . . well, come and see.

Paul gripped the steering wheel tighter as the Ford Pinto curved along the mountain road. Rain fell in heavy sheets, slamming against hood and pavement. The swish of the wipers played a dissonant beat to the drum of water on metal.

This is mad. We should turn back. Paul glanced at his wife, sleeping in the seat beside him. Maddie's breathing remained steady, her eyes closed. A deep snore drifted from her open mouth.

Paul smiled. Maddie hated it when he told her she snored. "It's not snoring," she'd say, "just strong breathing." Strong enough to be heard over the rain. Of course, she'd never believe him. One day, he'd record it, if he dared. His smile melted into a low chuckle. She'd never forgive him for that. At least not until he brought her a Hershey's bar — with almonds. The chocolate was no good, she insisted, without the almonds.

The rain quickened until the sound became a thunder on the rooftop. Paul leaned forward and squinted into the darkness. The car's headlights formed circles of yellow, reflecting off the rain in countless shards of light. He rubbed his eyes. He couldn't see the lane divider or the white line along the shoulder. Or the road that lay beyond the million falling diamonds blinking in the brightness.

The snoring stopped.

"Are we there?" Her sleepy question rose above the roar of rain.

"Not yet." Paul's knuckles whitened on the wheel. "We're going to be late."

"Told you so." The humor in her voice relaxed his grip.

He peeked over at her. A few curls of russet hair gleamed in the faint light. A smile touched her lips, curving into that funny half grin that he loved so much.

He reached over and brushed a strand of hair from her cheek. "Go back to sleep, smarty-pants. I'll get us there . . . eventually."

"It's too loud in here to sleep." Maddie raised her voice to a mock shout. "This rain is like listening to a bad rock band."

Paul slapped a tape into the player on the dash. "You just need the right music, that's all."

Maddie groaned. "Not that old tape again."

"What else?"

The strum of a guitar clamored against the rumble of rain. A second later, voices picked up the story of Puff the Magic Dragon just as Jackie Paper came no more. Paul sang along, adding another off-key note to the cacophony of sound.

Maddie reached for the volume control. "You know that song's about marijuana, don't you?"

"Urban legend. Can't be proved." Paul tapped his fingers on the wheel in time with the song's beat. "Besides, our daughter agrees with me."

"Mandy's only five."

"Exactly. No one knows more than a five-year-old."

Maddie chuckled as Paul sang even louder. He belted out a full stanza before she sat up straight and pressed her hand against the side window. "Turn it down, Paul."

"Aw, just because you don't like Puff."

"No, really." She leaned over and squeezed his arm. "Listen to that rain. It's coming down so hard the windows are shaking. Maybe we should pull over."

Paul ground his palms against the vinyl of the steering wheel. "The road straightens out just ahead. Besides, ten minutes and we'll be there."

"Promise?"

He downshifted as the Pinto approached a turn. "Nope. Might be fifteen."

The car lurched around the bend. The tires hit a pond in the road, sending a spray of water across the hood and windshield.

The wipers whooshed it away, revealing, for the briefest moment, a deer standing in the circle of the headlights.

The creature froze. Still. Wide-eyed.

Paul shouted. Brakes squealed. The Pinto swerved right. He jerked the wheel left.

Tires skidded across gravel as the car spun off the road into the trees.

Branches slapped the sides of the Pinto, scraped across the windows in a blur of water, leaves, and glass. He threw his arm across Maddie. The trunk of a pine flashed in front of him.

The car hit.

The steering wheel slammed into his chest. The dash rushed toward him, carrying with it a small square of color.

With sickening clarity, the colors took shape, and he recognized the Polaroid photo he'd taped there days before. A little girl in yellow pigtails. A crooked half-smile. And words scrawled beneath in childish script. Words he did not need to read to remember.

Drive Carefully Daddy.

1

Darkness rose from somewhere within her. Blackness, like a great, choking wave. Immersing her, drowning her, until she couldn't breathe under the weight of it. It flooded her mind, spilled down her back, and submerged her limbs in icy heaviness. She fought against it . . . and failed. Deeper. Darker. Until her world was nothing but a black river, crashing in currents of pain.

Help me . . . The words squeezed from her, unspoken yet real. They became a silent cry, like mist above the water, shimmering, then gone. Did anyone hear? Did anyone know? Was there someone listening out there beyond the darkness? *Help me. Don't leave me alone. Please* . . .

Time wavered. Stillness breathed. In. Out.

Then a voice dipped into the blackness. A single word, spoken from a world beyond her own. It came like a slender ribbon of light, rippling over the waves. "Maddie . . ."

15

I'm here.

"Maddie."

One word. And in it, hope.

I am not alone.

The water receded. A little.

"Wake up. I've come to take you home."

The blackness shivered, broke, then settled into a familiar gray. Her breath came again, steady and comforting.

"Can you hear me, Maddie?" The voice caressed her, embraced her in its gentle warmth.

I hear you. The answer formed in her mind but refused to be spoken. *Stay with me.*

"Come to me. Remember."

I can't.

Silence. Dreaded, awful silence.

Please . . . Don't leave me . . . You promised . . .

The dreariness of the hospital room pressed into Paul's consciousness more heavily than the Monterey fog pressed outside the window. Damp. Gray. Cold and unwelcoming. A moment, a lifetime, before he had laughed and loved, hoped and dreamed. But all that had tunneled into this one image — a flickering fluorescent light, the reek of antiseptic, and the woman he loved in the bed before him. His vision blurred.

"Maddie . . ."

The word fell and was lost in the buzz of the light, in the steady beep of the EKG machine. For so long he had sat here, with doctors and nurses going in and out, taking her blood pressure, scribbling on charts. He'd almost lost track of them all, as the day faded to twilight. As shifts changed. As visiting hours dwindled. But no one would ask him to leave. Not tonight. Because Maddie was doing much worse than anyone let on.

It was going to be a long night. And there was no way he was going to leave her.

So he sat here, watching the liquid drip incessantly through clear tubes, watching Maddie's chest rising, falling. And the fog blotting out all hint of the California sky. So long, yet nothing changed.

Outside the room a gurney squeaked, an intercom rumbled, footsteps hurried past and faded. Outside, the world went on. But here, in this tiny room, life teetered on the edge of darkness.

How had it come to this? To a hospital bed, a frayed chair, and an ocean of silence between them? All the years. All his love. All the memories of a lifetime past. All captured in this one woman, pale, shriveled, so different from the vital, lively girl who

17

shared his heart.

She lay there with her eyes closed, her breath ragged, her lashes dark against sunken cheeks. A single lock of hair, damp and dull, curled over her forehead. Tubes lined her cheeks, her arms, trailed over her chest. Rising. Falling. Breath rasping from lips once red, now the color of ash.

Why did it have to be like this?

"Maddie."

Did he speak aloud? No one heard. Did she? Could she?

Paul leaned forward. He reached toward her. If he could just take her hand, pull her back from the dark place where she'd gone. But he couldn't touch her. Not yet. She was too fragile, her life hanging by too thin a cord. "Wake up. I've come to take you home."

But Maddie didn't stir.

"Can you hear me, Maddie?"

Was that a sigh? Did her finger twitch? A shiver ran through him.

"Come to me." *It's time. Come out of the darkness. Remember.* He waited. A second. An eternity. Almost. Almost he had reached her.

A pen clicked. Shoes squeaked.

Paul straightened.

A nurse in hospital blue hurried to the far

18

side of the bed. "Blood pressure check."

Paul stood and moved away from the chair. "Not again."

The nurse pursed her lips and didn't answer. She just checked the levels of clear liquid dripping in the tubes, tapped the band around Maddie's arm, then glared in his direction.

Paul sighed.

The nurse stabbed her pen at him. Her forehead bunched.

Paul jumped to the side. "Oh. Oops." He had been standing in front of the EKG machine.

"Blood pressure's good." With brisk efficiency, the nurse reversed her pen and wrote something on her clipboard. Then she turned and paused. For a brief instant, her hand brushed Maddie's. Her voice softened, as if she knew, understood, how hard this night would be. "Hang in there. Won't be long now."

The words twisted through Paul's mind.

She clicked her pen again, shook her head, and rushed from the room.

Paul stared at the place where the nurse's fingers had touched Maddie's hand, so white against sheets that were whiter still. And her skin so thin that it seemed translucent. Delicate, frail. Yet, the freckle just below her left thumb was still there, reminding him that some things don't change. Some things are forever.

Warmth flowed through Paul. Perhaps, just once, he could kiss that freckle again. He'd done that, for the first time, years ago. Her hands were strong then, young and tan. But the freckle was still the same. He smiled. The kiss had been a joke, really. A prank done in passing. Yet he remembered it still. A simple gesture that changed everything. At least it had for him.

"Do you remember?" He spoke, knowing she couldn't hear him, knowing she was still too far away to understand.

"It rained that morning, before the sun came out."

Only the steady beep of the EKG answered him.

His voice lowered. "Come, Maddie, remember with me. Remember the day I fell in love."

Palo Alto, 1973
Paul smashed his racquet against the small blue ball. The ball thwacked into the front wall and zoomed toward the back corner.

Maddie raced left, her racquet extended. She slowed, pulled back, and swung.

Paul squatted, ready.

20

Air swooshed through the strings as Maddie's racquet missed the ball by a good three inches.

Paul relaxed.

Maddie's shoulder slammed against the wall. The ball dribbled into the corner.

"You all right?" He wiped his brow with his wristband. "That last chem exam gotten to you or something?"

"What do you know about exams?"

He grinned. "Not much anymore, thankfully. It's been a couple years."

Maddie grimaced. "Well, maybe if I had some fancy research job in a big pharmaceutical company I could joke about exams too."

Paul bounced the ball with his left hand. "I'm telling you, money's in research these days."

She rolled her eyes. "Blah blah. I think I'll stick to being a doctor . . . someday."

Paul chuckled. "I'll mix 'em, you fix 'em."

It was an old joke. And not a very good one. "Just serve, would you?"

"You sure you're ready?" He bounced the ball again.

"No."

"Here goes." He slammed his racquet into the ball. It hit the front wall and whizzed toward her. She swung. And missed. Again.

"Your game." Maddie twirled her racquet, then let it dangle from her wrist. "What's that? Four games now?" She scowled.

Five. Paul shrugged. "Who's counting?"

She put her hands on her hips. "You are. And don't pretend you're not."

Paul grinned, then sauntered over and picked up the racquetball. He popped it onto his racquet, making it dance there with small, precise bounces. "You wanna go again?" He tossed her the ball.

She let it drop. "I already owe you a pizza, a movie, popcorn, and a Coke. At this rate, I'm going to go broke."

"Normally, I'd say it's just bad luck. But . . ."

Maddie glared at him. "Go ahead, say it."

"Well, you gotta admit your game's off today." His voice turned to a whisper. "Really off. Can't blame that on a summer class."

"Thanks."

"So, what's wrong?"

"I don't know. It's like the ball just vanishes before I hit it."

Paul reached over and tousled her hair. He loved doing that. Her loose, short curls stood straight up when he did it just right. "Didn't I tell you? That's a new trick of mine."

Maddie chuckled and punched him in the shoulder. "Come on, let's quit while I'm behind."

"Way behind."

"Stop rubbing it in."

Paul slung his arm around her shoulder and turned her toward the glass wall behind them. A blonde in red hot pants crossed on the other side of the glass. The blonde was so different from Maddie. Where the girl was tall and slender, Maddie was, well, medium. Five and a half feet tall, not slim, not stocky. Somewhere in between. Athletic and built for racquetball. Usually, anyway. Just not today.

He paused. "She's new."

"You mean you haven't asked her out yet? Looks like I'm not the only one whose game is off today."

Paul scooped the racquetball off the floor with his racquet. "The day is still young, my friend."

Maddie shook her head. "What happened with the girl behind the soda counter?"

Paul opened the court's door for Maddie and stood back as she slipped out in front of him. "I think she found me too suave and debonair."

"Oh, yes, you're very swave." She purposefully mispronounced the word.

"All she did was giggle and talk about the Bee Gees. It was like she was fourteen." He pulled out a towel from his gym bag and wiped the back of his neck.

"She's nineteen. And everyone knows she's a huge Bee Gees fan."

"Well, you could have saved me a bundle on dinner if you'd told me before. I count on you for these things, you know."

Maddie slipped her racquet into its case and dug around in her bag. "Poor baby. I thought you said all girls eat is salad anyway. How expensive could that be?"

"Speaking of food, I'll take my pizza first, then the movie. The new 007 is out."

Maddie groaned. "Not another Bond flick."

"When you win, you can choose. Tonight it's . . . Bond, James Bond." Paul faked an English accent.

"Bond is supposed to be Scottish."

"Not any . . . Moore."

Maddie cringed at his joke.

"You aren't still crying about their replacing Sean Connery, are you?"

"It's not a replacement, it's a downgrade."

"We'll see."

"Your date is leaving."

"What?"

"The blonde."

Paul glanced over to the blonde. She was sipping pink liquid through a straw and moving toward the back door. He stretched out his arms and cracked his knuckles. "Okay, watch the master work."

Maddie sighed and rolled her eyes.

Paul strolled over to the blonde. She was pretty, he supposed. But a little thin. And her eyes didn't sparkle. She looked, well, bored. And boring. He could turn around now and forget it. He wanted to, but Maddie was watching. So he straightened his shoulders and sauntered up to the girl. Three minutes later, he walked back to Maddie. "Friday at seven. Easy as that."

"Hope she's a salad eater."

"She is. I asked."

Maddie laughed. "I don't know how you do it. Next time, get a date for me, will you? I haven't been out in six months."

Paul ran his fingers through his hair. "You find the guy."

"Okay, how about him?" Maddie shot a glance at a man heading toward the weight room.

"Nah, too short."

"That one?" She pointed to a guy at the check-in counter.

"Too old."

"Over there?"

"Too muscular."

"What?"

"Clearly he's obsessed with his body. You don't want that, do you?"

"Well, how about — ?"

"No. No. No." Paul jabbed his finger toward the remaining men in the room. "No one here's good enough for you." He cleared his throat, fighting to hide the strange dryness in his voice. "Besides, with that wicked backhand of yours, you'd scare off all these namby-pambies anyway."

Maddie raised her eyebrows. "Yeah, my backhand sure was scary today, wasn't it?"

"Admit it, you just wanted to see old Moore-baby."

"You be good, or next time I'm going to find the most syrupy-sweet romance playing, and I'm going to win."

"You hate those movies."

"Yep. But not as much as you do." Maddie grinned and batted her eyes at him.

Paul threw his hand towel at her. She reached for it midair but missed.

"I give up. My place, one hour. You're driving." She grabbed her bag and started toward the door.

"I'll order ahead. Pepperoni."

"Good." She paused at the door and glanced back at him. "I'm starved."

Paul slung his bag over his shoulder. "I thought girls only ate salad."

Maddie pulled open the door and flung a final comment over her shoulder. "How dare you call me a girl." She marched outside.

Paul laughed as she disappeared from sight. He stooped over and picked up the hand towel. He frowned at it, then stuffed it into his bag. Something glinted at him from the floor. Maddie's keys. He grabbed them and trotted toward the door.

Maddie stood outside her car with one hand digging through her bag. The summer sunlight glinted off her reddish-brown hair, making it look on fire. Or maybe it was just her mood. Even from a distance of a hundred feet, Paul could see her muttering to herself. He snuck up behind her and dangled the keys in front of her nose. "Missing something?"

She snatched them from his hand. "I seem to be missing everything today. First the ball, then the towel, and now this. Everything just disappears right before my eyes."

Paul spread out his arms. "Everything but me."

"What luck, huh?"

He smiled at the dry humor in her voice. She shook her head and attempted to insert the key into the keyhole. It slipped to the side instead.

He plucked the keys from her hand and slid the right one into the hole. "Good thing I'm driving tonight." He opened the door, took her hand, and helped her in. "Your ride, m'lady."

"Thank you, sir."

"Would hate for you to miss the seat." He grinned, lifted her hand to his lips, then kissed it. Right on that little freckle.

For a moment, neither moved. The shock of something strange and new flowed through him. Their eyes met. And he noticed in hers deep golden flecks against the brown, flecks that he had never seen before. He dropped her hand.

And there it was. An ordinary moment in what would be a lifetime of ordinary moments. A moment that nonetheless touched the edge of eternity.

Maddie quirked her lips into a smile and looked away. "Suave. Very suave. And I'm not even blond."

2

I remember . . .

The words slipped through Maddie's mind and echoed there with gentle insistence. She followed the sound of them, up through the dark mist, up and away from the black water.

Yes, I remember.

Pictures formed in the dark, like an old-fashioned movie playing against the shifting grayness. The white walls of a racquetball court, a spinning racquet, a blue ball, and Paul. Yes, Paul, young, with eyes sparkling in victory. She'd always loved his blue-green eyes.

The image faded. *Paul . . . Paul come back.*

A touch. A brush of skin against hers. Just for a moment, and then gone. Did someone touch her hand? Was anyone there?

Maddie tried to reach out, tried to move her arm, her hand, even her fingers. But the blackness pressed down again. And with it, sharp, gasping pain. It radiated through her — up her chest, her shoulders, twisting through her mind. Pain, and worse, fear. She tasted its bitterness. The helplessness. The terror.

No . . .

Did anyone hear her cry?

She listened.

Silence answered.

Where am I? Why can't I move? What is this pain?

From the edge of consciousness a sound came. Beep. Beep. Beep. Steady, incessant. And inhuman.

The sound quickened.

God, help me.

The waters rose.

No! The denial screamed through her. *I remember . . . You can't take that from me. I still remember . . .*

Don't I?

Fingers of ice gripped Maddie's chest. What was memory? What was dream?

"Maddie, come back."

The voice. Was it real? It came again. "Remember, Maddie."

Warmth.

"I would have kissed you that night, just to be sure it was real."

Paul?

30

"I planned to. In the darkness of the theater. All I needed to do was simply lean over, touch your chin, bring your lips toward mine. I wasn't sure then, not of your feelings, not of mine. I would have found out."

Where are you?

"I never got the chance."

No.

"You must remember."

And still the voice called to her, beckoning her from the waters, drawing her toward that day. Why? Why then? Why now? And then she knew. It was not a dream. She had been there. She had faced fear before. Faced it, and lived. She could do so again. She must. This one last time.

Her breathing slowed.

She had to remember. She had to go back.

No, Lord, I'm afraid.

"Remember . . . You are not alone . . ."

Water, bright, warm, soft, flowed over Maddie's body and drove away the clinging blackness. It spurted like a healing balm from the silver showerhead and dribbled down her chin and chest. She pressed her hand against the cracked white tile and breathed deeply the scent of Ivory soap and strawberry shampoo. She turned, allowing the water to run through her hair until only the smell of Ivory remained. She rubbed the rich lather covering her arms. Smooth, firm skin met her touch as the soap washed away.

Her roommate's voice called from the hallway. "Hey, Mad, are you still in there? Save some hot water for me."

Maddie pulled back the shower curtain and peeked out. "Be out in a minute."

Steam covered the mirror and formed heavy drops on the ceiling. One drop fell and spattered on the green linoleum. Maddie stepped from the shower and grabbed a pink towel. Pink was Kelli's choice. Maddie had always hated pink, but now, somehow she was glad to see it. She was glad to see everything, from the hairline crack in the lower right corner of the mirror, to the place on the floor where the linoleum was peeling up, to the face of Mac Davis, grinning from the poster taped over the toilet.

She wrapped the towel around herself and opened the door. Steam billowed into the hallway. "It's all yours." Her shout reverberated through the small apartment.

Maddie scooted to her room, opened her dresser drawer, and pulled out the top pair of jeans. Bell bottoms. She slipped into them and threw on her favorite T-shirt. Her finger traced the picture of faded daisies on the shirt's front as her gaze swept the room. Here, there were none of the brash colors that Kelli insisted on through the rest of their apartment. There were no dangling glass beads, no orange beanbags, no red shag carpet with fat, furry pillows scattered about. There was just a plain brown rug on a pea green carpet, her old checkered bedspread, and a couple photos hanging on the walls. One was a black and white of Yosemite's Vernal Falls. She'd always wanted to see it for real. The other was a funny picture of an elephant sniffing a chimp that she'd gotten at the circus when she was twelve. And around her mirror were stuck a dozen or so snapshots of friends. Kelli, Paul, some girlfriends from school. Definitely no Mac Davis.

Maddie picked up a brush and ran it through her hair. Fat curls formed around her face. She stared at the round cheeks, the plain brown eyes, the short brownish hair that would never look like Cher's sleek, black tresses. She combed her fingers through, pulling the strands straight. They bounced back the moment she let go.

A sigh escaped her. Long, straight hair was sophisticated, sensuous.

She, on the other hand, was neither of

those things and never would be. Even her hair knew it. So why bother? She made a face at the image in the mirror, and then laughed.

Kelli poked her head through the doorway. "What's so funny?"

"I am."

Kelli flounced into the room and threw herself on the bed. "So, you going out tonight?"

Maddie shook her head. "Not out — just a movie and pizza."

Kelli's eyebrows flew to her hairline. "Don't tell me, another NAD with Paul?"

"When are you going to stop calling it that?"

"When you admit the truth."

Maddie tied a yellow scarf around her neck, then frowned at it in the mirror. "It is Not A Date." She yanked off the scarf and tossed it back on the dresser.

"Exactly." Kelli rolled over on to her stomach, with her feet in the air and her legs crossed at the ankles. She grabbed a plain brown pillow and stuffed it under her chin. "Though how it's different from a date, I'll never know."

Maddie turned and stared at her friend. An image of Paul flashed through her mind. Six foot three. Slender. A bit lanky even, but strong. Sandy hair that curled just slightly over his ears. And in her vision, he smelled like soap. Just soap. She sighed. "You know how it's different. I've explained it a hundred times."

Kelli swept a lock of perfectly straight, shining brown hair behind her shoulder. "Please, not the perfume theory."

"Not perfume. Cologne. C-O-L-O-G-N-E. On a real date, the man wears cologne. Everyone knows that. No cologne. No date." She smacked her hands together in a that's-that fashion.

Kelli sat up and tossed the pillow into the air as she spoke. "NAD. Not A Date. I dig it."

"Besides, Paul is just a friend."

"I can tell."

Maddie frowned. "What does that mean?"

Kelli squashed the pillow between her palms and threw it back to its spot. "Well, no one would wear that shirt on a date."

Maddie glanced down and fingered the daisies again. "What's wrong with this shirt?"

"So ho-hum." Kelli gave a mock shudder. "I've got a really cute orange and brown one I just bought. Flare sleeves. Beads to match. And dangling earrings." She wiggled her fingers near her ears. "Very foxy." She cleared her throat. "But not too foxy, of course."

Maddie threw her a scowl. "Orange, with this hair? I'll look like a fox all right. The kind people shoot and put their skins on the wall."

"Eww." Kelli wrinkled her nose. "How about the earrings then?"

"You know what I think of dangling earrings."

"Don't say I didn't try." Kelli shook her head. "How about that dark green blouse you bought last month?"

"It's not a date."

"Of course not. But still, you don't want to be seen like that."

"Oh, all right." Maddie took out the green blouse from her dresser drawer and shook out most of the wrinkles. She pulled off her old shirt, folded it, and placed it back in the drawer. For a moment, she stared at it. Was it really that bad? Sure, it was a little frayed at the collar and a bit faded. But wasn't faded *in*? She didn't know. Who could keep track of these things? She sighed, shut the dresser drawer, and slipped the green shirt over her head.

"That's better. Now, how about I fix your hair?"

"Nooo . . ."

Kelli put up her hands in surrender. "Okay, okay. I guess I won't even suggest perfume."

"Don't you dare."

The ring of the doorbell cut off anything more Kelli would have said. She jumped off the bed and rushed toward the door. "I'll get it. You finish up." She paused at the doorway, glanced back at Maddie, and grimaced. "I'll tell Paul you'll be out in about three seconds."

Maddie picked up a pillow and tossed it toward the door. It hit just as Kelli slipped out.

The sound of Kelli's laugh floated back from the hallway. "There's always the earrings."

"Never!"

The doorbell rang again.

Maddie smoothed her hand over her shirt and glanced at the bottle of perfume sitting on her nightstand. Maybe. Just a dab. For fun. She crept over and squirted a tiny bit on her wrist and neck. After all, no one would notice.

She hurried out to the living room just in time to see Kelli in front of the open door. Paul stood outside, dressed in jeans and a tight disco shirt. He stepped through the doorway.

Kelli lifted her hand. "Wait. Gotta check one thing." She rose to her tiptoes and sniffed his collar. She clucked her tongue. "You're right, Mad. Nothing. You two are hopeless." She threw up her hands and strode back to the kitchen. The sound of her muttering continued for several seconds, followed by the bang of a door.

Paul glanced at Maddie. "What was that all about?"

"Don't ask."

He reached out and ruffled her hair. "Hey, you smell nice."

Her eyes widened. "Uh, thanks."

"Did I say something wrong?"

Maddie rubbed her thumb over the opposite wrist. "No. Nothing. Kelli's just being . . . well, Kelli; that's all."

Paul stuck his chin in the air. "No leftover pizza for her then. Not until she learns to be cool." He motioned toward the door. "Shall we?"

An hour later, with their bellies full of pepperoni and cheese, Maddie and Paul entered the theater. The smell of popcorn and spilled soda swirled around them. Maddie blinked in the dimness. "The lights are low today."

Paul shrugged. "Balcony or down front?"

"You choose."

Paul turned. "Balcony."

Maddie followed. Her toes hit the edge of the first step. She tipped forward.

Paul grabbed her elbow. "Hey, watch out. You're worse than a little old lady today."

"Sorry."

Paul guided her to their seats in the front row of the balcony. He pulled a box of Jujubes from his pocket. "Your favorite."

"Where did you get those?"

"Brought them from home. Shh. Don't tell." He put a finger to his lips and smiled.

The theater went dark. Maddie focused on the screen. The picture blurred. She rubbed her eyes. It didn't help. "Can't they focus the picture?"

Paul's chair squeaked. "It is focused. Sit back, relax." He touched her arm. "The show's about to start."

"I must have something in my eye."

"Here." Paul handed her a handkerchief. His hand brushed hers.

"Quiet down." The hiss came from somewhere behind them.

Maddie squinted as the typical James Bond opening appeared on the screen. Rifling swirled down the barrel of a gun, revealing the invincible Bond. The barrel followed him as he strode in long, confident steps. Suddenly, he turned and shot toward the camera. Music blared. Color like blood flowed down the screen.

But something was wrong. A small black circle marred the middle of the screen. Maddie looked left. The circle followed. She looked right. The circle moved again. Her mouth went dry. Her hands trembled. She glanced down at them, at the black hole that had formed between them.

Her world narrowed. On the screen, shadowed, silhouetted women began their seductive dance. The music crashed. *Live and let die . . . boom . . . boom.* But Maddie scarcely heard. Instead, all her attention focused on that black, empty spot in the center of her vision.

She reached out and gripped Paul's arm. Her fingers dug into his skin. She glanced up. "I can't see the middle of the screen. It's gone."

"Come on, Maddie, this isn't a racquetball game. Stop joking around."

"I'm not." A chill swept through her body. Terror, tinged in black. *I'm not. I'm not . . .*

3

The beep of the EKG machine quickened and became erratic. Paul rose, reached out.

Maddie's head thrashed on the pillow. Her eyes remained closed.

"Shh, Maddie. It's okay." He yearned to gather her in his arms, hold her close, whisper in her ear until her eyes opened and she knew he was with her. But the IV, the tubes, the bed rails, and the ragged edge of her breathing kept them apart. All he had were his words, the memories, and a love so strong she must hear it, even now. "Nothing can hurt you anymore, Maddie. All the fear is over. Even the darkness can't go on forever. Fight, Maddie. Don't give up. Please . . ."

Her head stilled. Her lashes fluttered.

Light blasted from overhead. Hospital light — cold and sterile. Not at all like the warm, welcoming light of home.

Her heartbeat sped on, fast, uncertain.

And the moment was lost.

Footsteps came then, quick and efficient. Irreverent. And the same squeak of the nurse's white shoes.

He turned.

The curtain flew aside. Its chain rattled and hissed as the blue-garbed nurse again strode to Maddie's side.

Paul leaned forward. "She just started thrashing."

The nurse glanced over the EKG readout and frowned. "It's okay. This is not going to happen. Not on my watch."

Paul waited, not moving, silent, listening only to the stutter of Maddie's breath, and the steady clucking of the nurse's tongue.

The woman's hand lowered to Maddie's wrist. Two fingers pressed into the delicate skin. Seconds dragged to a minute. And all the while, the harsh, awful beeping went on, too fast, too ragged, as the lighted line bounced in sharp jags.

The nurse slid a needle into line with the IV. "This will help. It's going to be okay."

You already said that. But it's not okay, is it? Not even close. Paul swallowed the words and stayed silent. There was no use speaking them. No use at all.

The nurse pressed the plunger, and clear liquid dripped into the tubing, meandering toward the vein in Maddie's arm. "There you go, honey." Her voice dropped to a whisper. "Hang on, now."

Paul shivered.

The nurse gave Maddie's hand a squeeze. Then she sniffed and turned toward the door. "That's all I can do." In two quick steps, she had reached the curtain but didn't pull it back into place. Instead, she paused and looked back. Her gaze rested on Maddie's face. "Life isn't fair, is it, honey?" She sighed. "Don't I know it."

The beep of the EKG slowed.

And for the briefest moment, Paul thought the nurse was about to cry. But she didn't. She shook her head and pushed the curtain all the way to the wall.

Her footsteps squeaked toward the door. He followed the sound of them until they mixed with the rumble of voices outside. A muffled question from the nurses' station. A quick reply. The creak of a cart. A loud cough. Then the sounds faded, and the silence came again, broken only by the slow and steady beep of the EKG.

Paul leaned forward and looked into Maddie's face. His gaze traced the tiny lines at the corners of her eyes, her pale cheeks, her mouth. He could almost see those lips, pink and full again, opened slightly — so slightly

— waiting . . . And her hair whipping around, dancing in the breeze. A tendril caught at the corner of her mouth. He reached out and brushed it back, as his eyes looked deeply into hers. And for a moment, for just a breath, he believed she saw him. But that was later, much later. The darkness came first. And the fear. And the longing. Just like now.

Maddie groaned in her sleep. Her lashes fluttered but didn't open. She was slipping away again. Drifting into a blackness where he couldn't reach her. A blackness tinged by her fear. "Don't be afraid."

Did she hear him? Did she believe? After all, he had been right before.

He remembered that day well. He had paced in front of her apartment door as twilight spit long shadows across the concrete walkway of the second floor. He thumped on the door again, beating it until his fist smarted.

She didn't answer.

Her appointment with the doctor was that morning. After over two months of excuses, denials, and avoidance, she'd finally agreed to consult a doctor. But that didn't mean she had to like it. She was supposed to call afterward. She hadn't. And that couldn't be good.

He flattened his hand and slapped the door again. "Maddie, are you in there?"

A thud came from the other side of the door.

"Maddie? It's me."

Silence.

He paced again, paused, then beat the wood once more.

Light spilled from under the door.

He stepped back.

The door opened. Kelli stood there with a pink towel piled up on her head like a fluff of cotton candy. She plucked the lollipop from her mouth and pointed it at Paul. "Be cool, man. You dig?"

Paul strode through the doorway and glanced over the living room. "Yeah, I dig. I dig that I called Maddie five times today, and no one answered. That's what I dig."

"That's heavy, man."

Paul spied Maddie's purse on the chair. "Where is she? What happened at the doctor's?"

Kelli dropped her hip persona. "Ooh." She exhaled the word. "I forgot all about that. She wasn't home when I got back. And I didn't think . . ."

He grabbed Maddie's purse and stuck his hand inside. He withdrew his fingers and dangled a set of keys in front of Kelli. "She couldn't have gone far." He started toward the door.

"Her roller skates are missing."

He paused. "Mem Chu." The church on the Stanford University campus was her favorite place to go whenever she got bad news. When she failed that exam in chem class last year, that's where he'd found her. And when she got the news of her grandmother's cancer, he'd discovered her in the front pew. And when she thought she'd have to leave Stanford at the end of her junior year, she'd gone there too and sat with hands clasped, eyes wide, staring at the stained glass window of Jesus ascending in the clouds. "That's where she'll be."

Ten minutes later, he found her, huddled on the side of the church, her head buried in her arms, her skates sitting on the pew beside her. He slid into the seat and waited. September sunlight streamed through the stained glass at the front of the church. Jesus holding a lamb, the garden of Gethsemane, a woman at Jesus's feet. Paul tipped his head back and stared into the domed roof above. *Well, God, what now?*

"I knew you would come." Maddie didn't look up.

He scooted closer. "How did you know it was me?"

46

"I just did."

"Bad news from the doctor?"

Finally, Maddie raised her head. "No."

Paul frowned. "But then . . . why?" He motioned toward the front of the church.

Footsteps sounded on the stone floor behind them.

"All he could say was that I have a hole in the middle of my vision. I knew that much."

"And?"

"And he wants me to see a specialist."

He put his arm around her shoulders. "Maybe it'll be something simple. An infection or something. A few eye drops and bang, you'll be seeing like an eagle."

"I think my eagle days are over."

He squeezed her shoulder and grinned. "Don't worry, I won't make you go see Bond again. I promise."

Maddie sniffed. "I like Bond."

"Sure you do. And lace and ribbon and dangling earrings too."

She smiled and leaned against his shoulder. "Thanks for coming."

"When I saw you here, I thought you were going to say the doctor told you something awful."

Maddie sat up and turned toward him. The smile slipped from her face. "He didn't say anything." She paused. "But he didn't need to. I know what's happening to me."

A chill drizzled down Paul's back. "How do you know?"

She turned her face away.

He reached over, touched her chin, and turned it back toward him. "Maddie?"

She blinked. "It's happened before. Just not to me."

He swallowed the sudden lump in his throat. "What do you mean?"

Her mouth opened. A hand touched Paul's shoulder, and he looked back.

A man with a fat black mustache stood behind him. "I'm sorry, folks, we got a wedding coming in now. You gotta skedaddle."

Maddie grabbed her skates and rushed toward the middle aisle. Paul followed. She was halfway to the door before he caught up with her. He grabbed her arm. "Wait up, Maddie. What's happening? And who did it happen to before?"

She pulled from his grip. "You don't want to know."

"Yes I do."

She stopped and glanced back. "My brother went blind. It started just like this. Difficulty seeing, a hole in his vision, and before long, the darkness. Nothing but darkness." Her voice skidded to a halt.

Blind? The word sliced through him and

left him breathless. Blind. *No. Not Maddie.* That was . . . it was . . . unthinkable. *How? What? When? . . . Why?* A thousand questions swirled through his mind and settled as a hard knot in his gut. Suddenly, he was sick.

Maddie watched him for a moment, then shook her head. "I told you so."

"I didn't know you had a brother." Stupid thing to say. Silly. But it came out anyway.

"I don't." She turned and raced down the aisle.

She was gone. Fled. Vanished without a backward glance or a touch or any explanation for how she knew what she knew. Gone. With her words ringing between them still.

Blind.

Paul slid into a pew and put his head in his hands. How tight his throat had become. How hot his hands were.

Blind.

What could a person say to news like that? And how did she know it was true? Was it? Or was it just her fear talking? He lifted his head. Sunlight glinted through the stained glass above him. Jesus. Kind. Confident. At peace. Ascending toward the heavens.

Blind.

49

No. Maddie hadn't spoken out of fear. He'd known her for three years, and never in that time had she shown fear. Concern, yes. Confusion, sometimes. But never fear. Not like this. He closed his eyes.

Maddie is going blind. He turned the words over in his mind. Ugly words. Bitter and cruel. What would it mean for her? For him? For them? No more racquetball. No more movies. No more anything that they enjoyed together. Could he love a blind girl? Love her, not just today, but tomorrow, and the next day, and the next.

God, God, what are You doing to me? To her? How could this happen? And why now, when I thought . . . I thought . . .

He scrubbed his palms against his forehead, as if to erase the images forming in his mind. A woman who couldn't see. A woman hanging on his arm, always clinging, always needing. A lifetime of leading, helping, darkness. Was there no hope of anything else? No hope for the happiness he had just barely begun to imagine?

Blind.

He took a deep breath. He couldn't do this again. God wouldn't ask him to. *It's not the same as Samantha. It's not the same at all . . .*

Behind him, someone coughed.

50

Paul turned to see a young woman coming down the aisle. Her arms were filled with white roses and myriad ribbons. She glanced at him and smiled.

He nodded and turned away. Maddie hated ribbons. Too girlie, she said. He sniffed. *If she goes blind, ribbons won't matter anymore. She won't be able to see them.* He frowned. Or maybe they would matter still. Whether she could see or not, Maddie would hate ribbons. Blindness wouldn't take that away. And it wouldn't take her. Not like with Samantha. Maddie would still be alive.

Paul straightened his shoulders and stared at the stained glass images above him. *She'll still be Maddie. My Maddie.* The same one who stuck her forefinger in his chest and told him he was a pig the first time they'd met. The same one who promised she'd mop the floor with him in a game of racquetball, and she did. The same one who'd stayed up all night to help him study for his last biology exam, who prayed with him before every job interview, who always knew when he was fudging the truth, when he was worried or tired. The same Maddie who had been the best friend a guy could have for three years now.

Sighted or blind, she'd still be the

same . . . sort of.

The girl with the ribbons had sectioned off the front pews with fat, sleek satin and was now hurrying back up the aisle with her hands full of thin strips of white. She paused beside Paul's pew and pointed a long, pink fingernail in his direction. "You're not wearing that for the wedding, are you?"

He looked down at his jeans and polyester shirt. "Oh, I'm not —"

"It doesn't matter. Curl these." She threw the white strands in his direction. They fluttered onto the seat and floor. She reached into the tiny purse hanging from her arm and withdrew a shiny pair of scissors. She tossed them onto the seat beside him. "You'll have to change later."

"I'm not —"

"Hurry up. The wedding starts in" — she checked her slim, diamond-studded watch — "twelve minutes. And I have to get the rest of the decorations ready."

Paul picked up the scissors in one hand and a few strands of ribbon in the other. He held them out. "I don't know . . ."

She heaved a heavy, but delicate sigh. "Chill, man, it's easy." She took the scissors and a strand of ribbon from his hand. "Like this." She pulled one blade along the ribbon until it bounced into a tight curl. "You can do that, can't you?"

Paul shrugged. "Sure." He took the scissors and curled a second strand.

The girl smiled. "Thanks. I owe you." She rushed to the front of the church and began arranging the roses along the steps that led to the altar.

Paul picked up another bit of ribbon. Pull. Curl. Set aside. He closed his eyes and tried it again. "Ouch!" He stabbed the scissors into his thumb. His eyes flew open.

"You okay back there?"

"Fine." He grimaced and glanced down at the tiny drop of blood on his thumb.

Blind.

It wouldn't be easy. Not for her. And not for him either. He curled another ribbon. A wedding ribbon. His throat closed.

In a little while, a man would stand in the front of the church and a woman would walk down the aisle toward him. They would gaze at each other and smile. And they would join their lives together. Two people starting a normal life. Two people without the threat of blindness hanging between them. Two people who could look, who could see, who could love.

"Maddie." Her name came out as a low groan. It could have been them, someday. It should have been them.

Maddie. Maybe it still could be.

He just had to fix it. Somehow. Do something so she wouldn't go blind. She'd sounded so sure . . . so hopeless. But maybe she was wrong. Maybe it could be stopped. Maybe, if God wouldn't fix it, Paul could. Or at least he could convince her that everything didn't have to end. Not yet anyway. Just not yet.

If he could only face her, convince her. Bury his doubts. The only problem was, he never could hide anything from her. She would see how unsure he was. See it, even through that hole in her vision. See it, and despise him for it. And with good cause. He gave a savage yank to the ribbon in his hand. It broke. The scissors flew from his fingers and clattered on the floor beside him.

The girl in the front glanced up.

Paul stuffed the broken ribbon in his pocket, grabbed the scissors again, and curled five more pieces of ribbon. No. He could do this. Make everything all right. At least for now. And sometime, between now and when Maddie graduated in June, he'd figure out what to do after that. He'd understand how to face this thing. And even if he couldn't tell her about his love, he could at least be a friend. A real friend. She deserved that much.

He dropped his gaze and continued to curl the ribbons. A few months. And in that time, he'd study up on her condition, whatever it was. He'd learn how to help her adjust to vision loss, if there was no cure. He'd do right by her. Then he'd know what was real and what was simply fear.

"Hey, thanks, man."

Paul jumped as the girl appeared in the aisle beside him. She reached out her hand.

He looked up and handed her the curled ribbons. She was blond, slender, and even a little foxy. Funny he hadn't noticed before. And now that he did, he didn't care.

She slipped the scissors back into her purse and flipped her hair behind her shoulder. The action reminded him of the blonde from the finance department at work. The blonde he was supposed to have a date with that night. He stood and glanced at his watch. "I gotta go."

The girl batted her lashes at him. "See you later, alligator."

Paul didn't give her a second look. Instead, he slipped out the other side of the pew and hurried out the door. For a moment, he paused and turned in the direction of Maddie's apartment. Ten minutes, and he could be there. He could talk with her. Tell her it would be okay. But it wouldn't. Not if he didn't have a plan. And so he'd stand there, not knowing what to say, not knowing what to do to help. Or he could just go get ready for that date with the blonde from work. He could go eat and laugh and forget what Maddie had told him.

Forget that the woman he loved might be going blind.

4

I'll never see a baby grin. I'll never see the sun rise. I'll never watch as the ocean crashes against the cliffs and colors dance in the mist like the gems of heaven's necklace. Never again.

Strange that those words, those thoughts she had years ago, would come back to her now, here in this darkness, as the water washed slowly, rhythmically, at the shores of her mind. *I'll never see a rose bloom.* Pain slid away. *I'll never again look into my own face.* Why now? Why after all this time? *I'll never look into his and see . . .*

Thoughts, fears, whispered sorrows. She thought she'd silenced those long ago. But they were here again, taunting her, calling her, forcing her to remember. They had come then too, like shards of ice, impaling her dreams.

It doesn't matter anymore. But it did. It always had.

She'd lived with the what-if-I-nevers ever since that day she'd roller-skated home from Mem Chu. The memory swirled in her mind and clarified.

It had started months earlier with a failed NAD and a movie she couldn't see. But that day, even Jesus in stained glass couldn't drive the questions from her mind. And so she ran — or at least skated — away from the church. Away from Paul. But not away from the what-ifs.

Paul hadn't followed. She knew he wouldn't. He wasn't one to push. At least not then. Besides, didn't he have a date with another blonde? They'd go out, have dinner at the local burger joint, listen to a little James Taylor on the radio, maybe even stroll down University Avenue and stop for gelato. Paul would get praline. He loved praline.

A lump formed in her throat. *Paul* . . . He'd find it hard to be friends with a blind girl. Besides, there had been that girl back in high school. The one he thought he'd marry. But something happened to her. She was never sure what, exactly. The only thing she knew for sure was that Paul had gone into medical research because of her. "It was Samantha's idea," he'd said. Or no, maybe he didn't say that exactly. Maybe he just said, "Because of Samantha." But whatever it was, their breakup must have hit him hard because she'd pieced together this much: After Samantha, Paul dated only blondes, only casually, and only once or twice before moving on to the next. She'd always been glad she wasn't a blonde.

But now it wouldn't matter. Not a bit. Oh, he'd stick around for a while, but soon enough, he'd come around less. And less. And less. Then once he knew he couldn't fix it, he'd vanish from her life as surely as her sight. And she'd almost, just barely, begun to hope that someday, maybe . . . She shook her head. She couldn't think about that now. She didn't dare.

No one, not even Paul, would want to be with a girl who couldn't look him in the eye. She'd have to get used to that. Get used to being alone. Dreams gone. Career. Friends. Hopes shattered. Lost. Just like Malcolm.

She shivered. Losing him had driven her toward medicine. She was supposed to become a doctor and help people like her brother before it was too late. That plan had kept her going through all those long hours of organic chemistry and human biology. But now, even that had become pointless.

"Oh, Malcolm . . ."

What happened to God? Didn't He remember that she was going to redeem what happened to Malcolm with her medical career? "All things work together for good" and all that? It was the reason she'd kept her sight — so she could help others. She'd been so sure that was God's plan. But God didn't make sense to her anymore. Not a lick.

Betrayed?

Yes. Maybe. It sure felt that way.

She grimaced. Blindness didn't just diminish physical sight. It dimmed spiritual vision as well. Once, it had all seemed so clear. Become a doctor, be a good Christian, heal people with skillful hands and faithful words. But hands couldn't be skillful with eyes that couldn't see. And faith, it seemed, was just as fleeting.

Oh, God, what have You done to me?

The same thing he'd done to Malcolm.

She rubbed her temples. She had to get the image of her brother out of her mind. Best not to think of him. Best not to dwell on what happened then. Besides, maybe it wouldn't be the same for her. Maybe things would be different. But oh, what if they weren't? What would it be like to live in darkness for the rest of her life? What would it be like to have the darkness spread until it swallowed everything she knew? It would drive her mad. It did him.

That night, Maddie sat up in bed for hours. Moonlight trickled through the window and cast a dull glow on the pea green carpet. She watched it, moving her eyes left, then right. But still the same dark place stained the middle of her vision. At last, she stood and strode to the mirror. And there it was again. A black hole in the center of her face and two eyes, wide, unblinking, staring back at her from either side of the blackness. She pressed her hand against the cool glass and moved her finger, tracing the fuzzy edge of the darkness.

I can't do this, God. I can't, I can't, I can't. This wasn't supposed to happen to me. I'm twenty-one. It's too late for Stargardt's. Don't You remember, I'm supposed to be free . . .

Tears welled in her eyes. She dashed them away. It was no good crying about what might be. What would be. *Still . . . I had thought . . . I had believed . . . not me.*

But God had let her down. Tricked her. Fooled her into thinking that she had escaped this curse.

She reached over to the window and pulled the curtains shut. She closed her eyes, put out her hands, and moved toward the dresser. One step. Two. In total blackness. Three. Her fingers brushed the dresser's surface. Four. She rubbed her hand along the edge. *I could do it. Maybe. If I had to. If it wasn't too bad . . .*

Her wrist knocked into something cold. It tipped. Her eyes flew open. The lamp. She grabbed it before it fell and set it upright. It wobbled once, then stilled.

She closed her eyes again and opened a drawer. *Think.* Her fingers touched cloth. *My sunflower shirt.* It was on the top. *And beside it . . .* She bit her lip. *The purple tie-dye? No, that was dirty. The brown tank top? Maybe.* She explored it with her fingers. *No. It isn't a tank.* She opened another drawer and felt inside. Bell bottoms. Two pair. And socks in the small drawer above.

She moved right and reached toward the highboy. "Ow!" Her shin banged against wood. She stumbled and fell. Her leg throbbed. She opened her eyes again and clutched her shin to her chest.

God, God, God, please don't let me go blind. Not like Malcolm. Please God, not like him . . .

"You all right in there?" Kelli's voice sounded from the other side of the door. A moment later, she opened it. Light flooded into the room. Light. Beautiful, clean light . . . marred only by that circle of gray-black, still in the middle of it.

Maddie looked up from her place on the floor to see Kelli in her pink satin nightgown with fake feathers around the collar. She tugged her tattered nightshirt down over her knees. "I'm okay. I just bumped my shin, that's all."

Kelli sauntered across the room and flicked on the lamp. "You spaz. Turn on a light, will ya?" She twirled a strand of hair around her index finger and studied Maddie. "Say, you aren't psyched out about that appointment with the specialist you got next week, are you?"

"Of course not. I'll be fine."

"You *are* worried."

Maddie got up from the floor and straightened her shirt. "No, really . . ."

Kelli slapped her hands together and motioned toward the bed. "Come on, we'd better pray, and then you'll feel a lot better. Or at least you'll maybe stop thumping around here in the dark. Groovy?"

Maddie grimaced. "Groovy."

Kelli flopped on the bed and sat cross-legged. Maddie sat too, her feet hanging awkwardly over the edge. Kelli reached over and took Maddie's hands in hers. Then she prayed some pink little prayer filled with "you dig" and "right on" and phrases from Mac Davis songs. Eventually, she looked up, grinned, and squeezed Maddie's hands. "You're going to be okay, Madison. I just know it."

Maddie leaned over and hugged her friend. "Thanks. You go on to bed now."

"You sure?"

"I'm sure."

Kelli flounced up, turned off the lamp, and trotted out the door. It swung shut behind her.

Then the darkness came again. Blacker. Heavier. And with it, the haunting whispers of I'll never . . .

Shallow breathing. Dim lights. Distant echoes. And the same, steady beeping.

Paul waited. And waited. And waited.

Nothing changed.

Come on, Maddie. Don't leave me here like this. Come on back. You can do it.

And then, shuffling footsteps in the hallway. The crinkling of paper. Voices, soft and low.

"They'll have to be told." A male voice, young, like Paul's had been not so long ago.

"Her family?" That was the nurse, her tone no longer brisk.

A long sigh.

And the nurse again. "Maybe she'll turn around. She responded well to the morphine."

Paul rose from the chair and moved toward the window. They didn't know he could hear them. And for the moment, he wished he couldn't. The window glistened with thick fog that obscured his view. And yet there in the distance, through the tall cypress trees, he could almost see the ocean. Could almost feel it as it pounded against the rocks and sprayed high against hidden cliffs. Or at least, he wished he could.

"Don't listen to them, Maddie. Life is out there. I promise. Even if you can't see it through the fog." He turned back around. "I've seen it. I know it's true."

Outside, a pen tapped on a clipboard. The doctor's voice lowered again. "There's not much hope now. There's nothing more I can do."

The room suddenly seemed cold. He'd heard those words before. It had always been the hardest thing to hear. *"I'm sorry. I've done all I can. You just have to wait and see. There is no cure. There is no hope."*

Paul moved back to the chair and settled in it. No hope. He didn't believe it. Not now. Not anymore. He knew that love —

real love — could live through the darkness. It had before. It would again.

He leaned forward and breathed a kiss on Maddie's forehead. "There's always hope. I haven't always been sure of that. But I am now. Believe it, Maddie. Believe everything you know to be true. Fight the darkness. Don't be afraid. There's always hope . . ."

Paul rolled those words on his tongue, tasting the memory of them, letting them draw him back to another day, another time. October 1973.

"Do you remember, Maddie? There was hope then too. Though we didn't know it. We were both blind then, in our own way. But hope was real. It was all we had . . ."

"She won't come out!"

Paul held the phone away from his ear as Kelli screeched from the other end. "Candy, Marisol, and even Ryan have tried to get her out. No luck."

Ryan. Paul bristled. He didn't trust that Ryan.

Kelli continued. "Locked. I can't believe it. She was fine during our group Bible study this morning. Then as soon as it was over, bang! She goes into her room and locks the door. Crazy, man."

"Did she see the — ?"

66

"I don't know. She won't tell me anything. It isn't like her."

"Did she say anything during the study?"

"No. 'Cept that *strengthen* doesn't mean 'strengthen.' It's apparently 'in-power' in the Greek, whatever that means." Kelli made a loud huffing sound. "I could use some in-powering right now to break down that door."

"Cool it. I'll be over in an hour."

"An hour? Are you loco? She's got a midterm in an hour."

"Well, maybe she's in there studying then."

Kelli's voice wavered, indicating that she'd switched the phone to the other ear. "Well, that's gonna be kinda tough since the book she's supposed to be studying is out here on the counter."

Paul heard two sharp thumps, as if Kelli had pounded her palm on the book's cover. "Look, man. You gotta get over here. Now."

Paul took a deep breath and gagged. He sniffed his lab coat and wrinkled his nose. He'd been at work all night, after another desperate call had interrupted his date with the blonde. Oh, he'd been thanking God then. But now . . . now he smelled as if he had gone fishing in a sewer. The sweat and stale deodorant were bad enough, but then this morning, a flask of hydrogen sulfide shattered and sprayed all over him. He'd smell like rotten eggs for a week. "I've got to go home and change shirts."

"That's not groovy. The clock's atickin'."

Paul adjusted the phone against his ear. "Fine. I'll be right over." Stink and all.

"Right on."

When Paul reached the apartment, Kelli flung open the door before he could even knock. "Thank God you're here. She's totally lost her cool, man."

Paul glanced at her. "Maddie? I don't believe it."

Kelli pressed her palms against her flushed cheeks. "See for yourself."

Paul strode to Maddie's door and rapped on it. "Hey, Maddie, open up. It's me."

A muffled voice answered from inside. "Go away."

Paul frowned.

From the far end of the hallway, Kelli raised her hands in an I-told-you-so motion.

Paul turned his back on her. "I've got tickets to the Eagles concert."

Nothing.

Kelli poked her head around the corner. "Psst."

He glared at her.

68

"Do you really?" Her whisper echoed down the hall.

He shook his head, then pressed his index finger to his lips to shush her. "Come on, Maddie, come out."

Something fell and clattered on the other side of the door. "Scram. I'm busy."

Paul cleared his throat. "I'm wearing cologne."

The door swung open. Maddie stood there with her hair sticking out at odd angles and a bead of sweat trickling down her cheek. She sneezed. "Liar."

He reached out and rubbed a bit of dirt off her cheek. "Got you to open the door, didn't I?"

She stood back and crossed her arms. "Yeah, well, you can just get out of here again. Like I said, I'm busy." She paused. "And you stink."

"Thanks." He stepped farther into the room.

She moved to block him.

He sidestepped around her.

The floor and bed were covered with piles of clothes. Old T-shirts, bell bottoms, socks, a few pair of shoes, and other things that Paul didn't want to look at too closely. He surveyed the mess, then glanced back at Maddie. "Call the newsroom. A tornado touched down." He moved toward a pair of pantyhose hanging from a lampshade. "And what are these?" He plucked the hose from the lamp and dangled them in front of Maddie. "You never wear this stuff."

She grabbed them out of his hand. "From my mother."

Paul motioned toward the clothes on the floor. "What are you doing in here anyway?"

She stuffed the pantyhose under a pile on the bed then turned back toward him. "Reorganizing. Isn't it obvious?"

"Now?"

Maddie raised her chin. "Of course, now. No time like the present."

"You've got a midterm in less than an hour."

"So?"

"So, what is Miss Sitting-In-The-Front-Row-Waiting-For-My-A doing reorganizing her drawers minutes before a midterm?"

Maddie shoved a pile of clothes off the bed and sat down. "Midterms aren't important anymore."

Paul did a fake gasp. "What's this I hear? Blasphemy!"

Maddie didn't laugh. Instead, she threw up her hands and glared at him. "Okay, Mr. Sitting-In-The-Back-Row-Hoping-To-Pass, tell me this: What good is a degree in chemistry going to do me now? Aren't you the one who's always saying I work too hard, I do too much, I ought to relax? Well, fine, I quit."

"You can't be serious."

Maddie drew her knees to her chest and clutched her arms around them. For a moment, she looked like a little girl who'd lost her favorite toy. "Really, Paul, think about it. Will I be able to see the measurements on the graduated cylinder? Will I be able to tell the color of the liquid in the beaker? Will I be able to read the printout on the spectrometer or the labels on the solvent jugs or the numbers on the powder scales?"

He came and sat beside her. "But what about med school?"

She turned her head and stared at him. "Get real. Who's going to want to be treated by a blind doctor? Even if I could pass the classes and navigate an internship. Even if I could get my MD before the blindness becomes complete. Those dreams are dead now. Those," her voice cracked, "and all the others too."

Paul laid his hand on hers and squeezed. "That's not true, Maddie." But she was right, he supposed. Still, he wouldn't admit it. Not here. Not in front of her. It wasn't fair. Something like this just shouldn't happen to a person like Maddie. He turned away and gazed out the window. Sunlight glinted through the pane and cast funky shadows on the carpet. Shadows she probably couldn't see. Even now. He rubbed his temples. *What are You thinking, God? How could You do this to her? To us.*

Maddie shook her head. Tears formed in her eyes. "What's the use of any of this? I've got Stargardt's. I'm going blind. There is no cure. There is no hope."

He stood and paced in front of her. "There's got to be something. We can fix this. Make it all right. Medicine, research . . ."

Her smile curved her lips but failed to reach her eyes. "You can't fix this, Paul. It should have happened to me sooner, in my teens. When it didn't, I thought . . ." She shrugged. "But it's caught up with me now, and it won't stop until it's taken everything I have. Until *she's* taken everything."

He paused. "Who?"

"Never mind." Maddie stood and grabbed a shirt from the pile on the bed. She folded it neatly and placed it in a drawer. "It's okay, Paul. I know how awkward this is. You've been a good friend to me these past years, but now . . ."

"Stop." Paul stuck his hand into his

pocket. Something brushed against his fingers. He pulled it out. A bit of silver ribbon caught his gaze. Broken ribbon, frayed at one end. *Remember, hide your doubts.* He twisted the ribbon around his finger. *She knows me too well.* The ribbon pressed into his flesh. *Try. I can't. You must.*

"Look, Maddie, I know this is hard. It's awful. But this is your last year. Classes are only for a few more months. Why not just stick it out and finish your degree?"

"Why?"

"Why not? Can't hurt, can it?"

She folded another shirt. "I don't know."

He walked over and took the shirt from her hand. His voice lowered. "Besides, sure beats spending the day reorganizing your drawers."

She grabbed for the shirt. "I like to organize."

He held it up, out of her reach. "I know."

She stood on tiptoe and stretched her hand toward the shirt. "Hey, that's my best blouse."

"Promise you'll get going and take that midterm."

She huffed and fell back to her heels. "Okay, I'll go."

He dropped the blouse on her head. "That's more like it. And you'll get an A

73

too . . . or else."

"I'll never get there in time."

Paul stepped over a hill of jeans and picked up her backpack from the corner of the room. "Sure you will."

She snatched the pack from his hand. "There's no hope of that. Not this late." She slung the pack over her shoulder and strode toward the door.

"Maddie."

His voice stopped her in her tracks. She glanced back.

"There's always hope. You know that."

For a moment, she didn't move. And he could tell that she knew he wasn't talking about the midterm anymore.

"You think so?" The words quivered from her lips.

He nodded. "Remember. 'I can do all things through him who in-powers me.' Just like it says in the Greek."

She gave him a rueful smile. "Yeah, maybe. If you say so." She shook her head, adjusted her pack, and picked up a pair of sunglasses from the table near the door. "There's hope for now. That is, until my mother finds out."

Just then, the phone rang.

5

The phone rang and rang, creating a discordant beat with the beep of the EKG. Paul didn't rise to answer it. There was no reason to. If he did, what would he say to the person on the other end? Maddie was dying? No. Maddie was lost in darkness. But she would come back to him. She had to. She'd done it before.

Maddie's eyelashes fluttered. A soft moan rose from her lips. Her fingers twitched.

Paul glanced at the phone. The red button blinked as it continued to ring. He turned toward Maddie. "I won't answer it. Not this time. I know better."

Sweat glistened on Maddie's brow.

Paul reached over but didn't wipe it away. "It's all right. It's not her. I promise."

The phone stopped ringing.

Maddie sighed and grew quiet again.

If only it had been so easy that other day. But it hadn't. Then, he hadn't thought twice about answering the phone, didn't know it would bring her more pain.

Paul reached for the phone.

"Don't do it. Don't you dare." Maddie paused, her hand on the doorknob. "It's her. And I can't —"

Paul didn't listen. He should have.

He picked up the phone and put it to his ear. His eyes widened as a string of French words met his ears. He turned toward Maddie. "How did you know?" he mouthed to her. He cleared his throat. "Oh, hello, Mrs. Foster."

Maddie rolled her eyes.

"Who is zis? Where is Madison?" Maddie's mother spoke with a French accent, even though, as Maddie had told him, she'd moved to Massachusetts years ago, when she was a teen. Maddie said she kept the French accent on purpose to avoid picking up "ze ugly accent" of taxicab drivers in Boston.

"Well, she's . . ."

Maddie shook her head and waved her hands in front of her face. "I'm not here. I've got a midterm. Remember?" The words came out as a low hiss.

Paul adjusted the phone against his ear. "She's just about out the door. Hurrying to an exam."

Maddie grimaced and swung the backpack from her shoulder.

"Put her on? I think she's late."

The backpack dropped onto the floor.

He glanced at Maddie. "It's important, you say?"

Maddie held out her hand toward the phone. "It's always important." Her voice turned sharp. "Or so she says."

Paul took a step back and motioned for Maddie to go. "I don't think she can talk now."

Maddie grabbed at the phone. "Oh, just give it to me." She scowled as he handed it to her then plunked down on the chair. "Hello, Mom. I've got to get to my test. I'm already late."

Paul moved toward the door. "Sorry."

She nodded as she pinched the receiver between her shoulder and ear. "Yes, I'm fine." She blew out a long breath. "No, it was just a, um, routine exam."

Paul stopped and looked back.

Maddie nibbled her lower lip. "Nothing's wrong."

She was lying. Maddie never lied. He stepped back into the room.

"Kelli told you I was at the doctor, did she? Great." She twisted a strand of hair around one finger. "Yes, I told you that. I need to run." She frowned. "No, I've gotta go."

She didn't hang up.

"I can't be late."

She stood. "No, Mom. Stop. I can't. Not now." The hand on the receiver trembled. "It's not like that." Her voice shook. "It's not like . . . him."

There was a long silence. Maddie's face turned pale. Finally, she spoke again. "No, don't." A pause. "You don't need —" She swallowed. "You can't. Mom!"

Maddie dropped the receiver into the cradle and buried her face in her hands. "I can't believe it."

Paul stepped beside her. "What's wrong?"

She bent, grabbed her backpack, and pressed it into her chest. Her eyes rose to capture his. Her voice turned cold, toneless. "Good-bye, Paul."

"Maddie?"

"You should have let it ring."

"Maddie!"

All was good, peaceful, quiet. Except. Something was there, something niggling at the corners of memory. Fear. And darkness. And . . . the faint sound of ringing. A phone.

Peace fled. Maddie groaned. She hated

that sound. Ever since she could remember, it had brought pain. "A blind girl should love the phone," her mom had always said. "After all, you don't have to see to use the phone." But Mom was often wrong. The ring was an ugly sound. Too often it heralded disaster. *"Your Grandmother has passed." "Your father and I are divorcing." "Malcolm has . . . Malcolm is . . ."*

And it hadn't ended there. There had been a lifetime, it seemed, of phone calls filled with questions, demands, and doubts. Calls that fed her fear, asked for answers she could not — would not — give.

Still, out there, past the dark water that splashed around her consciousness, past the heavy blackness that held her here in this strange place between darkness and light, the phone still rang. She focused on the sound of it. *Don't answer. Just let it ring.*

It rang.

Don't pick it up.

No one did. This time.

But there was another time. Yes, a long time ago. Paul answered then. He shouldn't have. But he did. And that changed everything.

The phone stopped ringing.

Maddie drew a long breath. And remembered.

■ ■ ■ ■

She dashed from the apartment that day with her mother's words still grinding in her ears. *"Do not lie to me, Madison Rose."*

Maddie threw herself down the stairs two at time. She knew that was foolish, especially now. But she didn't care. A scrape, a bump, a fall, what did it matter? Soon, she'd lose everything anyway. Everything, at least, that meant something, that made her life what it was. Everything that made it good. *Except God.*

Yes, except God. God was still there. God . . . who betrayed her. God, who let her believe everything would be all right, and then let *this* happen. Just like Malcolm. God hadn't saved Malcolm. God's existence hadn't even mattered — not at the end, anyway. All that mattered then was the darkness and the loss.

I can't let her do it. She can't know the truth.

Maddie bounded down the last step. Her foot twisted. She tumbled into the rail and caught her forearm against the stucco wall. Her knee scraped against a piece of rough metal. *It doesn't matter. Just get to class. You can figure this out later.*

She unlocked her bike and hopped onto

it. A moment later, she was peddling fast, down the sidewalk. *She can't. I won't let her.*

The bike picked up speed.

She will. She is.

A lump formed in Maddie's throat.

She's coming. And then . . .

The bike flew over a bump in the concrete. Maddie's teeth jarred in her head. Her breath came quicker. She slowed the bike.

It was almost as bad as going blind — having her mother come, having to hide the truth. For if she didn't, if her mother found out . . .

She swerved around a corner.

It would be worse than the darkness. It would be just like Malcolm.

No!

Her legs tensed. She pushed the pedals harder. Faster.

A bit of yellow flashed on her right. A shirt. A face. A body. A boy. She veered left. A splash of red. The handlebars twisted. She flung forward. Then came the sickening sound of bending metal. And air beneath her. The bike behind. Books and papers flew around her as her chin impacted the concrete sidewalk. Pain slashed through her cheek and radiated down her chest to her right elbow.

"You okay?"

She blinked and sat up. She rubbed her chin. It was rough, but dry. No blood. She swallowed. "Yeah, sure. I'm okay." Her voice wavered. "And you?" She stretched out her arm. Pain shot to her shoulder. She stretched it further. The pain sharpened, then faded away. "I'm so sorry. I didn't see you. It's just . . . I don't know how . . ."

The boy waved away her words. "It's cool."

She moved her jaw. It hurt. But not too badly. "No. No, it's not cool." She glanced up at him. His Afro stood out at least six inches from his head. She may have missed his neon yellow shirt, but she sure shouldn't have missed that 'fro. If she hadn't swerved. She shivered. "I could have . . . I almost . . ."

He gave her a toothy grin. "No worries, sister. You missed me." He grabbed one of the books that had flown from her pack and handed it to her. "You don't look so good, though."

She dabbed her elbow with her hand then glanced down at her fingers. A small smear of blood marred her fingertips. The fuzzy edges of her vision blurred further. "It's not too bad. I'll be all right."

The boy shook his head. "You were flying, man. Can't believe you didn't see me. I've been standing here for five minutes."

82

Maddie grimaced. A breeze ruffled the papers from her notebook. She snatched at a few loose sheets before they could blow away.

"Crazy." The boy put his hand down to help her to her feet.

Maddie struggled up without his help. Her ribs throbbed. Her elbow smarted. "You're okay. That's what matters."

"Your bike's a mess."

She looked down to see a haze of crushed metal. She squinted. "It'll be all right."

The boy reached down and picked up her notebook.

She took it and shoved it into her backpack. "I can do it. Thank you. Sorry I didn't see you."

"No skin off my chin. You've apologized already." The boy shrugged. "You sure you're okay?"

Maddie gathered the rest of the papers from the ground and pushed them into her pack. "I'm fine." Her voice caught. *I can do it. I can still do this. Without help. Without needing . . . Oh, God . . .*

God. He could have prevented this too. And didn't.

"All right. Be careful, huh? My ride's here." The boy stuffed his hands into his pockets and sauntered down the sidewalk away from her. In a moment, he began whistling a tune from the Jackson 5.

Maddie sniffed. *What was I thinking? What am I doing?* She dropped her chemistry book back into her bag, slung the pack over her shoulder, and picked up the bike. She slung her leg over the bike and wiped her nose. She blinked tears away. *I can still do this. I'll just go slowly. Really slowly.*

She gave the pedal a firm push with her foot. The bike stuttered and stopped. She pushed again. It wouldn't go. *Oh, come on.* She got off and squinted at the front tire. Then she felt it. The rim was bent, and part of the tire had slid off. She felt around some more. Spokes were broken. She licked her lips. They stung. The faint taste of blood tickled her tongue. She sniffed again. *No. I will not cry. I won't.*

With two hands, she lifted the front wheel from the ground and pulled the bike toward class. One slow step after another. Each one bringing the realization her vision was worsening. She could have hit that boy, and she would never ride a bike again.

And so began the long list of losses.

It's so still in here. So quiet.
Paul shifted in his chair.
No visitors. No laughter. No song. No

84

sharing of the mundane happenings of everyday life.

Sterile. Cold.

No wonder Maddie wouldn't awaken.

It had been like this before. The edge of darkness. The chill of loneliness. And the waiting, watching, while friends drifted away. He wouldn't have believed it, except he saw it with his own eyes, heard it with his own ears. And wished he hadn't.

It started one Friday evening. He stopped by her apartment on his way back to work. It had been a long week, and a longer day. Still, he wanted to see her. Her midterms were over. He thought she'd be glad, but she wasn't. She'd been quiet, withdrawn, tense. And tonight he hoped to find out why.

Voices drifted from her apartment as he climbed the outer stairs. He heard Marisol, Candy, and faintly behind them, Ryan. *Great, a crowd. It must be Bible study night.* Paul reached the top of the stairs and knocked.

A moment later, Candy pulled open the door and blinked out at him. "Good evening, Paul." She adjusted her thick glasses and straightened her shoulders. "You are here to see Madison, I presume."

Paul gave a stiff bow. "You presume correctly, ma'am. Is she in?"

Candy gave him a rare smile before her face fell back to its usual somber expression. "She is."

Paul stepped into the room, but before he could spot Maddie, he was engulfed by a brightly colored poncho with arms. He pulled a bit of orange yarn from his mouth and leaned back. "Hello there, Marisol."

Marisol twirled away, picked up a soda can, and saluted him. *"Hola, muchacho."* She winked at him, then tossed a heavy braid over her shoulder. "You come here to have some fun with us, *sí?*"

Paul grinned as her *y* came out as a *j*. "Are you calling me a Jew again, *muchacha?*"

She waved at him and cackled. "You no Jew. You a, what do they call it, *humorista,* comedian. Ha ha." She faked a laugh, then tossed him a soda can.

Paul caught it with one hand and set it on the coffee table just as Kelli burst from the kitchen wearing a bright pink tie-dye shirt and faded jeans.

"Paul!" She squealed his name. "I didn't know you were coming over tonight. Is it NAD night? Maddie didn't say a word."

"No, it's not. Is she — ?"

Before he could finish, Ryan sauntered out from the kitchen with a bottle of root beer in his hand and the words Make Love Not

War scrawled across the front of his T-shirt. His arm was flung around Maddie's neck, and she didn't look too happy about it.

Paul bristled.

Ryan pointed the bottle at him. "Hey, man, cool. How's it hangin'?"

"Good. Thanks." Paul fought to keep his voice steady.

Maddie wriggled out from under Ryan's arm, turned, and disappeared back into the kitchen.

Paul slipped around Ryan and followed Maddie into the kitchen. "You okay?"

She opened a bag of chips and dumped them into an olive green bowl. "Fine. And you can stop asking me that." She lifted the bowl.

He reached over and took it from her. "Hey, I just stopped by to say hi before I went back to work."

"Hi."

"Very funny."

"You're the *humorista*."

"So they say." He set the chips back on the counter.

A smile touched Maddie's lips, then vanished. "Really, Paul, you don't have to check on me as if I were a baby." She moved toward the counter, bumped into it, then reached up and opened a cupboard door.

Her fingers moved around until they contacted a plastic cup. She took it from the cupboard and closed the door. She felt for the faucet and filled the cup halfway with water. "Really, I'm fine." She took a sip.

Paul reached out and touched the scab on her chin. "Fine? Are you sure?"

The cup clattered in the sink.

"Hey, dude, cool it."

Paul turned to see Ryan leaning against the doorpost behind him.

"If the chick says she's fine, she's fine."

Paul scowled. "Back off, man."

Maddie huffed and pushed past him.

Paul turned with her.

She grabbed the chips from the counter and stormed into the other room.

Paul went after her. "Wait up."

She tossed the bowl onto the table and refused to look his way. She flopped into an orange beanbag chair.

Candy lifted her light jacket from the arm of the chair. She coughed and raised a finger. "Excuse me."

Maddie looked up.

Paul stopped.

"Shall we depart now? It's getting late."

Marisol whirled her arm in the air as if twirling an invisible lasso. "Let's go, *chicas*. And you *hombres* too."

Kelli heaved a sigh. "Coming, Mad?"

Maddie struggled out of the beanbag and straightened. "Where are we going?" She still wouldn't look at him. Wouldn't even acknowledge that he was there.

Paul edged toward the door. Maybe Maddie was right. She didn't need him after all. She was getting along just fine with her other friends. He'd been a fool to stop by. A fool to worry. "I'll just be going . . ." No one heard him.

Kelli popped a piece of bright pink bubblegum into her mouth. "There's that groovy new light show at the . . ." Her voice faded. Her face turned the color of the gum. "Oh."

The smile dropped from Maddie's face. She looked away. "Yeah, well, um, it's okay. You know, I'm kinda tired anyway."

Perhaps he was needed after all.

Marisol twirled a tassel on her poncho, her eyes fixed on a spot somewhere to the left of the door.

Ryan swigged down the rest of his root beer and set the bottle on the table.

For a moment nobody said a word.

Candy cleared her throat. "This is quite the awkward moment, isn't it?"

No one answered.

Kelli bit her lip. "Maybe, well, uh . . ."

Maddie picked up the root beer bottle and wiped the ring of water off the tabletop. "It's cool. I should stay home tonight anyway. I don't know what I was thinking."

Kelli pulled the gum from her mouth and plopped it back on the wrapper. "Stop jiving, Mad. You haven't been out in . . . forever."

Maddie's face turned red. "Kelli!"

Her voice lowered. "Well, it's true."

Ryan brushed the hair back from his forehead then swaggered over toward Maddie. "Come on. Come out with me. We'll do something someone like you can enjoy."

Maddie stiffened. "Someone like me?"

Her tone didn't faze him. He didn't even seem to notice the coldness in it.

Paul shivered.

Ryan patted Maddie's shoulder. "You know . . . something where it won't matter about your" — he motioned toward her eyes — "blind thing."

Marisol made a sharp sound with her tongue.

Paul longed to go to Maddie, put his arm around her, make this painful moment go away. But he knew she'd hate him for it, push him away. Reject him. So he didn't move. At least, not much.

Maddie removed Ryan's hand from her

shoulder and backed toward the kitchen. "No, thank you."

"It'll be good for you. We don't mind."

Her chin rose. Her jaw clenched. "Maybe not. But I do."

That was his Maddie. The strong, feisty girl he knew. Paul took a step toward her, then stopped.

"Maddie." Kelli's low hiss seemed to reverberate through the room.

Maddie glared at her, then at them all. "No. I don't need any pity parties. I don't want any pity dates. I don't need any pity at all." Her voice rose and cracked. "I can still see well enough to see the looks on your faces. And I know what you're thinking. 'Poor Maddie.' 'Sad Maddie.' Well, I can get along just fine, thank you very much." She was shouting now and seemed to realize it. Her voice lowered and grew hard. "Just go, all right? Get out. I'm fine."

Kelli put out her hands. "It's not like that, Mad."

"It is too." Candy's muttered words barely reached Paul's ears. He turned and glared at her. Her expression hadn't changed a bit.

Maddie pointed her finger at Kelli. "Not another word. Please. Just go."

Marisol pursed her lips. "Come on, *amigos,* we are not wanted here." She strode to the front door and flung it open. The others followed.

Paul heard their murmurs as they slid out the door.

"What's wrong with her?"

"Just trying to be nice."

"Pardon us very much for trying."

And then they were gone.

Paul stood in the corner, waiting, silent. Maddie collapsed on the couch and closed her eyes. Paul stepped forward. "Well, that was awful."

She started and sat up. "You still here?"

"Seems I wasn't invited to the show."

Maddie tossed him a quick half grin.

"Wanna go get some gelato?"

"No."

"Come on."

"No pity dates, remember."

"You're stubborn."

She jutted out her chin. "Yeah? So?"

"So, are you going to come with me or not?"

"You've got to get back to work."

"I've got a few minutes."

She crossed her arms and didn't answer. Seconds ticked between them. Finally, she sat forward and pressed her hands into her thighs. "This is how it's going to be from now on, isn't it?"

"How?"

"Awkward. Awful."

He grunted and plopped onto the couch beside her. "Probably."

She nodded. "Guess I'll have to get used to it then." She poked him in the chest with her finger. "Just as long as you don't start feeling sorry for me too. Asking me on dates. Patting my arm. Talking with some sickly soft voice." She wrinkled her nose. "Ugh. Promise me that, will ya?"

Paul's mouth went dry. And for a moment, he couldn't say a word.

6

It was raining that night, a slow, drizzly sort of autumn rain that lured you out, then drenched you all the same. Paul sat next to Maddie at the pizza parlor with Kelli and her newest boyfriend across from them. A neon Open sign flickered in the window. Two boys played pinball in the corner, and Neil Diamond crooned from the jukebox.

On the table lay a half-eaten abomination. Pizza. With olives and mushrooms, green peppers and onions. No meat. Pizza wasn't pizza without meat. But Kelli's newest beau was a vegetarian, so now she was too.

Paul leaned over and whispered in Maddie's ear. "Ten bucks if you go steal me some pepperoni."

"I wish." She hid her response in a forced cough.

But Kelli didn't notice. She was too busy making fluttery eyes at Rob.

Rob smiled down at her and flung his arm

around her shoulders. He reached for another piece of pizza.

Paul cleared his throat. "So, have you guys tried out the new burger joint on the — ouch!"

Maddie kicked him under the table.

Kelli shot him a look. "Hamburger is death on a bun, Paul."

"You take your death with cheese, if I recall."

Kelli's glance turned to a glare. "Paul!"

"Just kidding."

Maddie stifled a giggle.

Kelli snuggled against Rob's side. "You'd better be good, Paulie boy. Or else."

"Or else what?"

"Or else I'll tell the story."

Paul flicked an onion from his piece of pizza. "You wouldn't."

Rob stopped chewing and took a swig of soda. "What story?"

Maddie tapped her hand on the table. "You've got to tell it now."

"I'm leaving." Paul scowled.

Maddie's hand gripped his arm. "Oh, no you don't."

Kelli sat up straighter in the booth and wiggled her fingers at Paul. "He thinks he's so cool now, but you should have been there the first time Maddie and I met him."

"I was cool then too."

Maddie made a gagging sound.

Kelli waved her hands in the air. "So there we were at Tressider Union getting a —"

"Hamburger!" Paul flicked his napkin across the table at Kelli.

Maddie reached for it and missed. "We were not."

Kelli stuck out her tongue. "Getting sodas. At least Maddie and I got sodas. What's-her-name got Perrier." Her tone turned highbrow at the last word. "What was her name?" She turned toward Maddie. "She was your roommate."

"Deborah."

"Oh yes. Not Debbie, mind you, but Deborah."

Maddie nodded. "Deborah Elizabeth Wadsworth. Of the New York Wadsworths."

Kelli giggled.

Maddie grinned. "Imagine Paul dating her."

They laughed.

"Hey, it was worth a try." He took a bite of pizza and made a face.

Maddie rolled her eyes at him. "Even if you would have had the pedigree for it, you wouldn't have lasted one date. Trust me."

Paul set down his pizza and grabbed his glass of soda. "I can put my pinkie out when

I sip my tea." He stuck out his little finger and gulped his soda from the plastic cup, then grabbed a clean napkin and dabbed the corners of his mouth.

"Very genteel."

Kelli snatched the napkin from his hand and tossed it onto the table. "Don't distract me from the story." She tapped her finger-nails on the tabletop. "So, as I was saying, there we are sitting in front of Tressider Union sipping sodas and this guy," she nodded toward Paul, "comes sauntering over in his cutoffs and tie-dye T-shirt. He takes a look at the chemistry book sitting in front of Deborah on the table and drawls, 'Hey, good-lookin', you need some help with that? 'Cause I bet you and I could make some great chemistry together.' "

Rob choked on his pizza.

Kelli gave a short squeal of laughter. "And Deborah, she just sits there and stares at him."

Paul leaned back in his seat. "Come on, it was a great line for a chem grad student."

Maddie patted his arm. "Oh yeah, I'm sure that's what Deborah thought as she was sitting there with her mouth hanging open. No one ever talked to her like that in her whole life."

Kelli grinned. " 'Bout that time, I choke

and Maddie here snorts her soda right out of her nose. Then she reaches over and takes the book. 'It's my book,' she says. And she looks up with these big innocent eyes and yellow Mountain Dew still dripping out of her nose and says, 'Would you like to help me with it?' "

Rob laughed.

Maddie snickered.

Paul groaned.

"Well, Paul, he just stands there and starts sputtering, 'Uh, ah, well, duh.' And I can't help it, I'm laughing like a hyena now. And Deborah's shaking like a delicate daffodil in the wind. But Maddie hasn't cracked a smile. She just shakes her head all serious like and mutters, 'Pig.' "

Maddie took up the story. "So then Paul reaches into his backpack and shoves these fliers at us."

Rob frowned. "Fliers?"

"Yeah, he's inviting us to a *prayer* meeting of all things."

"No." Rob reached for another slice of pizza and stuffed a big bite in his mouth.

"Yes."

Paul shrugged. "See, I wasn't all bad."

"Did you go?" Rob spoke through a mouth full of vegetables.

Kelli raised her eyebrows. "Of course. If

anyone needed prayer, it was him." She jerked her thumb in Paul's direction.

Maddie smiled and placed her hand on Paul's forearm. "And we've been friends ever since." She reached for a napkin. Her wrist grazed her glass of soda and tipped it. She lunged for it. Too late. Dark, fizzy liquid sprayed over the pizza and poured between Rob and Kelli. They jumped up.

Maddie righted the glass. "Oh, I'm so sorry."

Paul grabbed a fistful of napkins and tossed them on the pizza. "No loss."

Kelli took a napkin and dabbed at the spots on her shirt. "That's the third time today. You've got to be more careful."

"I know." She looked at the large brown stain on Kelli's jeans.

Kelli shook her head, all laughter gone now from her eyes. "Not cool, Mad." She turned toward Rob. "Let's go, man. Movie starts in twenty minutes."

Rob flicked a drop of soda from his sleeve. "Groovy." He glanced at Paul. "Thanks for the pizza, man." And then at Maddie. "And for the shower."

Maddie's gaze slid to the floor.

Paul put his hand on her shoulder as Kelli and Rob strolled out the door. "Come on, let's take a walk."

"It's raining."

"Take my arm." He put out his elbow toward her.

She brushed it away. "I can do it myself."

"Maddie. Come on."

Her jaw tightened as she slid out of the booth. "No. I'm tired of this. I'm tired of spilling drinks. I'm tired of being treated like an invalid. I'm tired of the kid gloves, the concerned looks. Everything. Don't pity me, Paul! I can't stand it. I can still see well enough to get out that door by myself and walk across the street to your car. I don't need you to hold open the door, or to hold my hand, or to treat me like a blind baby. All right?" She stormed toward the door, flung it open, and bolted outside.

Paul grimaced. Women. Usually Maddie was different. But tonight . . . He raked his fingers through his hair and stepped toward the door. "Hey, wait up."

"I don't need your —" Her words cut off as the door swung shut, leaving him on the inside and her outside. He watched her throw her shoulders back and stomp toward the curb. She yanked her coat tighter around her shoulders and stepped into the street.

Then Paul saw them. Twin headlights flashing against the rain. A truck, swerving around the corner. Too fast.

Maddie didn't stop. Didn't see.

The truck came right at her.

"Maddie!" His shout ricocheted through the air as he plunged out the door. "Stop!" He dove toward her.

It happened in a blur. The squeal of tires. The flash of light and rain. Headlights blazing, blinding him. His arms around her, jerking her back.

The pickup roared past. Muddy water splashed over Maddie's front, dribbled down her shirt and pants.

"I didn't see it." Panic filled her voice.

Paul's fingers squeezed into the wetness of her coat. "Of course not, it's dark. You could have been killed."

A tremor ran through her. "I should have . . ."

"Waited for me." He spoke with force.

"No, please, no."

He drew her closer.

She buried her head in his chest. He could feel her trembling, her arms looped around his waist, her cheek over his heart.

"Oh, Paul, I don't want this. I don't want to go blind."

I know, love. He sighed, laid one hand on her head, and held her as the rain misted down and formed bright diamonds of wetness in her hair.

■ ■ ■ ■

Memory and mystery. They intertwined now until Maddie couldn't distinguish the two.

I hurt . . . That was now.

I'm afraid . . . That was now too, and then. Yes, she'd been afraid then too. And she had tried to hide it. Tried to hide so many things.

Was that what she was doing here now? Hiding on the edge of darkness and light? Of fear and courage? Of today touching tomorrow? On this shore, with the black water lapping at her toes. When the wind did not speak. The birds were silent. The very air held its breath. Only the water moved. Rhythmic. Quiet. Dark.

And she was afraid to cross it, afraid of what may lay on the other side of darkness. *God, if You're out there, send me help. Send me hope.*

But no one answered.

Not the wind.

Nor the sea.

Nor the clinging blackness.

But she knew where God was. He was out there, somewhere beyond the water. Somewhere beyond the night.

And between was this great gap of darkness, this great expanse of fear.

She had stood here before.

Shivering. Afraid.

Blind.

That night in the rain when she'd heard the truck roar past. That's when fear had come to dwell, to stay.

It had happened so quickly. And so slowly too. One day she could read the numbers on the spectrometer, the next day she couldn't. One day she could see the professor's diagrams on the chalkboard; the next they were a blur of gray. Colors came and went, flashes of blue and yellow against the green lawns of Stanford. But she could still see, at least that's what she made herself believe. The darkness hadn't come yet. Not fully.

Until she almost stepped in front of that truck. Then she knew. Life had changed. The darkness had come. And would keep coming, deepening, spreading. And with it, the horrible, haunting dread that Malcolm's fate would be her own. And Paul would be lost to her. For good. When all she really wanted was for him to hold her like he had, so close that she could hear his heartbeat. Forever.

Oh, God, don't let me fall in love . . .

They had driven long and far that night, up into the hills of Half Moon Bay. As the rain tumbled onto the roof of the car, and her dreams, her hopes tumbled into the darkness and couldn't be retrieved.

Paul drove with his hands tight on the wheel and his face set forward. She could still see that much, though barely.

"You may not lose all your sight," he was telling her. "I read that with Stargardt's, most people keep their peripheral vision."

She closed her eyes. "Most. But not Grandma. Not Malcolm. And probably not me."

"We'll face this then, together. It'll be okay. We'll make it okay."

She turned her face toward the window. She could feel the rain beating on the rooftop, could smell the dampness in the air. "Oh, Paul." She wanted to believe him. With all her heart. But it hurt too much. And he didn't deserve this. Not after what happened with his old girlfriend. The one she knew so little about. The one she couldn't forget. "You can't make it all right. No one can."

"I can try."

Maddie sighed. *Don't do this to me, Paul. Don't be kind and caring and make me ache for you. I can't depend on you. I can't depend on anybody.* She drew a long breath. "Do you know why my mother became a concert cellist? Do you know why she practiced until her fingers were raw?"

"What does that have to do with anything?"

"It does. So do you know why she did?"

"No."

"Because she was terrified, that's why. Because you can still play the cello when you're blind."

Paul shook his head. "Your mom's not blind."

Maddie smiled. "No, but she may as well be. She's spent her whole life preparing for it."

Paul drummed his thumbs on the wheel. "She should be able to help you then. To know what to do."

"Like she helped Malcolm?"

Paul swerved over to the shoulder and stopped. He turned toward her. "What happened to Malcolm, Maddie? What are you so afraid of?"

"Going blind."

"Tell me the truth."

She kept silent. The rain beat harder on the roof. Paul's breath came quicker. Harder.

"How could you keep something like that

from me? A brother. A blind brother. And you never even mentioned his name in three years."

Of course she didn't. It was too awful. Too painful. It was almost too painful now. But the time had come. Maybe it was time to remember, to voice her fears aloud. "He wanted to be a baseball player. I wanted to be a doctor."

"You still can."

Maddie snorted. Her tone turned sharp. "Get real, Paul."

"You can do something."

She pressed her finger against the cold glass and drew the outline of a cello. "Like what, play a cello?"

"No way. You're practically tone deaf."

She could hear the shadow of a smile in his voice. She sat up and rubbed out the image on the window. "To Mom's everlasting chagrin."

"She's coming in a couple of weeks, isn't she?"

Maddie nodded. "And if she finds out what's happening to me, I can kiss all this good-bye." She waved her hand in the air.

"Then we won't let her find out." Paul slapped his palm on the wheel.

Maddie turned toward him. "But . . ."

"Let me help you, Maddie. Like a friend

should. And more."

More? Her breath caught. *More than friends.* No, she couldn't let herself think that. Not ever. Never. Never. Never. *Remember that old girlfriend. Remember . . . Samantha.* She was the last girl he ever cared about. And that went wrong. Somehow. But she didn't pry. Didn't ask too much. Because she'd had her secrets too.

"You'll help me?"

"Of course."

Her hands balled into twin fists. "Okay then."

"Okay."

"I won't let her do to me what she did to him. I won't." She punched her thigh. "No matter what."

"No matter what." He paused, and she could see that he was holding out his hand. "Pinkie promise?"

She smiled. "Pinkie promise." She stuck out her pinkie.

Paul wrapped his finger around hers and shook it. Then he took her hand. "So, are you going to tell me? What is it that she did?"

Maddie stared out the front window and chewed her lower lip. Eventually, she spoke. "She killed him."

■ ■ ■ ■

The squeak of shoes caught Paul's attention. He turned as the nurse opened the door and walked in, carrying a potted plant dotted with white flowers. The pungent smell of gardenias filled the room. The woman smiled and placed the flowers on the table beside Maddie's bed.

She straightened and glanced around. "We normally don't allow flowers in these rooms, but in this case . . ." Her voice trailed off and she touched Maddie's forehead with her fingertips. "Not so warm anymore. Let's pull up your blanket, shall we?"

Of course, Maddie didn't answer.

The nurse gave the blanket a gentle tug, then tucked it around Maddie's chest.

Maddie sighed and smiled.

The nurse brushed a tendril of hair back from Maddie's cheek. "There's something special about you, isn't there, honey? I can feel it." She glanced up toward the far end of the room where Paul was now standing. "Doc said . . ." She paused and shook her head. "Well, it doesn't matter what he said. We won't pay no never mind to that." She placed her hand on Maddie's arm and squeezed. Her voice dropped. "I've said a little prayer for you. Don't you worry, now honey. You just enjoy your flowers and dream happy dreams." She looked back up. "She's going to be okay. I just know it."

Warmth filled Paul as the nurse gave Maddie one last look and walked out. She left the door open.

A voice drifted from the nurse's station outside the door. A spate of quick Vietnamese, followed by slower English. "You should not get so involved. 301 will be empty soon."

Paul moved toward the door — 301. Maddie's room.

The sound of shuffling papers interfered with the nurse's response.

The first voice spoke again. "You heard what doctor said."

Maddie's nurse moved farther away and lowered her voice. "Shh, she'll hear you."

The first nurse clucked her tongue. "She not going to hear anything. You know it."

"I don't know it."

"Why you say that?"

Paul listened as the nurse's shoes squeaked then stopped. She must be sitting, probably behind the desk. Next came the sound of computer keys tapping.

"You should not say that. There is no change with her."

Maddie's nurse raised her voice. "I see a change." Her tone softened. "I don't know what it is, but I tell you, something's going on in that woman. She knows what's going on around her."

"She no speak. She no blink. She no open her eyes."

"But she's present. She's there. It makes me think, wonder . . ."

"Think? Wonder? That for family. For friends. Not for professionals."

The nurse's voice dropped to a whisper, yet Paul still heard it. "I know. But it's real. I can feel it."

"You crazy talk."

"Maybe."

He heard a finger tapping something hard. "When she wake up and talk to you. Then you write that. She no do that. You no write."

"I'm writing it."

"Why you do that?"

For a moment, the nurse didn't answer. Then her words came again, wavering, slow. "There's just something about her . . . something in that room. It feels like . . . like hope."

"Hope, eh?" The woman's voice turned brittle. "For her, or for you?"

The nurse sighed. "Must be for her. It's

not for me."

"You could get pregnant on your own. I hear of someone —"

"Don't, please." The nurse cut her off. A chair squeaked. Then came footsteps again — a pair of them, fading, growing more distant. "James said . . ."

But Paul couldn't hear what James had said. The nurses had moved too far away. He looked at the door but kept it open, then moved back to the chair. Hope. It was a strange thing. Invisible. And real. Soft as a flowing stream, strong as a raging torrent.

Hope. Sometimes it was all a person needed in this life of pain and heartache, fear and sorrow. This life that people lived in the flesh. He once believed that if you just lived well, God would spare you from all that. He once believed that hope was in comfort, that a good life was one free of trouble. But Maddie taught him differently. Maddie taught him that God is in the sorrow. God works in the pain. She needed to remember that now. And so did he.

For the night was coming.

It was almost here.

7

Gardenias. She could smell them across the water. They beckoned her. *No, I don't want to go. But I don't want to stay.*

"*Come.*"

She touched the water. It flowed over her, through her. Black. Cold.

I'm afraid.

"*Remember.*"

She smiled, and the darkness drew back, just a bit. But enough to remember. Someone was out there, just beyond the shadows. If only she could reach him. Could he smell it too, the fragrance of memory? The scent of love. Everything changed that day. And nothing changed. Only she did. But in the end, even gardenias couldn't banish the darkness that was to come . . .

She was supposed to be studying that afternoon. She had her books in her backpack, her pencils and slide rule, and sheets full of formulas written in large black ink. Finals were coming. And she wasn't ready. But it didn't matter. Not today anyway. Today, the bus rumbled, road signs blinked by, and her backpack lay unopened on the seat beside her.

A dozen muted conversations buzzed around her. A guy with a voice that cracked on the high notes sang good- bye to Miss American Pie from the back of the bus. A mother tut-tutted her crying baby in a seat two rows up. An old man coughed and wheezed as he rattled the newspaper in front of him. But no one looked in her direction. Just as no one had noticed when she stumbled on her way to her seat. No one offered a hand then. No one offered a glance now. And that was just the way she wanted it.

After twenty minutes, the bus squealed to a halt. The doors flew open. Maddie grabbed her backpack. "Is this the nursery?" The vinyl upholstery squeaked as she leaned forward in her seat.

The driver removed his hat and stared back at her. "No, ma'am, this is the corner of Hill and Embarcadero. And that's the bank." He shook his head and muttered under his breath. "You blind or something?"

Maddie dropped her pack onto the seat

and swallowed past the sudden lump in her throat. "No. I'm . . . sorry."

He grunted. His voice continued in a harsh whisper as he closed the doors and threw the bus back into gear. "I gotta get me a different job. Old folks and idiots."

The man with the newspaper flicked it until it folded in half, then he glanced back at her over half-rimmed glasses. "The nursery is the next stop."

She attempted a smile. It fell flat. She clutched her backpack against her chest and stared out the window as the bus again picked up speed. The guy in the back began to chant about a stairway to heaven. Maddie sniffed. *I can do this. I have to. She's coming in two weeks. Just two weeks. I've got to be able to pretend.*

It was silly, really, what she was doing. Paul would say she was crazy if he knew. But she had to find out if it was true what they said about your other senses improving when your sight failed. And the nursery was the best place she could think of to put that theory to the test. If she could just walk through the rows of flowers — smell them, know what they were without looking — maybe she could convince herself that her mother's visit wouldn't be a disaster. Maybe she could smell, and listen, and feel, and her mother would never guess that her sight wasn't all it should be. Today would be an attempt to see without seeing.

Outside the window, images spun and blurred. A building of some sort, a yellow sign, a flash of orange. It made her head ache. "We're going too fast."

"I've got it at thirty-five, lady."

Did she say it out loud? She closed her eyes and tipped her head back. *Stop worrying. Your other senses will sharpen to compensate for your eyes, just like they say. What if they're wrong? What if I can't tell a petunia from a pansy, a rose from a rhododendron?* Maddie gulped. *What if I can't pretend?*

The bus lumbered to a stop.

Maddie didn't move. She didn't dare.

The woman with the baby got up, grabbed her bags, and tottered out the front door.

The driver swung around in his seat. "Whatcha waiting for, an invitation? This is your stop, ain't it?"

Maddie nodded, leaped up, snatched her backpack, and bolted for the front door. A moment later, her pack was flying from her arms as her toe caught on something and sent her sprawling across the aisle. This time, people noticed.

"You okay, miss?" The newspaper man reached down and helped her to her feet.

She forced a smile. "I'm fine. Thank you. Just going too fast."

The man patted her arm. "Young folks are always in such a rush. You forget that life's plenty long enough to slow down and enjoy the view."

Maddie trembled. "I wish that were so." She stepped forward, careful not to trip again, and picked up her pack. She gripped the handrail in tight fingers and made her way out of the bus. *If I fall like that when Mom's here . . .*

The doors slammed shut behind her. A breeze lifted a tendril of her hair and threw it across her face. She looked at the sign for the nursery above her. *I can still read that. I can still see it.* She straightened her shoulders and strode toward the open gate.

Once inside, she faced the riot of color around her. Reds, blues, yellows, pinks, all splashed in a sea of green and bordered by rows of black pots with their edges blurred and the colors fuzzy. A bright green hose drained water into the pot of a giant palm tree. A brown cart stood off to her left. She squared her shoulders and headed toward the flowers. Sunlight glowed through the plastic overhead as she reached the rows of color.

She paced the aisles, past begonias and

tulips and cute little Johnny-jump-ups. She went by daffodils and geraniums, touched the petals of pansies and the sharp thorns of a blooming cactus. She stopped and took a deep breath. *Okay, I can do this.* She shut her eyes. *Walk forward.* She took five steps down the aisle. *All right, name the flowers.* She breathed in. And out. And in again. She bit her lip. "Uh, lilies."

She opened her eyes, just a little. They were not lilies. She sighed. *Try again.* She moved to the next aisle, closed her eyes, and walked ten paces. There she stopped and breathed in again. "Pansies, no tulips, no . . ." She peeked through one eye. "Ooh, alyssum, and that was an easy one too." She grimaced. "One more try." She slammed her eyes shut and marched fifteen steps down the aisle. "Trees. I don't know what kind. And I don't care."

"At least you knew they weren't pansies."

Maddie opened her eyes and spun around. "Paul! What are you doing here?"

"Buying a suit." He made a face at her then motioned toward the parking lot. "I followed the bus from your apartment."

"What? All this way? Why?"

He quirked an eyebrow at her. "You don't remember? We were supposed to go shopping for that monkey suit I need for the conference. You were going to help me pick it out."

Her hand flew to her mouth. "Oh, I'm so sorry. I forgot." She walked toward him.

"Obviously. Unless you thought I look best in begonias." He picked up a pot of pansies and fluttered his eyelashes. His voice rose an octave. "Tell me, do they match my eyes?"

She punched him in the arm. "I said I was sorry."

"That's all right. We'll go tomorrow. What are you doing here, anyway?"

"Practicing."

He frowned. "Practicing what? Smelling flowers?"

She dropped her gaze. "No. Uh, well, okay already, I'll admit it. I'm practicing going blind, all right?"

He shrugged. "All right. But you may as well do it right, then."

"I can't. I tried."

"Close your eyes again."

"No."

"Stubborn."

She closed her eyes.

He took her hand in his. And then his voice was in her ear, warm and close. Too close. "Sure you can. Come with me." Paul placed her hand carefully on his elbow.

"This way. And don't look."

"I have to."

"No, you don't. Just keep your hand steady. The book said it's best if you get a good grip right behind the elbow."

"What book?"

"The *Flower Sniffer's Manual.*"

Maddie peered at him through the slit in one eye. "Smarty-pants."

"No peeking."

She shut her eyes again. Both of them. He led her forward. Her shoes crunched on what sounded like gravel as he sauntered down the next aisle with her at his elbow.

"Your arm is stiff. Loosen up."

She tried to think the tension from her grip. And failed.

"Trust me."

She took a long breath. "Okay. I do trust you. I do. Really."

His side jiggled.

"Don't laugh at me." She thought about the warmth of the sun on her face, how the earth turned from rough to soft beneath her feet, and the quiet in and out of her breathing. *I can do this. I can relax. I've walked beside Paul a hundred times. It's just like always. Nothing new. Nothing special.* But that was a lie. And she knew it.

"Told ya. I knew you could see in the dark."

See in the dark. If only he knew.

Paul led her to a turn and then walked straight for ten paces before turning again. He stopped. "Now, tell me, what do you hear?"

Maddie furrowed her brow. "Cars. Going by on the street."

"One car. It's passed now. What else?"

She touched her tongue to her upper lip to concentrate. "Voices. Far away."

"And?"

There was a bubbling sound, soft, closer, familiar. What was it? Ah, now she knew. "Running water. From the hose, I think."

"Good. What do you smell?"

That was easy. "Flowers."

Paul moved closer until she could feel his warmth against her side. "Come on, you can do better than that."

He led her forward again, but this time, she didn't resist. The sound of water came closer. The rumble of cars dropped away. She could hear him beside her, his touch soft and steady, his footsteps sure.

I could walk this way forever.

She hesitated.

"Trust me." His voice, gentle, quiet, tickled her ear.

Don't!

He stopped. His arm moved. Her hand fell away. "I'm bringing something near you. Tell me what it is."

"It better not be cow dung." She forced her voice to be light, joking. He was close. So close.

He was smiling now. She could sense it. "You never know."

Then came a scent, sweet and heady. "A . . . a . . . I don't know."

"Is it cow dung?"

She grinned. "Of course not."

"Then what is it? Focus. You can do this."

She drew a long breath. "Like a rose, but not so pungent."

"Feel it."

She did, gently. Tiny petals like bits of satin. "Miniature roses."

"Good! Now, what color?"

Maddie's eyes flew open. "No fair."

He reached over and ran his thumb along her chin. Goose pimples rose on her arm. She licked her lips. "They're red."

He dropped his hand. "See, no problem."

He tucked her hand behind his elbow again and led her down another aisle. This time, she could tell which were begonias and which were bottlebrush. She mixed up pansies and poppies but knew a juniper from a Johnny-jump-up. Paul took her down the last aisle and paused near the middle. "No touching. What do you smell?"

"Um . . ."

"They're red."

She laughed. "Roses again!"

He chuckled. "Full grown, this time. You're getting good at this."

She paused. Her voice caught. "If all I have to do is smell the roses . . ."

His fingers squeezed hers. "Someone ought to write a song about that."

"If they do, I'll buy it."

"And remember this day?"

For a moment she didn't answer. She couldn't. Then she steadied herself. "Of course."

"You promise?"

"Unless it's Mac Davis."

And for that second, for just a breath, she dared to hope that maybe, just maybe, she wouldn't end up like Malcolm after all. "Paul? I . . ."

A horn beeped. Loud and raucous.

She jumped.

"One more. Come. And keep your eyes closed."

He led her to the end of the aisle. And then she smelled them. Gardenias. In full bloom.

"Open your eyes."

She did and saw him holding out a fat pot of gardenias. She took it in her arms and breathed deeply of the heady fragrance. "My favorite."

"Happy birthday."

"It's not my birthday."

"I don't care."

Something painful lodged in Maddie's chest. *You can't! You've seen it happen before. A bit of hope. A thought. A chance. And then . . . No, don't let yourself dream, don't you dare begin to feel.* She touched a flower with her fingertips. "You know I have a brown thumb."

He plucked off a petal and held it beneath his nose. "You'll remember to water these, I promise. Tell me what they smell like to you." He dropped the petal.

She breathed in again. Sweet. Stimulating. Beautiful. "Heaven."

He stepped closer and lifted her chin until her face met his. "Hope." His thumb brushed her jaw line. "And don't you forget it. Ever." He leaned closer.

Don't pity me . . .

She stumbled back, away. And in that moment, the spell of the flowers was broken.

Paul stood at the hospital window and

watched the fog twine through the branches of a cypress tree. Bleak grayness pressed against the pane and swirled in dull eddies along the ground. He watched as a car backed from a parking spot below. Headlights flashed against the fog, illuminating a million minuscule drops of moisture.

In the hospital room behind, he could still smell the scent of gardenias, in full bloom and thriving. He'd seen them that way before. They were perfect that day long ago when he'd given them to her. And she'd kept them that way until Christmas. Perfect, blooming, watered. But then, everything changed.

Her mother came.

Paul focused on the glow of streetlights against the fog below. Behind him, the door creaked opened. But there was no familiar squeak of shoes. Only the click of heels. Sharp. Firm. Striding in perfectly measured steps. He knew that sound. He'd never forget it.

"Maddie, she's here." The words fell, unheard. For a moment, he didn't move, didn't turn. He didn't need to.

Then she spoke. Not to him. Never to him.

"I have come, Madison. Mama is here." She still had her French accent. Even now, after all these years.

He turned then and saw her. Isabelle Foster. Dressed in flowing black. Elegant, as always. He looked closer. So little had changed. And yet, she was different too. Her black hair had turned gray, and she no longer swept it into a bun behind her ears. Fingers that had wielded the cello with such grace were bent now, the skin wrinkled and dotted with age. But her back was still as straight, her shoulders held with the same stiffness.

Then her shoulders seemed to sag. Just a little. "Madison?" She stepped across the room toward Maddie's bed. With a smooth movement, she removed her glasses and set them on the small end table. She reached her hand toward the bed, but paused there before touching Maddie. "They did not tell me —" The words choked to a halt. She drew a shuddering breath and dropped into the chair that Paul had been sitting in earlier. "I would have come sooner, but . . ."

Paul frowned.

But she didn't turn, didn't glance his way. She had eyes only for her daughter, only for Maddie, who could not answer, would not. For Isabelle, Paul didn't exist. Some things never changed.

Her fingers brushed Maddie's arm. "I

should have come right away." She lowered her head close to Maddie. Tears filled her eyes. Real tears. The first Paul had seen there in a long, long time.

"Oh, *cherie,* I am so sorry."

Sorry. The word echoed through the room and dissolved in a sigh.

Paul moved closer.

And still Isabelle didn't look up.

Instead, she took Maddie's hand in her own. Hers trembled.

Maddie didn't stir. Only her chest moved up and down, her breath still coming in low, rasping whispers.

Isabelle sniffed and shook her head. She took a tissue and carefully dabbed her nose. She spoke again, her words stuttering, stopping, broken by her tears. "I would have saved you from all of this, if I could. I tried, *ma petite cherie.* Then. Now. Always. But I could not. *Non.* I never could." Her lips quirked into a sad smile. She dabbed her eyes. "You knew that, did you not? You knew it all along."

For a moment, Paul thought she would look up at him and say something. Anything. But she didn't. So he moved back to the window and turned toward the glass. But he could still see her there, reflected in the pane. Could still hear her. Could still remember all this woman had done. But that was years ago. A lifetime. An eternity. And yet it mattered still. To Maddie. And to him.

Again, her voice came, soft, gentle, strange. "It is all I ever wanted, to save you from pain. I spent my life . . . No, I will not say it. You did not believe me then. You will not believe me now. But *je t'adore.* I love you, Madison Rose. I only wanted to keep you safe." She folded the tissue into equal quarters and placed it in the trash can. "What good is it to say it now? It is too late. Look at you, my *belle,* my *fille.*" She closed her eyes.

Paul turned around, but he wouldn't intervene. Not yet. Not now. He had learned, over the years, to wait until the time was right.

In a minute, Isabelle leaned over and kissed Maddie's hair. "You were so beautiful. Did you know that? You always were. Always will be." She looked up and blinked. "*Oui,* even now." She choked back a sob. Her face turned away from Maddie. Her voice became no more than a whisper.

And still, Paul heard it.

"Why, why my Madison? Why, God in heaven, why did You let this happen to my baby?" She paused, as if expecting a response.

But God wouldn't answer. Not that question. Never that question. Paul knew it. And so did Isabelle.

"It is too late, is it not, Madison? Too late to talk of the past. But perhaps you do not care. Perhaps it has been too long for it to matter anymore."

Heat rushed through Paul. It was not too late. It was *never* too late.

"Forgive me, *cherie*."

Forgive? Paul moved forward.

But Isabelle ignored him. She could see only Maddie. Only the daughter who lay, motionless, in the bed.

Forgive? Maddie would do that. And so would he. He had to. He had. Years ago, he had done what he must. He had found a way to be free.

"She forgives you, Isabelle. We both do."

Isabelle lifted Maddie's hand and held it to her lips. She muttered something Paul didn't hear, and then she fell quiet. For a long time, she sat there, silent, beside Maddie's bed, while shadows grew deep and cast their gray fingers through the fog. She didn't speak again, nor did Paul.

Together they waited. Together they watched the woman they both loved. Together, for the first time in so many years.

It hadn't always been that way. It never would be again.

Paul stood by the chair.

Isabelle stroked her daughter's hand.

And then, Maddie moved.

8

The water turned black, threatening. It held her here, in this eerie in-between place of darkness and light. Where Maddie could see the water and know it was a lie because she saw it. Dimly, darkly. Black waves against a gray sky. But it was there, when she hadn't seen anything for a long, long time. Water calling, whispering in folds of darkness. A place with fear, but without pain. Where tomorrow touched yesterday, and caused her to remember.

Those were dark days too. Before the blackness, before the light. In between. Hidden in folds of desperation and crevices of gray doubt. Those days, when her mother came. And the world tipped. And the dimness deepened in ugly waves.

No. Not that. I won't remember that.

But the memory came anyway. It floated above the black water. Came with the sound of heels clicking on a tile floor. And a voice.

And a touch. And an image of a face she hadn't seen in years.

She raised her hands. Batted it away.

But the image still came. It reached out, surrounded her. And sank into the water.

She could feel it then, the wind on her face as she stepped from the car and moved toward the door of the restaurant. The door swung open, and she went inside.

"Come, Mom." Her own voice, trembling, just a little.

Her mother followed. The click of heels. The lifted chin. The firm strides that could belong to no one else.

Kelli closed the door, then took the lead. "I knew it. Crowded, just like always. Good thing I called ahead." She squeezed up to the hostess and held up her hand. "Bredlin for three."

The woman behind the counter inclined her head, then motioned for them to follow.

Maddie swallowed and clenched a fist. *I can do this. Without tripping. Without bumping into anyone. I've done it dozens of times.* It was one reason she and Kelli had picked this restaurant — Maddie knew it well. Her chopsticks would be in precisely the place she was used to. And her glass would be just left of the top of her plate, where she expected it. No surprises. No stumbling

131

blocks. Here, she wouldn't make a mistake. She'd be able to keep her secret.

Maddie took a deep breath, then wound her way past the potted palm, past the rows of bamboo, past the brightly colored fish in the huge aquarium. She listened to the buzz of voices around her as she slipped past the images of women dressed in cheongsams and followed Kelli's hot pink–flowered shirt to their table.

Behind her, her mother's heels continued to click.

Finally, they reached their table, tucked in a back corner. Maddie blinked at the white tablecloth covered by gleaming glass. She slid into place. Kelli and Maddie's mother took their seats on either side.

Her mother picked up her set of ivory chopsticks and examined them. "I did not know you like Chinese food, Madison."

Kelli held out her hand as the hostess handed her a menu. "It's our favorite restaurant. Discovered it freshman year."

The hostess handed Maddie her menu, just as always. Maddie turned her head a bit and attempted to glimpse the fat red dragon on the menu's front. All she needed was to be caught holding the menu upside down. She'd never be able to explain that.

Apparently, Kelli was thinking the same

thing. She reached over and plucked the menu from Maddie's hands. "Oh, let me. I love to do the ordering."

Maddie's mother flicked her napkin onto her lap and opened her menu. "Rather costly for Chinese, is it not?"

Kelli handed the menu back to Maddie. "Maybe you should choose something after all. You know what your mother will like."

Maddie's mom closed her menu and placed it neatly on the table before her. "It is quite the sacrifice, I would think, for those who are still students." She sipped her water. "Or perhaps your parents give you a generous allowance?"

Maddie could feel Kelli squirming in the seat beside her. "My mother is dead, Mrs. Foster. And my daddy ran off with another woman when I was eight. So, no, there is no generous allowance for me. There's no allowance at all."

Mom dabbed her lips with the napkin. "Then however do you — ?"

"We sacrifice for what we love, don't we, Mrs. Foster?"

She stared at Kelli for a moment. "*Oui.* That is what I have always said."

"And I do love Chinese."

Maddie cleared her throat. "How about the mu shu then?" She pointed to where she knew it was on the menu, though she couldn't actually read it anymore. "They have the best plum sauce here."

Her mother clucked her tongue. "I dislike cabbage, Madison. You know that."

Maddie pursed her lips. A figure moved into the side of her vision. A flash of white, a splash of black. She turned toward it. The waiter. But she couldn't make out who. Was he the same one who normally waited on them? Or someone new? She didn't know. Not quite. Not yet.

Then he spoke. "Hot and sour soup very good tonight. You have that?"

Maddie smiled. Ah, it was Huang Fu. Good.

Kelli closed her menu and tapped it on the table. "Hot and sour it is then. And almond chicken, rice, and . . ."

Maddie straightened. "And the mu shu pork, please. With extra plum sauce."

Her mother glared at her. She couldn't see it, but she knew. She felt for her napkin and placed it on her lap. "How was your flight out here, Mom?"

"Bumpy, hot, and *très* unpleasant." Her voice sharpened. "And there was a terrible, portly man sitting next to me who insisted upon snoring in the most awful manner."

Kelli coughed and giggled.

A tiny Chinese woman hurried toward the table, bobbed once, then set down a pot of tea and three minuscule cups.

"Allow me." Kelli grabbed the pot and the cups from in front of Maddie.

Maddie turned her head back toward her mother. "And the Christmas concert?"

Her mother sniffed. "*Oui.* I must be back in time for it, of course."

"Of course."

"I am to meet the maestro Bergenheimer while I am here. He has written me about an antique cello he insists I must see. Only I can do it justice, he tells me."

"Hmm."

"He believes it was crafted in the fourteen hundreds. I, certainly, have my doubts. And yet . . ." She continued for some minutes on the possibility that the cello was indeed an antique, when the maestro had obtained it, why she was the only one who should play it, and how he'd lent it to the symphony anyway. Maddie stopped listening halfway through.

The meal was going well so far. Everything was normal, controlled, boring. Just as she'd planned it. Her mother wouldn't know a thing. She wouldn't suspect. And in a week and a half, Mom would go back home to Boston and Maddie would be safe again. A week and a half. She could survive that long. She could. One day at a time. One hour. One minute.

"Madison? Madison! Are you paying attention?"

Maddie jumped. "What? Huh? Oh, I'm sorry, Mom. That cello sounds wonderful."

Dishes clanked as the busboy cleaned the table next to them.

Her mother's voice tightened. "I was asking about your doctor visit. What exactly — ?"

"Soup! Hot. Sour. Good." The waiter slapped a giant soup ladle on the table and plopped empty bowls next to it. He motioned vigorously to a smaller man standing behind him.

The little man placed the soup next to the bowls, bowed, and backed away. Behind him, a woman came with the almond chicken and mu shu.

The waiter tapped the ladle on the table again. "Extra plum sauce coming. Mustard, sweet sauce, ketchup." He pointed to three small bowls in turn.

Maddie pulled the mu shu toward her as the waiter dished up the soup.

Kelli placed Maddie's soup next to her plate at exactly the two o'clock position, just as they had discussed. Then she reached for her own bowl. "It looks wonderful, Huang Fu."

Maddie smiled. "Perfect, as always."

Huang Fu bowed. "Extra plum sauce here." He took the bowl from the smaller man, who had just returned, and set it on the table. He turned and walked away.

Maddie plucked up a thin pancake and placed it on her plate.

Kelli leaned forward and placed her hands, palm up, on the table. "Shall I pray, or would one of you like to?"

Maddie's mother scooted up in her seat. She did not place her hand in Kelli's, but rather folded them discreetly in her lap. "You may do so. Quickly."

Maddie hid her grin.

The three bowed their heads as Kelli said a short prayer. "Thank You, Lord Jesus . . ."

But Maddie was again not listening. *Please, God, don't let me mess this up. You haven't taken away my blindness. You haven't even slowed it down. But I still think You're out there. Somewhere. So You can do this for me. This little thing. At least You can do that. Don't let her find out the truth. It would kill her. It would kill me. Help me, please, God. I just want to be normal. I just want —*

"Amen."

Maddie lifted her head. "Thanks, Kelli."

She reached for the mu shu and sprinkled the mixture onto the pancake on her plate. "And how is Poppette, Mom?" Poppette was her mother's obnoxious pet Pekinese.

"Ugh, I had to rid myself of him. He would not be quiet."

Maddie dipped her spoon into the plum sauce and dropped some onto her food. A sharp pain shot up her leg as Kelli's shoe impacted her shin. "What?"

Kelli reached over and took the plum sauce out of her hand. "I'll have some mustard too, Maddie. Thank you."

Maddie gulped. Hot mustard. How could she mistake mustard for plum sauce? She hated mustard. But there was no turning back now, or her mother would notice. She'd have to just eat it that way.

Kelli's voice took on a falsely happy note. "And here's the extra plum sauce you ordered." She placed it directly into Maddie's hand. It was in a different dish than usual. A cup rather than the normal small bowl. No wonder she'd mistaken it.

Maddie could almost see her mother's sharp eyes taking in the exchange. Or maybe she couldn't see it. Maybe she just imagined it. "Thanks, Kelli." She heaped the plum sauce onto the mixture, folded the pancake over, and took a tiny bite. Sweat broke out on her upper lip. She wiped it away and forced herself to take a second bite.

"Madison, are you well?"

She coughed. "Yes, Mom, I'm fine."

"You look terrible."

"Thank you."

"Pale."

"Please, Mother."

"You are ill."

"Oh, look." Kelli's arm shot out as she pointed to a group of people just being seated at the table opposite them. "It's, uh, Frank Sinatra."

Maddie's mother glanced back at the group. "Do not be ridiculous, child. That man, he looks nothing like Frank." She started to swing back around.

Then it happened. Maddie reached for her glass and knocked over her cup of tea. It spilled over the table, the liquid rushing in a steaming line toward her mother. Maddie felt it move, as if in slow motion. Closer. Closer. She wouldn't be able to get around it now. Her mother would ask a hundred questions, would probe, would suspect. She had to. Maddie opened her mouth to say something, to make some excuse.

But before she could formulate anything sensible, Kelli snatched up the cup and a napkin. Her voice rose to a squeak. "Oh,

I'm so sorry, Mrs. Foster. I'm the worst klutz. It's a wonder Maddie puts up with me."

Maddie caught her breath.

Her mother scooted back. "I thought Madison —"

Kelli shook her head. "No, no, it was me, as always." She grabbed another napkin. "Let me just mop that up. Glad I didn't get anyone wet." She smiled and piled the soggy napkins next to her plate. "I can hardly get through a meal without a spill. Maddie should have warned you."

"No need for apologies, *cherie*." Maddie could hear the coolness in her mother's tone. "My mama, Madison's *grandmère,* was one to spill something at every meal as well." She picked up her tea and daintily sipped it. "Of course, that was because she was going blind." She lowered the cup and looked at Maddie. "And speaking of sight, how is yours these days, Madison?"

"Uh . . ."

Kelli gasped. "Oh groovy! They've brought the little cookies with the almonds in the middle. I love those! Cookie, Mrs. Foster?" She grabbed the small plate and thrust it at Maddie's mother.

"No, thank you."

Maddie reached for a cookie and dropped

it on her plate. It hit the mu shu. "We'd better get eating. I have a test tomorrow." She picked up her chopsticks. But even as she did, she noticed the sharpness of her mother's glance, a look she couldn't miss, even now.

And it told her that Mrs. Isabelle Foster had not forgotten the question about her daughter's sight.

Something was happening. Something Paul didn't understand. Maddie was sweating now. Drops of moisture dotted her forehead and upper lip. Her lips were moving. He leaned forward.

He caught her mumbling. Words. Barely audible. Spoken in mutters. Laced with fear. "The symphony. Not the symphony. No."

He glanced at Isabelle. She hadn't heard. Or if she had, she gave no indication. Instead, her eyes were closed, her own lips moving. Paul looked closer. She wasn't . . . no, she couldn't be. He moved to the far side of the bed until the light fell so he could see better. Yes, she was.

One hand held Maddie's, the other was clenched around the corner of the sheet. Isabelle was praying. Truly praying. And in English, not in French.

"Father in heaven, spare her. Heal her.

Make her whole." Isabelle opened her eyes. "What will I do without you? I cannot. You must know. Oh, God." She looked down, let go of the sheets, and pressed her fingers against her lips. "Just let her know that I love her. That I care. That I will be here if she needs me."

Paul straightened. "She doesn't. Not now. Not anymore."

"Save her . . ." Isabelle rose, gulped in a quick breath, and rushed from the room.

Paul watched her go. He waited. And waited. She did not return.

"She's gone, Maddie." It was strange, almost impossible. Isabelle Foster had come, had stayed, had spoken. And then she left, without demands, without controversy. She had been, well, almost kind. At least to Maddie.

Paul sat beside his wife again. He gazed into her face, noting how her forehead was still etched with worry, and sweat still glistened on her brow. "People change, love. Sometimes, anyway." He glanced at the door. "Sometimes they do what we least expect."

But this wasn't the first time Isabelle Foster had surprised them. This time, the surprise was a good one. But then, it had been for Maddie a nightmare come true. It started so simply, so innocently, with two tickets to the San Francisco Symphony. A gift, and no more.

He'd brought them to Maddie that night as a gesture of friendship toward her mother. It seemed so simple — an evening of music and dimmed lights, where Maddie could spend time with her mother and yet still hide the failing of her sight. At a symphony, a person didn't need their eyes; they only needed their ears. Or so Paul had thought.

Stupid. He knew that now. But at the time, he'd only wanted to do something nice. He remembered how he pulled the tickets from his pocket and put them directly into Maddie's hand. "Tickets to the symphony for Friday night. I thought you and your mother could enjoy it together."

Maddie held them in her fingers. Behind her, the lava lamp bubbled and oozed on top of the television. A radio spat a static-filled waltz in the background. The light in the hall clicked off.

Maddie squeezed his arm and gave him her funny half grin. "Thanks, Paul. That was so thought—"

"Who is that, *cherie?*" Isabelle strode into the room with her chin held high and her eyes flashing. Her hair was pulled into a tight bun, which made her jaw line appear even more rigid.

Maddie turned. Her hands trembled. "Just Paul, Mom. And look, he's brought us tickets to the symphony."

"The symphony?" She turned to Paul. "You know that I am a member of the Boston Philharmonic, do you not?"

Paul stiffened. "Of course, that's why I —"

"You do not understand."

"Mom!"

Isabelle pressed her lips into a thin line. "I see. You meant to be kind. What night is it?" She glided over and snatched the tickets from Maddie's hand. "Friday. It is not possible for me. I am meeting with the maestro on Friday evening. I cannot possibly reschedule. I am sorry." She looked closer. "First Tier. Center. They are reasonable seats, at least." She dropped the tickets onto the table. "It is regrettable that I cannot attend, Mr. Tilden. Please do not think me ungrateful." She inclined her head slightly toward him. "Perhaps that little pink floppit can go with her so your tickets will not be wasted?"

Maddie stepped forward. "Kelli?"

"Yes, of course."

Maddie frowned. "She's out of town this

weekend."

Paul grabbed the tickets from the table and shoved them into his pocket. "I'll take her."

The scowl dropped from Maddie's face. "Oh, Paul, what about your conference? Your new suit?"

"I can wear the suit to the symphony. And the conference will still be going on Saturday."

"Paul." He heard the warning in Maddie's voice. That almost-imperceptible sting that meant something wasn't right.

Her mother sniffed. "Well, I am certainly glad that is settled."

Maddie spun toward her. "The carrot juice is ready in the kitchen."

"Thank you, cherie." With a click of her heels on the linoleum, Isabelle turned and left the room.

Paul walked around the table to Maddie. He stopped in front of her and crossed his arms over his chest. "Okay, so what's the matter?"

She glared up in his direction. "No pity, remember."

Paul grimaced. "Don't worry, it's not pity."

She huffed and shook her head. "Oh please. I can't even get a date with my own mother. How pathetic is that?"

He looked over to where Isabelle had disappeared through the kitchen door. "Count your blessings."

"Paul!"

"Well?"

"Okay, if it's not pity, then what is it?"

He smiled. "Spite."

She tried to hide a grin but failed. She chuckled. "All right. But she'll get you back for this, you know. She'll make you pay."

"Why? I'm the nice guy here."

Maddie raised her eyebrows. Her look softened. "Yeah, you are." For a moment, he thought she'd say more, but instead she turned away. "Just remember, no good deed goes unpunished. Especially by my mother."

He thought she was joking, but she'd been right. He did pay. Those two symphony tickets almost cost him everything.

9

Nineteen seventy-three. San Francisco in winter. And Maddie in a dress of deep blue. It fluttered around her ankles, soft against her skin. Strange and out of place against the blinking neon above her.

Paul stopped in front of a narrow doorway. The sound of clanging pots echoed from the inside.

Maddie touched his elbow. "What's this? It can't be —"

"Au contraire." Paul flung his arm toward the open door. "This just happens to be the most famous eating establishment in all Chinatown."

"This place? With . . . what are those?" She squinted and turned her head until the sight became clearer. "With chickens hanging in the window?"

"Of course."

"My sight must be worse than I thought. It looks like a hole in the wall." She squinted again at the greasy window, then at the laundry on one side and the luggage shop on the other. "It's gotta be, what, ten feet wide?"

"Oh, it's at least fifteen. Come on."

Maddie hesitated. "You're kidding, right?"

"I'm not." He gave a mock bow and motioned inside. "Welcome to Sam's."

"No way."

Paul took her hand and led her inside. Dishes clanged, spoons scraped against the sides of woks, knives thudded on chopping blocks, a half-dozen people jabbered in rapid Cantonese. Steam blurred her vision even further, but not before she saw that they had walked right from the sidewalk into a skinny kitchen. "Are you sure about this?"

Paul tucked her hand behind his elbow and against his side. "Of course I am. Guy at work said you can't come to Frisco without eating here. It's famous."

"For what?"

He pressed a finger to her lips. "Hush, and just enjoy. You said this wasn't a date, remember?"

"Certainly."

"Well, would anyone bring a date here?"

Maddie grinned. "You got me there."

"See." He squeezed her hand. "You've got

to learn to trust me." Paul raised his arm and spoke to a woman stirring a large pot over the fire. "Two, please, for dinner."

The woman waved toward the back of the building. "You go. Third floor. Chop, chop."

Maddie narrowed her eyes and just made out the skinny steps at the back of the room. "Up there?"

Paul took her hand again and led her to the stairs. They were so narrow that she could navigate her path even without Paul's help. But she left her hand in his as they made their way up one flight and to the next. Finally, the steps twisted again and ended in a tiny room with seven rickety tables surrounded by short stools. Paul guided her past another couple who occupied one of the tables. She glanced at them, though she couldn't make out their faces.

"At least we're not the only ones here."

"I told you, this place is famous."

"Sure."

"Let's take the table by the window." He led her to the last table and pulled out a stool.

Maddie could tell that the floor was scuffed and worn, and the table and stools were as well. "Famous, huh?"

"I told you, great place for a NAD."

She laughed. "Yes, it is."

Outside, neon flashed in colors of bright green and yellow. Something fluttered. Chinese lanterns, maybe, from the shop across the way. The high-pitched yip of a dog added to the sharp ring of a bell from the street below.

Paul swung his stool closer to the window and looked out. "Just a boy on a bike, I think."

"This late?"

Paul cocked his head toward the street. "Can't tell. Too far down to see."

Maddie leaned across the table. Outside was a blur of colors and light. "I can't tell either. Are those sheets fluttering from those windows over there or lanterns?"

"Looks like a nightgown, hung out to dry."

"I'm not dressed right for this place."

Paul laughed. "You look fine to me."

Just then, the sound of heavy footsteps pounded from the stairs. A moment later, a large Chinese man lumbered into the room, paused, and shouted some unintelligible words down the steps, then stomped over to the couple at the other table. The tiny room echoed with a string of angry words in quick Cantonese.

Maddie's gaze flew to the waiter still standing beside the other table. She couldn't make out his expression, but he was jabbing his finger toward her. No, toward the window behind her.

The waiter's jabber turned to English. "You see sign, fat man? This Chinese restaurant. No Coke. No Pepsi. Tea. Only tea. Hot. No sugar."

The couple scooted their stools closer to the wall. They mumbled something Maddie couldn't hear.

The waiter's voice rose. "No. No tea now. Only water for you. You get yourself." He threw his arm toward the counter along the far wall, then grabbed their menus and stormed toward Paul and Maddie.

Paul cleared his throat as the man came to a stop by their table. "We'll have tea, please. No sugar."

He threw the menus onto the table and gave a loud "humph." Without another word, he strode over to the far counter, snatched up a teapot and two cups, and marched back to the table. He slammed them down, yanked a pen from the pocket in his apron, and jabbed the instrument at Paul. "You eat?"

"Yes, please."

"Humph." He switched the pen to his other hand.

Maddie noticed that he had no paper. Apparently, the pen was for gesturing, not for taking down orders.

The waiter wiped his palm on his stained white apron and glared down at them. "Speak up. Tea get cold."

Paul opened the menu. "We'll have mu shu. And —"

The waiter slammed his hand down on the menu. "You read? No mu shu." He flicked his pen under Paul's nose. "You have house special chow fun."

Paul scooted back. "Okay. And soup?"

The waiter shoved the pen into the pocket of his apron. "You have chow fun, won ton soup, fried rice." He snatched the menu and threw it onto the table next to them.

Paul slapped his hands together. "Sounds good." The man glowered at them for a moment longer, then walked over and shouted down the dumbwaiter. He thudded down the stairs.

Maddie giggled. "Wow, that was something. Did your friend at work warn you about him?"

Paul shook his head. "I guess the walls are right."

"The walls?"

Paul motioned toward some writing Maddie couldn't read. "No Booze. No Milk. No Coffee. No Fortune Cookie. No Jive."

"Does it really say that?"

"Would I make something like that up?"

Maddie smiled. "Yes."

Paul ruffled her hair. "You know me too well. But in this case, I'm only reading."

"This place really is something. It's like watching a show for free. Or almost free."

Paul shrugged. "Some show. But it's plenty cheap. I got a glimpse of the prices before that guy grabbed my menu."

"Do they really not have mu shu?"

"Who knows?"

Maddie giggled again. "Oh no, here he comes again, I think. Look out."

Footsteps pounded up the steps. Then the waiter appeared. The dumbwaiter creaked. A shout echoed from downstairs.

The waiter opened the door of the dumbwaiter, took out three bowls of food, and plopped them onto the table of the other couple. He turned toward Paul and Maddie. But before he took two steps, the man at the other table raised his arm. "Excuse me. Sir?"

Paul moved forward and whispered in Maddie's ear. "You'd think he'd know better."

"Shh. Listen."

"I asked for brown rice." The man's voice turned nasally.

The waiter stopped short. Slowly, he turned back to the other table. "You want brown rice?"

A stool squeaked. "Yes."

Maddie watched the waiter stroll back to the other table and pick something up. She squinted. The soy sauce. It must be.

He was holding it now, unscrewing the cap. Then he poured it over the rice. "There. You got brown rice."

The man at the table didn't say another word.

The waiter strode over to Paul and Maddie again and scowled. "Napkins there." He pointed to a pile of white on the counter. "Get yourself."

Paul nodded. "Of course."

He crossed his arms over his chest. "Chopsticks only. No forks." He uncrossed his arms and jabbed a finger at Maddie. "Girlfriend want fork?"

The smile froze on Maddie's face. Her throat closed. "Oh no. I'm not. Not his girlfriend."

The waiter stared at Paul for a long moment without saying a word.

Maddie's heart thudded. *It's not a date. No one would take a date here. He should know that. He shouldn't think . . .*

Finally, the waiter scowled. "No girlfriend." He clucked his tongue. "What wrong with you? She pretty. She nice. She not sister?" He waved his hand in the air.

Paul shook his head. "No."

"Stupid man."

One of Paul's chopsticks fell and clattered on the floor. He reached down to get it.

The waiter turned on Maddie. "He not good enough for you? Huh? Too cheap?"

Maddie forced a grin. "No, it's not that." *Not at all.*

"Ah, you wait for handsome Chinese man." He threw out his chest and patted it. "Wise woman."

Maddie laughed, for real this time.

The loud squeak of the dumbwaiter announced the arrival of more food. The waiter walked over and retrieved a soup tureen and two bowls from the hole in the wall. He returned and dropped the bowls onto the table and put the soup next to them.

Maddie raised her eyebrows as the waiter dished out a bowl of soup and placed it carefully before her. Then he filled Paul's bowl and held it up. "No soup for stupid man." He marched away with Paul's bowl.

Paul watched, silently, as the waiter disappeared down the stairs. "I'm gonna kill that guy at work."

"Ah, come on, it's not that bad."

"Yeah, well, you have soup."

"And it's very good." She dangled her spoon in front of Paul's face.

"You're cruel."

"Hey, that's the closest I've come to getting asked out in a long time."

"Gimme a break."

She giggled. "I told you you'd have to pay."

"But not with my soup. I'm hungry." He raised his hands in the air in mock surrender. "Had I but known the price would be so high . . ."

Maddie slurped a spoonful of broth and licked her lips. "At least it can't get much worse, can it?"

Paul groaned. "Unless a stupid man can't have chow fun either."

"You're not stupid. You're just —"

Paul pressed his finger to her lips. "Not another word. The waiter was right."

And in that moment, more than anything, Maddie wished she could see the look in his eyes when he said it.

It was quiet here, on this side of the water. No voices, no sound. Just the mist and the dampness and swirling eddies of darkness. It should have been soothing. It should have been peaceful. But something was eerie in the silence. Something wasn't right. She had forgotten something important. It nagged at her, scratching at the corners of her mind, digging in the blackness, calling.

"Remember."

Paul is there.

He was there.

Now.

Then.

He can't save me.

He did.

Not then.

Yes, then it was dark, like now. With hope dim, wavering. Gone. And the darkness came like a black wave. Filled with truth and lies. Exposed.

He had seen it all.

She had lived it.

"Remember."

Why? I don't want to go back. Not then.

"Remember."

Leave me alone.

"Remember."

Don't leave me alone . . .

Maddie closed her eyes and let the music flow over her, soft, deep, poignant. Violins, a bass, trombones played gently in the intervals. She recognized them all. And then the cello, haunting, longing. She opened her eyes.

The theater lay in folds of darkness. Paul sat beside her. She could feel him there, sitting stiffly, though she couldn't see his face. Was he thinking about the music or the waiter at the Chinese restaurant? Or was he recalling the way the lights twinkled over the city as they had stood at the lobby window before finding their seats? He'd described every light to her — the twin globes of taxis bobbing up and down hills, the shimmering beacons of boats out on the bay, the fat yellow of streetlamps, and far away, the glow of the Bay Bridge, like a diamond necklace against the black velvet of the night.

"Would you like to live in the city someday, Maddie?"

She stepped closer to the window and placed her hand on his arm. "No. I'm a country girl. You know that." She frowned and glanced up at him, suspicious. "Hey, was that a line?"

He grinned at her. "Was it a good one?"

She slapped him on the shoulder. "Oh, you!"

They'd gone to their seats, then. And he'd described the folds of red cloth on the walls, the precise seating in the orchestra, and the types of instruments he saw. And, from what Maddie had heard since, he hadn't missed one. Which was a good thing, because tomorrow, her mother was sure to grill her about everything she'd seen.

The music changed to an eerie wavering of violins. Sad and soulful.

Yes, I feel it. The longing. The loss. The knowledge that what could have been will never be. What should have been was gone forever. *Oh, God . . .*

But He wasn't there. Not in this darkness. Not in this yearning. She had lost sight of Him too. In feelings of betrayal. In questions that could not be answered. But the feelings had faded a little, and the questions had become but a murmur in the distance. Because that's what God had become. Distant. Out there, somewhere beyond her reach. Once, she loved Him. Maybe she did still. But it was hard to be sure in the pain, the loneliness. Hard to be sure when it seemed that He'd turned His back and walked away. *God?*

The violins silenced. A piccolo trilled. Maddie swallowed and tried to push the music from her mind. But she couldn't. She never could. Her mother could sit for hours, listening to the lilt of the piccolo, sitting perfectly straight and still as the violas swayed and the clarinets hummed. She would study every nuance, every strum, every vibration of string. But for Maddie, music always mixed with darkness. And the questions came, the doubts, ever since she was a little girl and her mother would snap her fingers, point to the sheets of music on the stand before her, and demand she follow along.

"You must hear it in your head, Madison. You must sense it. Make it your own." Her mother's hands would tremble, just slightly, as if a chill had passed through them and was gone. "Focus, Madison. Because someday you may not have the sheets to read anymore. All you will have is the *musique.*"

And the darkness. Her mother would never say the final words, but Maddie heard them anyway. Always. On the edges of the music rode the fear.

And now, someday had come.

And all Maddie had done — from sniffing gardenias, to rearranging drawers, to practicing walking in the dark — none of it mattered. Not really. None of it had done a thing to beat off the fear. But still she tried. She planned, believing it would make a difference. But it didn't. The music told her that. It sang to her of dark truth. Sang and skittered away, mocking her.

It was ironic, really, how blindness had passed her mother, who had prepared her whole life for it, and settled instead on Maddie. And Malcolm. Malcolm hadn't wanted to be a musician either. All he'd ever wanted was to play ball.

The melody soared around her as the bass deepened, the violins began again, and a flute warbled like a sparrow falling from flight.

God, how could this happen to me? Why? Wasn't Malcolm's fate bad enough? Wasn't his loss enough for us all? I don't want to lose everything too. I don't want to go home to Boston. I want to stay here and live. I want to do the things I've always planned. Finish school, drive a car, climb to the top of Vernal Falls at Yosemite. God, do You even hear my cry? Or am I alone? All alone in this darkness.

Maddie sighed as the music rose to a crescendo, then fell to a single instrument. A cello played slowly — throbbing, aching with sound.

Mom should hear this. She'd love it. Maddie shivered. *But I just want to get out.*

Paul moved closer to her and whispered, "Are you okay?"

She nodded.

"Cold?"

She shook her head.

Then it was over. The music stopped. The lights went up. Intermission. Finally. She had survived half a symphony without going mad.

"You look like you're going to be sick."

She grimaced. "Thanks."

"The Chinese food giving you indigestion?"

Maddie rubbed her nose. "It's not the chow fun. It's the cello."

"What?"

"All right, I'll admit it. I don't like the symphony, okay? I hate it, I always have. Not very cultured of me, I know. But there you have it."

"Why didn't you say so?"

"In front of my mother, Mrs. Professional-Cellist-I-Live-For-Zee-Musique? And after you'd already bought the tickets? How awful would have that been?"

"Awful. You're right." He squeezed her knee. "But we don't have to stay. Come, let's go do something fun. I hear they have tea dancing at the Hyatt. Or we can take a walk along the wharf. What do you say?"

For a moment, Maddie allowed herself to imagine dancing in Paul's arms to the sound of a big band, or walking along the bay with the breeze feathering her hair and the sound of sea gulls above her. "Oh, that

162

would be wonderful." Her voice flattened. "But of course we can't."

"Why not?"

"Mom will know."

Paul made a sound in his throat. "She's not here."

"It doesn't matter. She'll make me tell about everything. Recount every last detail of every last moment. She always does."

Paul sighed. "I'm sorry. I didn't realize."

She rested her hand on his arm. "I know. It's just . . ."

He nodded. "I understand. We'll stay. You just wait here." He dropped his hand from her knee and stood.

She looked up. "Where are you going?"

He paused a moment before answering. "Come on, Maddie, do you have to know everything?"

Then she understood. Heat flushed her face. "Sorry. I thought only girls needed potty breaks."

Paul chuckled. "I'll be back in a minute." He ruffled her hair again.

"Stop that!"

"Sit tight." He stood, then disappeared up the aisle.

Maddie sat back in her seat and listened to the quiet rumble of voices around her. She focused on none but instead allowed her thoughts to wander up the aisle after Paul. He was a good friend. Kind. Thoughtful. He always had been, even as he was making dates with a dozen blondes, beating her at racquetball, or making fun of the way she always did her homework days in advance. She was lucky to have him, especially now. Maybe, if things had been different — if she hadn't been going blind, if there wasn't the specter of that old girlfriend hanging over them — their friendship could have turned into more. Maybe. Someday. She'd never let herself dwell on it. Their friendship was too precious to waste on wishful thinking. But sometimes she wondered if he knew how she felt, how she'd always felt. Would that have made a difference? It wouldn't now. Not anymore. It would only send him running.

She closed her eyes and tipped her head against the back of the seat. *Thank You, God, for Paul. And for his friendship, even though it can never be more. He is Your gift to me. I know that. And, maybe, with friends like him, and like Kelli, I can be okay. I can survive going blind. I just need Mom to never find out. Or at least not for a long time. A really long time. That's all I'm asking of You, okay? Just that. You can do that for me, can't You?*

The seat next to her creaked. Maddie

opened her eyes. "Paul?" She saw a flash of shimmering black. Heard the tap of a shoe on the floor. It wasn't Paul. It was a woman. A stranger.

Maddie sat up in her chair and faced the woman. She couldn't see her features but knew the woman was looking her way. She cleared her throat and pasted on a friendly smile. "I'm sorry, ma'am, that seat is taken."

The woman spoke in a voice that was not the voice of a stranger. It was familiar. Too familiar. Cultured and perfectly modulated. With a strained French accent. "You lied to me, Madison."

Her breath stopped. "Mom?"

10

No one answered.

But someone was there. Not a stranger, but her mother. Maddie knew it by the way she breathed. Deep, firm, and fierce.

Her mother's hand grabbed her arm. Pressed. Hurt her.

Betrayed. Again.

"Come."

A single word. The last one she wanted to hear. Or obey.

But she did obey. She had to. Her mother stood, her hand still tight on Maddie's arm. She stepped into the aisle and dragged Maddie behind her. The seats were nearly full again. Maddie could hear the rustle of taffeta, the sliding of silk, as stragglers moved down the aisle past her.

Maddie tripped, stumbled.

Her mother slowed. Her grip trembled. And fear became a tangible thing. Both hers and her mother's. It twanged between them, louder even than the first strains of music that rose behind them. Notes, soft and creeping, chased her from the room as her mother flung open the door and pulled her into the lobby.

The door swung shut, muffling the music.

Then her mother was there in front of her. Facing her, all voice and hands and heat. "How dare you!"

"Mom."

Fingers pinched her arm again and shook her. "How dare you lie to me about this. This! Of all things." She swore in French. "Did you think I would not know, would not find out? I am your mother, Madison!" She dropped Maddie's arm and paced in front of her. "What shall we do? We must plan. You have seen the specialist, yes?"

"Yes."

"And it is Stargardt's. There is nothing he can do."

Maddie didn't respond. She didn't need to.

Her mother's voice raced on, quieter now, but just as agitated. "You were supposed to be past the danger point. I believed . . . I hoped . . ." She rounded on Maddie again, her voice raised. "How long has this been going on? When did you first notice? It is progressing. How quickly?" She battered

Maddie with questions, coming in quick succession. None of them answered. Most of them barely heard as Maddie stood, numbed, before the onslaught.

Her mother reached out, shook her again, and threw her hands in the air one last time, as if beseeching the heavens. "Ah, *ma cherie,* why did you not tell me zis? Why did you not confide in your own mother?"

A figure appeared behind her mother in the lobby. A figure that Maddie recognized. Paul. It could only be Paul.

He came closer.

Was that . . . ? It was. A splash of green and red. A single red flower in his hand. A rose. For her?

Maddie's throat closed.

"Answer me!"

Maddie blinked. It wasn't real. It couldn't be. Not her mother standing before her with fire in her voice. Not Paul with a rose trembling from his fingers. Not the city lights or the music or the too-rapid beat of her own heart. *Wake up.*

But she didn't awaken. The muffled music still played, the lights still twinkled, and her mother still stood there, breathing heat, oozing hurt.

Paul stepped up beside her and laid a hand on her shoulder. "Is something wrong?"

What could she say? How could she answer? The world is ending? The sky is falling? All my hopes are dead? Instead she said nothing, nothing at all.

Her mother was not so silent. "You stay out of zis, young man. Zis has nothing to do with you." Maddie saw a flash, a hand perhaps, moving toward him. "Zis is between Madison and me."

Maddie trembled. "Yes, it always has been, hasn't it?"

Paul didn't move. "Maddie?"

Her mother stepped closer. "How long has it been going on? You must tell me."

Paul cleared his throat. "What?"

"Madison?"

"She means my sight."

Paul shifted beside her. "Why are you here, Mrs. Foster? Didn't you have a meeting tonight?"

"Why? You have the gall —" She paused. She was shaking now. Maddie could hear it in her voice. "You want to know what I am doing here? I am finding out what my daughter has been hiding from me. Finding out that my daughter — my daughter! — is a liar. *Une menteuse!*" She choked on the last word.

Paul's arm dropped around Maddie's

169

shoulder. "I thought you were seeing about that cello."

Her mother sniffed. Was she crying? No, she couldn't be. Not Mom. She never cried. She rarely laughed. And yet, there was still that strange waver in her voice when she spoke. "*Oui.* I was. I am." She waved her hand in the air. And sniffed again. A sad sniff.

Maddie caught her breath. She *was* crying. She had to be. Mom, crying for her. Maddie reached out.

"The maestro insisted I hear the cello in action. It is being played tonight." Her mom's voice steadied. "It was supposed to be a pleasant surprise to see me here." She turned again toward Maddie. "But you could not see me, could you, Madison? Could not tell my face from the face of a stranger." She paused, and when she spoke again, her voice was strained, filled with a hurt that was like a knife in Maddie's soul. "It has happened, what we have feared your whole life. How, how could you not tell me?"

Because of Malcolm. How could you not know it was because of him?

Maddie lowered her chin, studied the floor at her feet, and tried to discern the patterns of darkness and light. "No, Mom, it's what you've feared."

"And I was right to fear."

Maddie fell silent. Wisps of music drifted through the closed door. A woman stacked programs behind her. She listened to the tap of paper on glass. Beside her, Paul squeezed her shoulder, but he didn't speak. No one did.

Had she been wrong? Maybe, but fear was a strange thing. It whispered of what-if and what might be. It painted pictures and called them truth. It lured you in, held you captive. It had held her mother captive, and Malcolm, and her. And now it came again, choking, overwhelming, drowning, and tinged with guilt.

A hand touched Maddie's arm. Fingers cold and shaking. And then she could feel her mother straightening, stiffening. She knew what was coming now, knew it before her mother opened her mouth and spoke the next words.

"You are coming home. *Immédiatement.* We will deal with this together. I know what to do."

Maddie stepped back. "No."

"I shall speak with Joshua Freeburg. You can work at the factory, counting inventory, or some such thing. You can do that blind, at least." She nodded. "We will get through this. We will be okay."

Maddie folded her arms and turned away. "Like Malcolm?"

Her mother drew in a hissing breath. "That was different. Do not mention your brother. How could you? I loved your brother. And I love you."

Maddie's breath came in heavy spurts. She steadied it. "He didn't want to count widgets either. But you made him."

"I did not make him. I gave him opportunity, a chance for a real life."

Maddie lowered her voice to a whisper. "Is that what it was?"

"Must we discuss this here? *En publique?*"

Maddie trembled. "There's no one here but Paul. And that lady behind the counter."

Her mother snorted and seemed to shake her head. "How do you even know it is a woman?"

Maddie smiled, a tight, cold smile. "She's wearing pink."

Her mother sighed. "I know you wish to stay here. I know you wish your life to just go on, as it has been. But you cannot pretend, Madison. You must face the truth and do what is best. You have to come home."

"No."

"You cannot do this alone. You know that."

"I'm not alone."

Her mother's tone sharpened. "Oh, do not be a fool about this. You cannot think to saddle this boy and that roommate of yours with the care of a blind girl. How long do you think that will last?"

"Mom . . ."

Paul stepped forward. "Mrs. Foster, listen —"

She cut him off. "I know this is hard to hear. I am not trying to be cruel."

Paul whispered, "You are cruel. And —"

Her mother turned on him, her voice now hard and fierce. "This is not your place. I am her mother. You are, what?" She waved her hand at him. "A boy who used to play racquetball with her?"

For a moment, Paul didn't answer. And when he did, his voice was quiet. "A friend. I'm that, at least."

"*Un ami?* And you think to replace a mother?" She turned back to Maddie.

"You have no money, no job, no way to take care of yourself now."

Maddie raised her chin. "I have school. I'm almost done. Are you saying you won't pay my tuition anymore?"

"What use is that degree to you now?"

Maddie had said the same words herself, not so long ago, but coming from her mother's lips, they sounded so chilling, so final.

Paul squeezed her shoulder again. "I'll pay."

Maddie glanced up at him but couldn't discern his expression. "No, Paul. I can't —"

Paul backed away and faced her. "What? You've put in all this time and work to get your degree, and you're going to quit now? You can still see well enough to finish your classes. Don't give up, Maddie. Not when you're so close to finishing."

She could feel the pressure of his gaze, the tension in his words. And she could feel her mother's too. Both watched her, waiting. Both tugged at her and insisted she do the impossible. Insisted she be either blind or seeing. But not in-between. Not this awkward place where darkness still mixed with light. It was all confused and muddled and gray. That's what life was now — gray. Paul still lived in the white. Her mother in the blackness. And here she stood, stuck between.

Maddie looked at her mother, looked without seeing. "How could this happen to me?"

"You know the answer to that. We have always known."

Maddie turned away. "I just want to live. I just want to see, like a normal girl. Like everybody else. I want to graduate and get a job. I want to marry and have kids. I want to parasail and kayak and climb a waterfall. I want to do a hundred things that will never happen in Boston."

"Shall we pity you, then? Would you have him pity you?" Her mother motioned at Paul.

Maddie stiffened. "Pity only lasts so long." She said it by rote.

"And then real life is upon you."

Maddie sighed.

So did her mother. "I do not wish to say these things. They are harsh, I know. But they are true. Life changes, Madison. We must live it as it comes to us, *n'est-ce pas?* To pretend otherwise is to fool yourself." She turned toward Paul. "You must see that. You must understand. This is not something we play at. I know this."

"How do you know?"

Her mother's voice changed as she glanced away. "Because I have failed before."

Paul was pale, and he rubbed his chin. "But I'm not playing. We aren't playing."

Her mother crossed her arms. "Are you not? Are you going to get groceries for her, cook them? You cannot drop even a sock, move a piece of furniture. She will not see when you are happy or angry or sad. Are you going to shop with her? For everything? Bras, panties, perfume?"

"Maddie doesn't wear perfume."

"What is she going to do all day when you are at work? Sit there in the dark in her apartment and wait for you to return? What kind of life is that?"

Paul didn't answer.

Maddie waited. Her mother was right. Paul was good and kind and thoughtful. But he wouldn't stick around. All those other girls had found that out. A date or two and Paul moved on. Always. He wasn't one to stay for the hard stuff. He liked to play, have fun, and enjoy life. And there was nothing wrong with that. He deserved it. And he didn't deserve a burden like her. Not him. He deserved better.

Her mother's voice came again, this time soft, resigned. "You are not prepared to befriend a blind girl. You cannot be prepared to care for her as I can."

"But . . ."

She raised her finger and jabbed it at him. "Do not lead her on. Do not dare."

Her mother touched Maddie under the chin and lifted her face until Maddie could feel her mother's breath on her cheeks.

"Graduate, Madison. And then come home. It is best this way."

Maddie trembled. "And then?"

"You know."

"Paul?"

But Paul didn't answer. He didn't say another word.

11

Dozens of fat bulbs shone from the branches of an equally fat Christmas tree. It was extravagant, too much for the little apartment. It should have cheered her. After all, she could still see those lights, blurred and missing in the middle of her vision, but they were there, red, gold, green, and blue.

Maddie gripped her mug tighter until the heat penetrated her palms. Yes. She would enjoy everything while she could: the warmth, the smell of pine, the way the morning sun peered through the slats in the shutters and cast ribbons of light across the packages beneath the tree. It was Christmas. A day of promise, of hope, of — she drew a deep breath — of not worrying about what would happen next week, or the week after that. Today was a day to etch into memory every sight, every color, every image that would last her for the years to come. And today was a day to remember a Baby wrapped in rags, lying in a manger. Remember, and be thankful.

She took a sip of cocoa, then lifted her mug toward the nativity scene on the bookshelf near the door. A cheap thing, it was, plastic with bits of peeling paint. But it was hers. And by next year she wouldn't notice the paint peeling or the cheapness of the plastic.

"Happy Birthday, Jesus." She murmured the words, then stretched her legs across the couch. The scuffed toes of her slippers peeked back at her. She wiggled them and tightened the tie on her bathrobe. From the radio in the corner, Nat King Cole sang about chestnuts roasting on an open fire.

She sighed and glanced at the two red stockings hanging from the windowsill. The apartment had no fireplace, but it wouldn't be Christmas without stockings. Even though hers would hold only an orange, a pair of fingernail clippers, a mini calendar, and a book, just as it did every year. But still, there was something about starting Christmas morning with cocoa and stockings. It was a tradition she had hoped to someday pass on to her own children. But now . . . well, now she would be satisfied with just one more year of seeing the stockings hang, of watching the tree's lights glow, of noticing how the lights glinted in a dozen bright shards off the glittering silver-wrapped presents.

"Mom, are you coming?" Maddie called over her shoulder into the kitchen behind her. Mom had stayed for Christmas, despite the concert back in Boston. Stayed, not because she wanted to, but because her daughter was going blind. Maddie grimaced. At least Mom would be going back soon. Maddie needed the break.

"A moment, *s'il vous plaît.*"

The sound of a spoon tapping ceramic resonated from the kitchen. Then came the firm click of heels on the linoleum floor. A moment later, her mother appeared in the kitchen doorway with a steaming cup in her hand.

"What took you so long?"

"I brewed some Earl Grey. You know I cannot abide cocoa."

"It's tradition to drink cinnamon-spiced chocolate on Christmas morning."

Her mother frowned and took a quick sip of tea. "Cocoa was your father's tradition, God rest his soul." She smoothed her hand along the pleat of her immaculate turquoise skirt.

Maddie raised her eyebrows. Mom had a few favorite English expressions from her many years in Boston. This was one of them. She frowned. "He's not dead, you know." She said the words too softly for her mother to hear. It didn't matter, though. Her mother wouldn't have answered, even if she had heard. To her mother, running off to Italy with some "floozy dancer" was just as good as dead. Especially since John Foster had never come back. She glanced back. "You know, Mom, it's only us. You didn't have to dress up."

"One should always look one's best." She turned, and Maddie glimpsed the end of her mother's skirt caught up in the back of her pantyhose.

Maddie smiled. So Mom was human after all. She reached out and flicked the skirt free.

Her mother whirled. "What . . . ? Oh!" Her voice colored. *"Merci."*

Maddie tucked her scuffed slippers beneath her, leaned back on the couch, and took another sip of cocoa.

Her mother perched on the edge of the fluffy chair next to the couch. From the radio, some woman with a deep contralto began to sing about the little town of Bethlehem. Mom set her teacup on the coffee table. "There are two stockings filled on the sill. Did you do that, *ma chère?*"

Maddie nodded. "Of course ol' Saint Nick wouldn't forget you, Mom." She winked.

For a while, her mother didn't say a word. Then she spoke again, her voice quiet, thoughtful. "I was not expecting you to . . . not this year, with everything . . ."

"Santa can still shop."

"Of course. Thank you."

Maddie grinned. "Maybe you'd better see what he brought you first." She finished her cocoa and put her mug on the table. It clanged against the glass. She stretched out both hands to steady it. "Sorry."

Her mother stiffened.

Maddie grimaced. "Come on, let's open the stockings." Her tone was too high, unnatural. She cleared her throat.

Her mother stood. "I can get them, Madison."

Maddie's jaw tightened. "No, Mom, I'll —" She paused. Her mother was already at the sill, lifting the stockings. Maddie's voice lowered to a whisper. "I always pass out the stockings. Every year."

Her mother returned and laid a stocking carefully in Maddie's lap. "It does not matter."

It does to me.

Her mother went back to her seat and placed her own stocking on the table before her. "Things change. You will adjust."

Not yet. Not so soon. Maddie twisted the loop from the stocking around her finger and refused to look up. *And especially not today.*

"Soon enough others will have to do for you. It is the way it must be. I know."

Of course you do. Maddie shivered. Dependent. Needy. Helpless. The words slithered through her mind and twisted in her stomach. "Can we not talk about this today? I'm not blind yet, you know."

"You never wish to talk about it."

"It's Christmas."

"And suddenly your sight is restored?"

Maddie folded her arms across her chest and plunked her feet to the floor. "Let's just open the stockings, okay?"

Her mother pursed her lips. Maddie couldn't see it, but she knew the expression was there all the same.

Maddie reached into her stocking and pulled out a round, firm orange. She held it up and smelled it. At least some things didn't change.

Her mother followed suit, taking an orange, a pair of clippers, a copy of *Two From Galilee* by Marjorie Holmes, and a refrigerator magnet in the shape of a cello from her stocking.

The snappy voice of Bobby Helms burst from the radio as he sang his famous "Jingle Bell Rock." Maddie tapped her toe.

Her mother cleared her throat. "The garbage they put on the radio these days." She rose, strode to the table in the corner, and clicked off the radio.

"That's an old song, Mom."

"One I have never liked."

"If it's not classical, it's not music."

"I have never said that."

Maddie's lips turned in a wry smile. "Haven't you?" She bit her lip. She'd promised herself they wouldn't argue today. Not on Christmas. Not if she could help it. "Sorry, Mom." Maddie felt around inside her stocking for the clippers that must be in there. She touched the smooth cover of some book, then wiggled her fingers down into the stocking's toe. "I can't find the clippers."

"There are none this year."

Maddie withdrew her hand. "What? Why?"

Her mother neatly folded her stocking and placed it on the side table. She sighed.

And Maddie knew. Her mother planned to clip her nails from now on, and fix her hair, and pick out her clothes. Something solid and heavy, cold, settled in Maddie's gut. She reached in her stocking and pulled out the book. Its cover was plain except for a few rows of tiny bumps. She opened it. Inside, there were no words, only the bumps again. *Of course, Braille.* She slammed it shut.

"It is *Pride and Prejudice.* Your favorite." Her mother took the empty stocking, folded it, and placed it on top of her own. "I thought you would —"

Maddie shoved the book beneath a pillow on the couch.

"Do not pout, Madison. It does not become you."

Maddie didn't answer. *It's Christmas. Christmas! Maybe my last . . .* She turned away. It didn't have to be this way yet. Blindness as the center of life and identity. Every minute of every day. Nothing being as it was before. Nothing ever being good again. That's what happened to Malcolm. But it wasn't going to happen to her. Not like that. And not today.

Oh God, I can't do this. I can't. I won't.

But life came. It happened, and you took it as the silver-wrapped gift that it was. Pain in a pretty package. Darkness wrapped with loss and topped with a shiny bow. Did it really have to be that way today? Couldn't they just forget the fear, live as if tomorrow would stay away? Couldn't Mom give her that?

Please, Mom, it's still Christmas. The lights still shine on the tree, the air is still spiced with the scent of pine. Can we pretend today? For this one day. Please?

"Let's just open the presents, okay?" Maddie reached for a pink-wrapped parcel. She opened it to find a pair of bright pink mittens from Kelli and a Mac Davis 8-track. Next, she opened a box of Thin Mints from her aunt and a checkered hat and scarf from her Grandpa Ed.

Her mother opened the gold brooch that Maddie had picked out for her and a matching box of mints from her sister.

Maddie breathed out a long sigh. Everything was going to be fine now. Just like always. Mints from Aunt Melda, scarves from Grandpa, and if she guessed right, two or three bookmarks with Bible verses from Mrs. Tobias, her old Sunday school teacher. Tension oozed from her shoulders as she opened the narrow envelope and pulled out two shiny bookmarks.

"Here, Madison, let me."

The bookmarks vanished from Maddie's hand.

Fingernails tapped on plastic. "This one says, 'Cast all your care upon him; for he cares for you, 1 Peter 5:7.' And there is a picture of a tiny orange kitten held in a man's palm. The kitten's eyes are closed and —"

"And there are black paw prints all along the edges. Yes, I know."

"But . . ."

Maddie held out her hand. "Mrs. Tobias sent me the same one last year."

Her mother placed the bookmark on her outstretched fingers. "Now, the second one —"

"Let me see it." Maddie wiggled her fingers. "I can read it."

"Be reasonable, Madison."

"I can try."

Her mother reached out and lowered Maddie's hand. "Now this one has a picture of an angel with arms outstretched in the night sky. Shepherds are standing below on a hillside. The verse reads, 'Fear not. For, behold, I bring you good tidings of great joy. Luke 2:10.' The writing is very small. You will not be able to read it." She handed the bookmark to Maddie.

Maddie held the bookmark to the side of her vision, squinted, then turned for better light. But Mom was right. She couldn't read the writing, couldn't even make out the images of the shepherds and angels. She dropped the bookmarks on the table. "It doesn't matter."

Her mother remained silent.

Maddie picked up the next gift, a tiny package from Paul. He'd brought it the day before he'd left for his parents' house in Pacific Grove. She peeled back the paper to reveal a small glass bottle filled with pale liquid. She clutched it in her hand and felt the smooth glass press into her palm. Perfume. But why? Could he . . . ? No. Not after what happened at the symphony. Perfume didn't mean anything. Not any-more.

Maddie tucked the bottle, unopened and untried, into the pocket of her robe.

"One more, *cherie.* From me."

Maddie took the long, slim package from her mother's hands and carefully slid her finger beneath the taped seam. "What is it?"

"Open it."

Maddie smiled and pulled the paper from the packaging. She opened the box and folded back the tissue paper. Her breath stopped in her throat.

There, in the folds of smooth tissue, lay a shiny, all-white cane.

It should have been the perfect Christmas. It could have been, if he had only done what

188

was right. A fire crackled in the big stone fireplace. Multicolored lights twinkled from the big Douglas fir in the corner. Wads of shiny red and green paper lay scattered about the floor. He picked up a ball of paper and tossed it into the fireplace. For a moment, the flame roared up, then simmered back to a gentle burn.

He watched it, grabbed another wad of paper, and closed his eyes. He threw it into the fire. Light flared before his eyelids. He could still see it, could still tell when the fire went from bright to dull. He squeezed his eyes tighter. There. He bent down and reached for another wad of paper, felt with his fingers along the carpet until he found one. He lobbed it toward the fire. He heard it bounce against the stone and fall back. He reached out again, found it, and adjusted his throw. This time, he could not see the light change, but he could feel the heat. It fanned his cheeks and forehead, then diminished. And in his mind, he pictured the flames rising, leaping up, then falling back, just as they'd done before.

He opened his eyes and sighed. It would be awful to go blind. To have to only imagine a fire burning, a sun setting, a flower blooming. But a person could find a way to live through blindness. To survive. To even thrive. A person could feel the heat without seeing it. Maddie could feel it. He knew she could. He kicked a ball of paper toward the fireplace. It skittered and stalled inches from the hearth.

Paul turned his back to the flame. Blindness was bad, but it wasn't the end. So, why hadn't he told Mrs. Foster that? Why had he listened to her words and said nothing? What kind of man was he? What kind of fool?

Laughter echoed from the next room. Paul glanced through the doorway to see his brother, Pete, holding a square something in his hand and pushing it toward their father. Pete tapped a finger on the slim gray box. "Won't even introduce them until later next year. Prototype, this is. Look at it. Beautiful."

Paul moved away from the fireplace, toward the doorway. His brother was always going on about some new gadget he was designing at Hewlett-Packard.

"Look at this." Pete lifted the box and dropped it into his shirt pocket. "That's a first."

Paul leaned against the doorjamb. "Hey, bro, so who's this new love of your life?" He nodded toward the bulge in Pete's oversized shirt pocket.

Pete frowned and extracted the box. "It is not a joke. This calculator will change the world."

Paul held out his hand. "Well, let's see it then."

Pete studied Paul's hand for a moment, then slowly extended his own. "May I present the first programmable pocket calculator, the HP-65." He held it out like a jewel in a velvet case. "Don't touch."

Paul shook his head. "I wouldn't dream of it. So, how's this one any different from the last one you brought home?"

Pete widened his eyes and stared at Paul. "How's this different? Weren't you listening? It's *programmable*." He drew out the word in a long breath. "The HP-35 was the world's first handheld *scientific* calculator."

"Making the slide rule obsolete." Paul made his voice sound like a commercial.

Pete ignored him. "But this . . ." He drew the calculator closer to his chest and caressed it with one finger. "This is a whole new world."

Paul coughed. "So, how long have you two been dating?" He glanced at his father, and the man stifled a laugh.

Pete scowled and stuffed the calculator back in his pocket. "Longer than you've dated anyone, at least."

This time, Dad laughed out loud. "He's got you there, boy." He rose from his chair and clouted Paul's shoulder. "I'm as likely to get grandkids out of that there piece of machine as I am outta you." He shook his head. "Sorry state of affairs. Pitiable. And here I am, one foot hovering over the grave."

Paul and Pete both rolled their eyes.

"Same old wheeze." Paul crossed his arms.

"Same old whine." Pete patted the calculator in his pocket. "Long as you don't go get a steady girl, Paul, I'm safe. So don't be letting me down."

Paul swallowed the sudden rock in his throat. "I won't." He turned and walked back to the family room.

His brother's voice followed him. "Hey, what's wrong with you?"

He didn't answer. Instead, he wandered over to the window and pulled back the curtain. Outside, red poinsettias glowed in the circle of the porch light, a green lawn ran toward the street, and beyond that, the ocean crashed against jagged rocks. A few people in windbreakers with collars turned up meandered along the path beside the ocean. And beyond, a flock of gulls swooped toward the waves.

Paul let the curtain drop back into place and turned toward the Christmas tree.

There, his brand-new racquetball racquet sat propped against the bottom branches. He'd wanted this model — sleek, light, made of high-strength aluminum alloy — since it was first introduced in '71. Now, he wished he'd never gotten it. But he couldn't tell Mom that. He couldn't tell anyone.

Beside the racquet lay a new green sweater, a mug with the words *Hewlett-Packard* stamped on the side, and a box of Shrinky Dinks. Why he'd want plastic pictures to color and put in the oven to shrink, he didn't know. But his twin sister, Jenny, was always getting him some crazy new thing for Christmas. "It's to make up for Pete's boring gifts," she'd always say. Two years ago, she'd gotten him a whole set of Weebles, and last year she'd given him a little round beanbag that she called a Hacky Sack. "It's going to be all the rage, you just wait and see if it won't," she claimed. He liked the Weebles better.

He smiled and picked up the box of shrinky things. Maddie would have really liked Jenny. He'd always meant to get them together, just to see what schemes they'd come up with to torture him. But now things were different. A lot of old plans would have to be put aside.

"Eggnog's ready." Paul's mother stepped

into the room with a pitcher and a tray filled with paper Christmas cups. She set the tray down on the side table, then smoothed her hand over her short, frizzy hair. "A splash of real vanilla and lots of nutmeg. Just like you like it, Paul." She turned her head toward the kitchen. "Come on, Jenny. Paul wants you to play some carols for him on the piano." She winked at Paul.

He frowned. "Mom. You know —"

"Shh." She put a finger to her lips. "She'll play if she thinks it's you asking."

Jenny strode into the room wearing the cashmere hat he'd given her for Christmas. It clashed terribly with the bright orange pajamas she'd been wearing all day.

Paul almost smiled. It was good to be home. Even if his heart was only half here.

Jenny's strawberry blond ponytail swung beneath the hat as she jammed her fists into her hips and gave him a long stare. "Hey, grumpy."

"Be nice or I'll tell your friends about that ponytail and bunny slippers."

She stuck her tongue out at him. "They wouldn't believe you anyway."

That was probably true. Jenny may look cute with those fuzzy slippers and tiger stripes on her jammies, but she was fierce when crossed. Or when someone crossed her twin brother. Plenty of her friends had learned that. The hard way.

"So, are you gonna play with me?" She jerked her thumb toward the piano in the corner.

Paul grabbed a cup and poured eggnog to the rim. "No, I'm going to drink Mom's famous 'nog."

"Party pooper."

Mom settled onto the couch. "Play, 'O Come All Ye Faithful.' It's my favorite."

Jenny plunked the first couple notes. "I know. Is Dad coming?"

"Once he and your brother finish fiddling with that pocket thingy." She turned toward the doorway and raised her voice. "Honey. Jen's playing. Come on."

No one answered.

She huffed and stood up. "That man!" A moment later she stormed into the next room.

Jenny turned to Paul. "Listen, I'm meeting Lisa, Jodi, and her brother at the beach tomorrow night. We're gonna have a bonfire. Joe's bringing his guitar."

Paul gulped the last drops of eggnog from his cup, then set it on the table. "So?"

"Wanna come?"

"No."

"Jodi's blond."

"So?"

She snorted. "So, what's gotten into you?" She plunked her fingers down on the keys all at once. "You're gonna just sit around and sulk all week, are you?"

Paul poured himself a second cup of eggnog and took a long drink. "Yep." He crumpled the empty cup in his fist and tossed it into the trash.

"No Frisbee yesterday, no golf today, no beach tomorrow. You're a downright bore. You sick or something?"

"Who's sick?" Mom bustled into the room.

Sick? Yeah, maybe he was. Sick over what happened at the symphony. Sick over the way he'd let her down. Sick that he left her. There, with her mother, in that little apartment. That was enough to make anyone sick.

Mom hurried over and reached toward his forehead. "Do you have a fever, dear? Come, sit down."

He batted her hand away. "I'm fine, Mom. Jen's just joking."

Mom wrinkled her brow. She still looked young, despite the touches of gray in her hair and the wrinkles starting at the corners of her eyes. Laugh lines, she called them. But there weren't any laugh lines now, just those deep wrinkles in her forehead as she stared up at him. "I should have known when you didn't eat the snickerdoodles I made for you last night. They're your favorites."

"I'm not sick. It's just —"

"A girl?" His father's deep bass voice boomed from the doorway.

"Dad!"

Jen whirled toward him and stared.

His mother sighed. "Well, it would be about time." She patted his arm. "Is it a girl, dear?"

He stepped back.

His father crossed his arms. "Well, boy? You gonna prove that brother of yours wrong?"

Heat rose in Paul's face. "It's not like that. She's just a friend."

"Better be." Jen breathed the words so low that only he could hear her.

Mom's face brightened. "Oh, is it that sweet girl we met last year? What was her name? Maggie?"

"Maddie."

"I liked her. How is she?"

"Going blind."

"Oh no." Jen gasped. Heavy silence fell in the room, broken only by a single, minor note played by his sister.

He stared into the fire.

They waited.

He lowered himself to the edge of the couch. And then slowly, painfully, he told them about Maddie, about the symphony, about her mother's plans to take her back to Boston. He told them how he failed her in the end.

As he finished, his mother came and sat beside him. "Is her mother still here?"

"She goes back tomorrow, I think."

"Why don't you invite Maddie here, dear? For New Year's."

Jen turned from the piano.

Paul glanced up, saw the paleness of her face, and the look of warning in her eyes.

She stared at him, then at their mom. "Mom. I don't think . . ."

Paul dropped his gaze, then clenched his hands together in front of him. "She won't want to sit around and play bingo with us anyway."

His mother slapped his arm with her fingers. "Pish posh. Why ever not?"

Paul straightened. "Didn't you hear me, Mom?" His voice rose and cracked. "She's going blind. She won't be able to even see the numbers on the cards."

"What kind of fool boy did you raise there, Mama?" His father's voice rattled from the chair near the doorway.

Paul's head shot up.

His father sat back in the chair and glared at him. "Been playing bingo at New Year's since you were knee-high to a gnat. Should know by now that it ain't about putting buttons on numbers. It's about having a good time together. She can still do that, can't she? Well?"

Mom put her arm around his shoulder. "He's not an idiot. He's just a little slow." She ruffled his hair. "Now, go call the girl, dear, and invite her over."

"She'll think I'm pitying her."

Jenny banged on the piano keys again. "Think, Paul."

He scowled. "Whaddaya mean?"

Pete sauntered in. "Just do something, already, man. Or we won't be able to stand you."

Paul grimaced and stomped into the other room. He glanced at the phone on the wall. Mustard yellow, with numbers worn off from dialing. He stared at it for a full thirty seconds. Then he turned and walked away.

12

It took Paul five days to pick up the phone and call Maddie. Five days that strung out like an eternity. Days of his mother tut-tutting, his sister's baleful glares, his brother's loud calls from across the room to "be strong" and "hold out" as Pete continued his affair with the programmable calculator. But finally, Paul gave in. He gripped the phone tight and shoved it against his ear. It rang a half a dozen times before someone answered.

"Maddie?"

A moment of silence. Then a voice, high and strained. "Paul? Thank goodness it's you."

"Kelli?"

"I've been calling your apartment ten times a day. Where are you?"

Paul caught his breath. "What's happened? What's wrong?"

"I knew something was going down. Her

mother was meeting with people at school, department heads, and I don't know who all."

"Is she still there?"

"No. But she's coming back next week."

"So soon. Why?"

"She's graduating."

"Who?"

"Maddie. Did you know?"

He frowned. "Of course. In June."

Kelli's voice grew louder. "Not in June. Now."

Paul pressed the phone against his ear. "But . . ."

"I tried to call you."

Paul swallowed. His head spun. He pressed his hand into his forehead and forced himself to focus. Kelli was wrong. She had to be. Maddie couldn't be graduating yet. She had a whole two quarters to go.

Kelli's tone sharpened. "I'm telling you, there's got to be some jive going on 'cause as soon as her mother leaves, first thing Maddie tells me is that she's graduating, then she spends half the night baking."

"Baking?" Sweat broke out on Paul's palms. "Maddie doesn't cook."

"Don't I know it. But I've got three cakes, a loaf of bread, and half a dozen doughnuts that say otherwise."

He wiped a palm on his pant leg, then switched the phone to his now-dry hand. "That's serious. Where is she now?"

"In her room again, with the door locked."

Paul paced in front of the table that held the phone. "She's not reorganizing drawers again, is she?"

"Hardly. She went out this morning and returned with more bags than she could carry. Something's up. I thought you ought to know."

"I'll be there in a little over an hour. Maybe two."

Silence answered him.

"Kelli?"

He heard her hesitation. Then she spoke. "I don't think she'll see you, Paul."

His thoughts shot back to that night at the symphony. But no, Maddie wasn't like that. Maddie wouldn't hold a grudge. "She'll see me. Even if I have to beat down the door."

Paul dropped the phone back in the cradle and strode toward the front door. Halfway there he paused and grabbed his keys off the hook in the hallway. A few stray notes plunked from the piano in the family room. Paul raised his voice to a shout. "Mom. Dad. I'm going out. Be back tonight."

His dad sauntered out of the kitchen and

stopped in the hall. "Going to get that girl, are you?"

Paul spun toward him. "You a mind reader now?"

His dad chuckled. "Naw, just a jack rabbit. Long ears, you know." He tapped a finger to his left ear. "Besides, I've a bet on with your mom." A grin split his face. "Looks like I'm getting rhubarb tonight." He rubbed his hands together, turned on his heel, and headed back to the kitchen. "Honey, fire up the oven. You've got a pie to bake."

Paul twirled the keys on his finger, then headed toward the door. Those two — married thirty-three years and they still made each other laugh. No wonder he never dated anyone for more than a couple weeks. His parents had set the standard too high. For a few dates, he could get by on the thrill of emotion, the newness of a pretty face. But then reality set in. Discomfort and irritation, like the feel of a shoe that will never fit right. His parents, though, they fit together. Comfortably. As if the shoe had been fitted specially to the foot that wore it. Only God could do that. And time. And a love that was worn around in the everyday comings and goings of life, not just brought out on special occasions. He'd never thought he could feel that way with anyone. Except Samantha. Until Maddie. And now . . . He grabbed his coat, shoved open the front door, and jogged to his car.

Paul slipped his key into the car door and stopped. He rested his forearm against the roof and stared out over the ocean. Of course. That's where he'd been wrong. Love wasn't an emotion that helped one through the trials of life. It was a bond, a way of being, a force that was built from the very breath of God, built on the ordinary, commonplace ins and outs of daily life.

Isabelle Foster had tried to scare him with her talk of trips to the grocery store, of lonely apartments, of counting steps from door to car. And she'd succeeded, for a time. But, with God's help, those moments would not be burdens to threaten love but would be the very threads from which the fabric of love would be woven. That was the truth of it. It wasn't trials or hardships or difficulties or even blindness. It was the weaving of lives together. His and Maddie's. That's what mattered.

Paul banged his hand on the top of the car, then flung open the door and swung inside. He backed the car from the driveway, then shot forward down the road with a squeal of rubber on asphalt. A mile later, he slowed. Maddie would think he'd lost his mind if he barged in on her like this. Or worse, she'd think it was pity. No, he'd have to take it slow, easy. They'd been friends for a long time. To be more would be tricky. Especially now.

By the time he reached Maddie's apartment, Paul had composed his thoughts and emotions. He'd barely rung the bell when the door flung open and Kelli practically pounced on him before he could enter.

"I thought you'd never get here. What took so long?"

Paul glanced around the apartment. The Christmas tree was still up, though the branches looked dry. An empty mug sat on the coffee table, and Mac Davis blared from the 8-track player in the kitchen. "It's a long drive from Pacific Grove."

"Well, if she'll listen to you, it'll be worth the drive. I mean, why would she do it?"

"What?"

"Graduate early. Heaven knows she doesn't want to go back to Boston. What's she thinking? Wasn't she trying to get a job? What happened? You guys didn't have an argument, did you?" Kelli spoke so fast that her words ran together in a blur of sound. "Maybe it was something her mother said. That woman's strung so tight I could play *her* as a cello. Seriously." She twisted the end of her pink belt around her finger as she followed Paul through the hall, jabbering the entire time.

The sounds of Mac Davis faded as the music of James Taylor roared from behind Maddie's door, drowning the last of Kelli's questions. Paul paused and glanced back at Kelli. "Okay, I'll take it from here."

Kelli remained at his elbow.

"I mean, you should go."

"Oh, yeah." Kelli nodded, let the belt untwine from around her finger, and hurried toward the kitchen. "Good luck." She called the last words over her shoulder, then disappeared.

Paul pounded on the door. "Maddie, you in there?"

"Paul?" A rumble sounded from behind the door, followed by quick footsteps. The door swung open.

He didn't know what he'd expected, but it wasn't this. He'd prepared for blotchy cheeks, red-rimmed eyes, or perhaps the stony silence of anger. But instead, Maddie stood there with her favorite daisy shirt covered in splotches of multicolored paint, her feet bare, and a paintbrush in her hand. She smiled up at him. "What are you doing here?"

"I, um, well . . ."

She strode over, turned off James Taylor, and returned to the door. "So? Why are you here?"

Paul rocked back on his heels. "Well, I guess I'm finding out if the rumors are true."

"What rumors?"

He rubbed a bit of paint off the end of her nose. She was so like . . . so like . . . Maddie. Just regular, normal, fun Maddie. He licked his lips. "Kelli said you're acting weird."

"That why you came over? To see the weirdo?"

Paul's face turned hot. "Uh . . ." He straightened. His eyes narrowed. "Wait a minute. She said you've been baking."

Maddie glanced down. She scuffed her toe over the carpet. "You caught me. But I'm not baking anymore."

"Aha!" He searched her face. "Looks like Maddie. Sounds like Maddie." He sniffed. "Sure doesn't smell like Maddie though. Might be an alien invasion."

"Oh, you." Maddie stepped back and flicked the paintbrush at him. A narrow spray of paint dotted his shirt. "Oops, sorry."

"Clumsy like Maddie." He studied the

expression on her face. It was Maddie all over, except . . . except she was different too. There was something forced in her laughter, something dark behind her eyes. She hid it well. If he hadn't known her for so long, he would have missed it altogether.

She scowled at him. "I am not clumsy."

He touched a finger to a speck of blue paint on his sleeve. "Really? It's Paint Paul Night, is it?"

"If you say so."

He rubbed a line of blue paint across her cheek. "I don't."

"Well, come on in and see for yourself." She moved to one side and made a sweeping gesture with the paintbrush.

Paul stepped into the room.

This, definitely, was not like the Maddie he knew. A dozen or so paintings, if you could call them that, were propped against every surface. A tall canvas on the bed; two small watercolors on the dresser; some black sheets, marked with something that looked like colored chalk, were scattered on the floor under the window. And on the chair, two small canvas paintings sat at odd angles. He walked over and picked one up. The picture resembled a lopsided tomato riding a horse. He glanced at it, then back at Maddie. "What's this?"

She strode over and waggled the thin paintbrush under his nose. "What do you think? It's art."

He threw her a sidelong glance. "Is that what you call it?"

Her lips turned up in that funny half-smile he loved. "Yes, I do. And that one" — she stabbed her brush toward a picture of a lumpy, brown mass with something the color of carrots sticking from its top — "is of you."

Paul swallowed and made a face. "What happened to me? Did I melt?"

She stuck out her tongue at him. "Haven't you heard of Picasso? Besides, I'll have you know that these will be very valuable someday."

"As what? Archery targets?"

Maddie folded her arms across her chest. Her tone softened and grew quiet. "As the final efforts of a blind girl, of course."

The smile faded from Paul's face. Here it was then — the truth, or at least a glimpse of it. His voice lowered to a whisper. "Come on, Maddie. Don't say that."

She moved to the edge of her bed, sat down, and looked into his eyes. "If I'm going to paint, I've got to do it now."

"And bake?"

"Now."

"Maddie . . ."

She held up her hand to stop him. "You know I'm right, Paul. What other chance will I have? Do you think there will be any baking or painting or walks by the ocean or even trips to the store once I'm back in Boston? There will be nothing." She turned her face away. "Nothing that matters anyway."

He sat beside her. "It can't be that bad."

"How would you know?"

He sighed. "I don't. But there's got to be something we can do. I could —"

"Shh." She turned back and touched a finger to his lips. "Don't."

Paul fell silent. He knew she was thinking of the symphony. And so was he.

"Kelli told you I was graduating early."

"Yes." He choked on the word.

"And you want to know if it's true. And why."

"Yes."

She stood and moved away from him. "It's true. I have to. I can't see the pages of the books anymore. I can't tell what I'm writing. I can't see the professors' notes on the board, even from the front row. The darkness is growing. I can't stop it. And I don't have time to mess around with another quarter."

"But . . ."

"Mom worked it out with the school. How I can graduate now. I've done all my core classes already anyway."

"But . . ."

"They're making an exception for me because of, you know." She wiggled her paint-covered fingers in the direction of her eyes.

"But . . ."

She spun back toward him. "What does it matter to you? What's another few months to you? Huh, tell me that."

He searched for something to say, something that sounded strong and convincing. *I love you and never want you to go.* She would never believe that. *I want you to stay, forever.* She'd think he was crazy. *We could be like two old shoes.* She'd know he was crazy then. *I'll take care of you.* That would come across as pity for sure. Or worse, a lie. He glanced up.

Her gaze slipped down, away. "Or shall we pretend June will never come? Would that be better?" Her voice grew soft, pained. "We'll go on with our lives, me taking classes, you busy with your work. We'll eat pizza, study late, and make midnight runs for ice cream."

Yes. Exactly. Except . . . He couldn't speak

the words. Not out loud at least.

She dipped her paintbrush and made a long black stroke across the canvas. For a moment, she glanced up at him, and he saw something in her eyes. A longing. Yearning. And something more. "Maddie?" He breathed her name, willing her to confirm what he saw, praying that she'd tell him the truth. Just this once. *Maddie, do you love me?*

She closed her eyes. "Those days are gone. I can't go back. I wish . . . No, I can't."

"We'll find a job for you." It sounded weak, stupid, even to him.

Maddie didn't even favor him with a look. "You know my mom is right about that. No one will want to hire a girl going blind. Do you think I haven't tried already?" A sad smile, straight and not lopsided, brushed her lips and then was gone. "So, shall we pretend, Paul? Shall we forget that I'm going blind?"

He sat on the edge of the bed. "No, Maddie. But still . . ."

"She's coming back for me. And then everything will change."

He pushed the heels of his hands into his thighs and straightened his elbows. "But she's not coming back today, right?"

Maddie looked up, startled. "No."

Paul nodded and stood. "Then we still have today. And tomorrow. And the day after that. Let's not waste them. Come on."

"Where?"

"To my parents' place in Pacific Grove."

"What?"

"For New Year's."

Maddie tossed her brush into a cup of colored water. Her eyebrows rose. "You've got to be kidding me. All this talk, all for a New Year's invitation?"

He shrugged. "You coming?"

"All right." She stood there for a moment without moving. Then she took the lumpy carrot picture and held it out to him. "Here, this is for you."

He stared at the awful painting. "Thanks."

"You're welcome."

He took the painting and balanced it on one finger. "So, you think you'll get rid of me just by giving me one ugly painting?" He relaxed and put his arm around her shoulders. Yes, this was the Maddie he knew. This was the Maddie he loved.

She moved closer to him. "What? You want more?"

"Of course I do." *You have no idea.*

It was coming. The thing she feared and hated. The thing that almost cost her every-

213

thing. It swirled in the blackness, breathed in the darkness, called her to remember.

No. I don't want to go back. I don't want to recall.

But it didn't matter what she wanted. It hadn't then. It didn't now.

She drew a breath. Rattling. Searing. A half-breath and no more.

I'm drowning.

In her own breath. And in the threat of memories she didn't want to recall.

Why? Why must I relive it all?

But she knew why. This darkness that pressed around her now, this murmuring water, this swirling black, was brother to the darkness then. They were the same. And there was something she must remember, something important that happened then that mattered, even now. What was it? There was nothing then but fear. And Paul. And an ocean filled with black doubts.

And denial.

Yes, there was that too.

She had been so close. To freedom. To truth. To love. If only she had known.

The water rose around her. Suffocating. Icy.

Lord, help! I can't breathe! I can't fight my way through the waves.

Something cold pressed into her chest.

Pressed and held.

Another labored breath. A stab of pain.

Lord!

It came then. A voice from far away, outside the darkness. So slight, so distant, and yet she could discern the words. A man's voice.

"There's nothing more we can do. Her lungs continue to fill with fluid."

Fluid. Of course.

The waves swelled and broke over her.

13

Paul leaped from the corner of the hospital room. "Maddie, no!" He rushed forward.

Maddie coughed, sputtered, gagged on her own breath.

"Lift her." The doctor's voice penetrated Paul's senses. "Tilt her head."

The nurse jabbed her hand behind Maddie's neck and pulled her up. A few inches. So little. Yet enough. Maybe.

Maddie's chin angled up. She coughed again. Spittle peppered her lips. Another breath shredded the air.

Paul shivered. *Maddie . . .*

"Easy." The doctor stepped closer and listened to her breathing. His brows furrowed. His jaw tightened.

Not like this, Maddie. Don't go like this. He couldn't speak the words aloud. Instead, they echoed in his mind. Echoed, and fell silent.

The nurse reached down and jammed a

finger into the bed's controls. "Endotracheal tube?" A harsh squeal filled the room as the bed adjusted upward.

Paul hovered at the foot of the bed, watching, waiting, not daring to voice the questions that raced through his mind. He reached out, then drew back.

The doctor glanced at Maddie, then back toward him before he spoke again. "Not yet. Increase the oxygen. It may be enough. For now."

The nurse nodded. Her lips thinned. "Don't worry. We'll keep a close eye on her."

Paul moved closer. "She'll be okay?"

The doctor stepped back. "Her breathing still isn't as smooth as I'd like." He took out a notepad, scribbled something on it, tore off the page, and handed it to the nurse. "Give her this if her breathing worsens. And call me."

"Of course, Doctor."

The doctor turned on his heels and left the room, but the nurse stayed. She held Maddie's hand and gazed into her face. She spoke, softly, quietly, as if Paul weren't even there. "Don't give up, honey. You've got people to live for. Just hang on a little while longer. You can do that, can't you? I'll be watching. Don't you worry about a thing." She placed Maddie's hand back on the bed, then smoothed the sheets over her.

Then something strange happened. Something Paul did not expect. The nurse gripped the railing on Maddie's bed. Her eyes closed. Her mouth moved. No words came, but he could hear them anyway. Hear them as clearly as if the woman was shouting in his mind. "Have mercy, Lord. Spare her. You're her only hope now. Only You can save her. I can feel her fear. I can feel mine. I don't know why it matters to me. But it does. Only You can take away the fear."

The word echoed between them. *Fear.* It kept him from Maddie now. Just as it had done before. So long ago. Too long. Not long enough.

The light is coming, Maddie. Don't fear the dark. Not anymore. But his words were useless. *Don't you remember? Everything could have changed that night. If only you would have let it. If only you'd not been afraid . . .*

The water receded. A little. Enough. And Maddie could breathe again. And remember. Yes, she could remember too. A wilting Christmas tree. A warm fire. The smell of baking bread. And corn. She remembered corn. The feel of the rough husks in her hand. The sharp whoosh of them stripping from the cobs. Tiny strings wrapping around her fingers. And behind her, the steady scrape of a spoon in a wooden bowl. Steady and calming and peaceful.

Then it came, whispering through the years. Tugging her back. Beckoning her to remember. And once again, she heard the voice of Paul's mother, a gentle rumble in her ears.

"So glad you decided to join us for New Year's, dear."

Maddie smiled and continued to shuck the corn. "Thanks for inviting me, Mrs. Tilden."

"Call me Rhena. You're doing us a favor, you are. Made that son of mine bearable. Should have seen him stomping around here with that long-faced scowl, refusing to have any fun."

Maddie shook her head. "Paul? I don't believe it."

"Well, we're just glad you're here. Practically had to twist his arm to get him to give you call, though."

Maddie stopped shucking. Her voice caught. "He didn't want me to come?"

Rhena snorted. "Heavens, no, I mean yes. Well, what I mean is that he wanted you to come very much. It's us he was worried about." She flicked her spoon toward the door. "Oops." She whistled.

A yellow lab trotted through the kitchen door, then stopped to lick up the bit of stuffing that had dropped onto the linoleum.

Maddie listened to the smack of the dog's lips and the whoosh of its tongue across the floor. She grinned. Never in her life had she heard a dog lick the kitchen floor. It was a messy sound. Full of wetness and primitive pleasure. It soothed her.

Maybe Paul did want her here. Maybe he didn't just invite her out of pity because she was going blind, her mother had found out, and her life was ending. Not just because all her hopes, all her dreams, were dead. Or maybe that was precisely why he'd asked her to come. She picked up another ear of corn. "Why did he invite me?" The words slipped out, quiet and trembling.

The spoon stopped scraping the bowl. "Oh, my dear, I don't need to tell you that." Rhena tapped her spoon smartly against the countertop and waved her hand toward the door. "Out you go, Rosie girl. No more messes to clean up here."

The dog wandered out.

Maddie peeled back another husk. "I thought, maybe, you know . . . he felt sorry for me?"

Rhena jabbed the spoon back into the bright yellow bowl. "Sorry? Whatever for?"

"You know." Maddie touched a finger to the side of her eye.

Rhena paused. "We aren't supposed to talk about that."

Maddie stopped shucking. "Oh."

"He's afraid we'll say something to embarrass you, of course. And probably we will. But you'll just have to forgive us. 'Cause truth is, Paulie didn't invite you out of pity." She chuckled. "Oh no, not by a long shot. And you can quote me on that."

Maddie smiled. "I told him I didn't want any pity."

Rhena dropped the spoon onto the counter then moved the bowl to a far spot on the kitchen table. "Why ever not?"

For a moment, Maddie didn't know how to answer. The question was so strange, unexpected. "I . . . well . . . I just want to be treated like normal, that's all."

Rhena laughed. "Normal? Who's normal? Take pity when you can get it, I say. 'Cause sooner or later we're all gonna need it."

Maddie twisted the corn in her hand. "What do you mean?"

Rhena pulled a stack of bowls down from a cupboard. "Hard things happen to all of us, this side of heaven. No one gets off easy. So, a little compassion, a little understanding, even a little pity can be a good thing."

"But . . ." Rhena didn't know, didn't understand. Pity was an awful thing. The worst. It . . . it . . .

Paul's mother walked over and placed her hand gently on Maddie's shoulder. "Just not all the time, right?"

Maddie shook her head. "Not all the time."

"Don't you worry, dear." She patted Maddie's arm. "God's got big plans for you."

"Big plans for a blind girl?"

"Jesus made the blind to see."

"He hasn't healed me yet."

"No, not yet. But He will. Someday. You just wait."

"And see?"

Rhena laughed. "That's right, dear. Wait and see."

Wait and see. Could she do that? Could she still believe that God could have plans for her? Even now? After all the unanswered prayers, or prayers that were answered in the opposite? Could she just trust? Believe? Probably not. But somehow, when she listened to the lilt in Rhena's voice, she wished she could.

Footsteps sounded in the doorway. "Dinner ready yet?" The voice of Paul's father boomed across the room.

Paul's mother heaved an exaggerated sigh.

"Oh, Earl, for heaven's sake."

"What?"

Rhena came closer to Maddie and whispered in her ear. "And in the meantime, dearie, count your blessings. Believe you me, there are some things you don't want to see."

Earl grunted. "Don't listen to her, girl. I'm a fine specimen of a man. Don't look any different than when I was twenty."

"You hush up and button your trousers." Rhena shook her head. "Lord help us."

Earl sauntered closer. "I'm just getting ready for the big meal." From the corner of Maddie's failing vision, she saw him pat his belly.

"And tuck in your shirt." Rhena looked away and muttered words only Maddie could hear. "Honestly, some days blind would be a blessing." She raised her voice. "No wonder Paul was afraid to bring Maddie here. Good thing she can't see what I can. Same as when you were twenty?" She snorted a laugh. "Maybe your pinkie toe. Probably not even that."

Maddie snickered.

"Thank the Lord I didn't marry you for your washboard stomach." She turned toward Maddie. "Should have seen him when we married. Right out of the military.

Spit shined, clean cut." Her tone grew louder again. "Wouldn't have needed to unbutton your pants back then."

Earl chuckled. "It's all your good cooking that's to blame."

Rhena waved at him and shooed him out. "I've heard it all before. Now go clean up before you scare Paul's girl away."

Paul's girl. Maddie dropped the corn in her hand. "Oh, I'm not . . ."

Rhena shushed her.

Maddie swallowed and fell silent. *Paul's girl. If only . . .*

"That's a good girl."

Maddie picked up the ear of corn and broke it in two. She gathered up the corn, carried it all to the sink, and dropped it into a large pot.

Paul's girl.

She pushed the words from her mind. And yet, all through dinner they still rang in her ears and made a hollow ache in her heart.

"B-2."

"Wait, Dad, we're not ready." Pete pulled out the chair next to him and patted the seat. "Sit here, Maddie. I've got your bingo card all ready."

Paul set down his cup of eggnog and hurried to the table. Too late. Maddie was already sitting next to Pete.

Pete grinned at him. "You had her for dinner, man. Besides" — he shifted toward Maddie and spoke in a stage whisper — "he can't be trusted, you know. If you aren't careful, he'll cheat you out of your rightful paper clips and bars of soap."

Maddie's eyebrows rose. "Soap?"

Pete laughed. "Prizes, of course. For the winners. If you're lucky, you might get a pack of Alka Seltzer." He rubbed his stomach and deepened his voice. "I can't believe I ate the whole thing."

Paul pulled out a chair opposite them. "Just make sure Dad can see her card."

"Of course. I know how the game works."

Dad coughed. "If you two jokers are ready, we'll get started."

Mom hurried in from the kitchen, carrying a tray of popcorn, pretzels, and a plateful of snickerdoodles, even though they'd just eaten. She spread them out on the table, then took a seat next to Paul.

Jenny sat at the end of the table with her bingo card ready. "Hurry up."

"Did you write in the box top, Earl?"

He downed a swig of eggnog. "Course I did."

"Let's see."

Jenny grunted. "Aren't we going to play?"

Paul shot a glance at her. "What's wrong with you?"

"Like you don't know."

"B-2." Dad's voice drowned out Jenny's answer.

"Wait, I want to see what you wrote." Mom snatched the box top from the bingo game and turned it over to the inside.

"I-59."

"Earl!" Mom swatted his arm with the box top.

Jenny huffed.

Dad dropped the bingo marker back into the bottom of the box. "Oh, all right."

"Hey, I had that one!"

Pete sat back in his chair and tilted toward Maddie. "Dad writes a few sentences in the box top every year. Just stupid stuff, like who was with us, what the weather was like — things like that." He glanced at his dad. "If it were me, I'd mention something about the new HP-65. First programmable pocket calculator ever. And here it is." He patted his shirt pocket. "The prototype shown to you before the rest of the world sees it." He scowled. "But no. Instead he writes about the sunshine and the fog." Pete gave a long-suffering sigh. "As if we don't get fog and sun every year."

Mom flicked open her glasses and placed

them on her nose. "We had rain last year. Says so right here."

Pete grimaced.

Mom pushed her glasses further up the bridge of her nose and tapped a spot on the box top. "You forgot to mention how sweet Maddie is. And she's such a dear." She stretched her hand toward Dad and wiggled her fingers. "Here, give me the pen."

Jenny groaned and jabbed her elbows into the table. "Come on, Mom."

"Do you have somewhere you have to be tonight, Jen?"

"No."

Paul sank lower in his seat. What would Maddie think of this crazy family of his, arguing over the start of a bingo game? As if dinner wasn't bad enough, with Mom telling that ridiculous story of him dressing as a daisy for his first-grade play, then dancing all over the stage because he had to go number one. Dad piped up with an excruciating description of Paul's first attempt at a mustache. Pete spent the whole time poking at that silly calculator of his and telling Maddie she "just had to try it." Only Jenny had been quiet.

Paul looked at Maddie. She was staring down at her bingo card, moving her head slightly to the left, then to the right, as if attempting to find an angle where she might be able to see the numbers.

The pen stopped scratching on the box top, then Mom looked up. "Ready."

Jenny scowled. "Finally."

Mom tossed her a snickerdoodle. "Not a good way to end the year, dear. Maybe some sugar will help."

Jenny sighed. "Sorry." She tried a smile. "It's just . . . well, never mind." She glared at Paul, then quickly looked away.

Dad raised his voice. "For the third time, B-2. And that's the last time I'm going to say it."

Paul pointed to Maddie's card. "She has that one."

Pete batted his hand away. "I know." He turned to Maddie. "He's a little overprotective, wouldn't you say? Is he like this up there in Palo Alto?"

Maddie grinned. "Not usually."

Paul growled.

"N-40."

He peeked at Maddie's card. She had that one too. But Pete didn't say anything. Paul tapped his fingers. Shuffled his feet.

Pete chuckled, then whispered something in Maddie's ear.

She picked up a small, round disk and placed it on the N-40 square.

Five minutes later, Paul's mother threw her hands in the air. "Bingo!"

Jenny jumped up and dug into the bag in the corner of the room.

Mom tilted back in her chair. "Kitchen sponges, please, dear." She looked at Dad. "Tell me somebody remembered to get sponges."

Jenny pulled a package out of the bag and waved them in the air. "Just like every year."

Mom pressed her hand into her chest and breathed a long sigh. "Thank goodness."

Dad grunted. "And you doubted me?" He slapped his hand on the table. "Clear your cards." He dumped the called numbers back into the bottom of the box and mixed them around with his hand. "Free one on the free one."

"That's the middle square."

"Paul!" Pete rolled his eyes. "She knows."

Maddie placed the tiny disk onto the center square without help.

"O-72."

"Second from the top." Pete muttered the words, then raised his eyebrows at Paul.

He looked away.

"I-22."

After ten more calls, Paul heard a low "pssst" followed by, "Bingo, you've got bingo."

"Bingo!" Maddie called out the word.

Jenny popped up again. She returned with a cheap framed photo of Monterey Bay and a chocolate bar. She handed them to Maddie.

Maddie took them, her fingers feeling the frame. "What's this?"

Paul glared at Jenny. How could she? What was she thinking?

Jenny turned red, her gaze refusing to meet his. She knew! What was she playing at?

Paul rose.

The others fell silent.

Slowly, Maddie's hands traveled over the picture. She felt the frame, the back, the smooth front. Then she touched the chocolate bar. Her brow furrowed.

Paul waited. His stomach twisted.

"I don't want this."

No one answered.

"Didn't Paul tell you?"

Heat crawled up his neck. His fists clenched.

"I only like chocolate with almonds."

Pete guffawed.

Mom giggled.

Dad slapped the table again. "Get the girl an Almond Joy. Don't want our guest dissatisfied with her candy bar."

Jenny said nothing. She only looked at Maddie. Hard.

Paul glanced at her, then back at Maddie. Maddie was smiling. Really smiling. And in that moment, Paul knew he had never seen anything so beautiful.

The night was clear but for a few high clouds. The air was crisp, but not cold. Maddie wore that fuzzy blue sweater. And her face shone in the moonlight.

After all the bingo prizes were won, the cookies eaten, the eggnog drunk, they had gone out on the porch — just him and Maddie. The moon shone in a thin crescent, casting shimmering light onto the lawn and tipping the ocean's waves with bright silver. A bicyclist rode by with a light shining from his handlebars. The breeze rustled the dry lilac bush beside them and made the clouds drift south.

Paul sat on the bench and beckoned Maddie to sit beside him. "You ought to see it." His whisper fell between them and drew her closer. He flung his arm across the back of the bench behind her.

She tucked one foot beneath her, then leaned back into him. She closed her eyes. "Are the stars beautiful tonight?"

He dropped his arm over her shoulder.

"Close your eyes, and maybe you'll see."

She grinned and obediently closed her eyes. "Tell me."

"The stars are shining like a thousand diamonds on a blanket of black velvet. The moon is just a sliver tonight, yet it glows like a shaving of silver light. And the ocean," he paused, "the ocean looks like someone sprinkled a million pearls over its surface. And . . ." He grimaced. "I'm not very good at this."

She opened her eyes and smiled up at him. "Go on, I can see it. Almost. Tell me more." Her eyes fell closed again.

He licked his lips. He didn't want to talk about the sky or the ocean or the stars. But he could describe the way the moonlight touched her cheek, how it glowed like golden ribbons in her hair. How it made her mouth look like . . . He stopped, his eyes riveted on the fullness of her lips, parted ever so slightly as breath escaped them. She was close, so close. So beautiful. If only . . .

She opened one eye. "You *are* bad at this. Here, let me try." She squeezed her eyes tightly shut and tilted her chin toward the sky. "Stars, scattered like dewdrops from the shores of heaven. So close that it seems like you could reach out and touch them.

And if you did, they'd be as cold as ice, and just as hard. But that one" — she pointed to a random spot in the sky — "isn't a star at all. It's an airplane."

"There isn't an airplane."

She stuck out her tongue. "Humor me. And look!" Now she pointed west. "There's a shooting star."

"Where?"

"Right there. I see it. Don't you? Make a wish. Quick."

A wish. Paul stared into the night sky. *Make a wish.* He glanced down. And then he wished. A great big, bold, impossible wish.

The door slammed open.

Maddie jumped.

Paul pulled back. His head whipped around to see Jenny standing in the doorway. He frowned. He should have known better than to wish on a fake star.

Jenny stared at them, her eyes narrowed, her fists jammed into her hips. "Come on. They're about to do the countdown on TV."

He blinked. "Countdown?"

Jenny scowled. "New Year's, silly. Times Square? The big ball?" She raised her hands and wiggled her fingers. "Lots of lights?"

Maddie sprang up.

Paul followed.

In the family room, the television blared.

Dick Clark's face beamed from the screen.

Jenny plopped onto the couch and tossed him a paper horn and a kazoo. He handed the kazoo to Maddie.

"Ten. Nine. Eight . . ." The numbers boomed from the television. His family joined in the count. "Seven. Six. Five . . ." He moved closer to Maddie. "Four. Three. Two . . ." She raised the kazoo to her lips. "One. Happy New Year!"

Everyone yelled out the words. Except him. And Maddie. She blew the kazoo. He swung her into his arms. Her chin tilted. His lowered. And he knew he would kiss her. Finally.

But at the last moment, she turned her head away.

14

I believe in heaven. I believe in Jesus. And yet, I dread the darkness. Even now. Even after I've lived with it for all these years. I still long for the light. God, where is the light?

The thoughts came to her, washed through her, soaked into her like a wave in the sands of memory.

She was afraid then too. So many years ago. Afraid of the darkness she did not understand. Afraid that though God said He loved her, He didn't really. Afraid that the blindness proved that He didn't, that He'd let her down, betrayed her. That somehow, He had lost her in the shadows that crept over her mind. Yet the shadows still came. Despite the doubts. Despite every effort she had made to beat them back.

Yes, she had faced these fears before. They had a familiar flavor. They tasted like ocean spray . . .

■ ■ ■ ■

The waves of Monterey Bay hit the rocks beneath Maddie and splashed up to wet her platform sandals. A flock of sea gulls squawked from an outcropping a hundred feet from the shore. Farther out, she could hear a group of scuba divers splashing as they swam past a line of floating kelp.

She wanted to do many things in her life — ride in a biplane, white water raft, snowshoe in Yosemite, see the northern lights. She shivered. Many things she had hoped for, planned for, but scuba diving — going beneath that cold, black water — wasn't one of them. Especially on a day like today, when all was dim, dark. The water like night that never ends. She could tell that much at least. Gray sky. Black water. And cold. Damp. It soaked into her skin, beaded on the brown poncho she wore over her shoulders.

Another wave threw itself into the rocks and sent a spatter of spray onto her arm and face. She touched the place on her cheek where the wetness kissed her. As Paul had kissed her. Just last night. Almost anyway. His lips barely brushing her skin as she turned away. So simple. So gentle. So innocent. And yet even that had undone her.

She removed her fingers and let the ocean's kiss remain. Let it linger, mock her. Just like his. He hadn't meant it that way. He hadn't meant anything at all. But oh, how he'd made her heart throb . . .

Maddie pulled up her knees tight against her chest and wrapped her arms around them.

Oh God, why did You let this darkness come? And why haven't You taken it away?

He could have, so easily. Could have . . . but He didn't. Why? Because the Bible spoke of love but didn't really mean it? Or because some were loved and others . . . well, others went blind? Had God really left her, abandoned her to this darkness? And if He had, would she leave Him too?

She stared out over the water and saw only the glint of sunlight off the surface hurting her. She squinted. Maybe God was like that. So bright that even a glimpse through the darkness was enough to overwhelm the senses. If so, she would never know the answer to her questions of why. Not fully anyway. So what would she do? Trust or turn away?

She dropped her gaze. The glimmer of light slipped away. It was too hard to trust in this darkness. But it was also too hard to turn away. "To whom will we go?" the disciples once said to Jesus. "You have the words of eternal life." And that was still true. She didn't understand, didn't know why God had led her on, only to let her down. But to turn back, to give up faith entirely? She couldn't do that either. So she wandered here, in the wilderness of doubt and fear. She sat on the edge of its waters and let the wetness lap her toes.

And the darkness spread, the waters rose. And one by one, her dreams fell into that darkness. Fell and were lost. Until last night, when one was tossed up to taunt her.

She dropped her chin onto her knees and tilted her head sideways. *I shouldn't have come. What was I thinking?* It was hard enough to be near Paul like this. Hard enough to feel his lips on her cheek. But to be here with his family, experience their kindness, know their love — it was like a wound that could not heal. Would not.

She lifted her gaze and spied a flash of white on the horizon. A sailboat maybe. She couldn't tell. And then came a seal's bark. And a splash. And the faraway slam of a door.

Maddie again buried her face in her knees. *You can't blame him. He didn't mean it.* He didn't mean to remind her of what could never be. Should never be. He was a good man. And they were but friends, after all. Friends. How could he ever know she had hoped for more? So much more. And now . . .

No. You know what the doctor said.

But . . .

No.

There's always a miracle.

A miracle?

Yes.

It would take that. And more.

Two weeks ago, she'd seen the doctor again. He looked into her eyes with his ophthalmoscope for what seemed like a half hour. He tested her with a series of tiny lights, asked a million more questions, and looked into her eyes again. And then he'd sighed. She'd never forget the sound of that sigh. Or the words that came after. "It's progressing faster than we had anticipated. A year maybe, and then your central vision will be gone." A year. Once, that had seemed like an eternity. Now it was no more than the blink of an eye. One year.

The doctor had suggested training with a guide dog, learning Braille, getting used to walking with a stick, listening for traffic, and hearing what could only be seen. Maddie nodded. She would do all those things.

Maybe. Later. But not now. Not yet.

"My mom has set that all up for me in Boston," she had said.

"You'll be going back soon then?" The doctor tapped his file and set it on the exam table. "I'll have Cindy prepare your records."

Soon. Too soon. Maddie didn't answer. Instead she stood and headed for the door. Paul was in the waiting room. Like always. He'd driven her to half a dozen of these appointments. And he knew by now not to ask too many questions.

One year. *Why did this have to happen to me? Why now?*

More why's that couldn't be answered. Wouldn't be.

She had swallowed the news that day. Swallowed it and put on a brave face. Just like always. But she didn't feel brave today. Not here. In this place. Sitting beside an ocean she could smell, hear, touch. But barely see. Knowing that everything she once loved would be lost. Was this how Malcolm felt before, just before he . . . ?

She lifted her head. Light came up from the water's surface and sprinkled into her eyes. She blinked. The fog was lifting. The dampness receding. But it was still cold. Still wet.

Malcolm always hated the ocean. He said that if you sat still long enough, it would come and sweep you away. The ocean. The unknown. Maybe he was right.

Malcolm's blindness had come quickly too. Too quickly for him to adjust. One day, he was heading for the minor league; the next, he was back in Boston — shut up in his room, taking classes on Braille, using a white stick, and living blind. Just like she was supposed to do.

Mother took him to the classes, and he learned, a little, how to read, how to walk, how to find the phone when it rang, to recognize the sound of streetlights and footsteps, to arrange furniture and utensils, and to forgive people who talked too loud because they thought you were half-deaf too. But they didn't teach him how to leave behind every dream, every hope, every vision of what life could have been. No one said a single word about that.

One day, Maddie had come home from school to find Malcolm polishing his baseball bat. He was just sitting there, rubbing it with a cloth. Back and forth, back and forth. Steady, methodical, slow. His eyes were open, and he was staring but not seeing. Never seeing. By then, he could only see along the very outer edge of his vision. But he knew it was her.

"Hey, Malcolm."

"Hey, Mads." He always called her that.

"Why ya doing that?"

"I don't know." He kept rubbing, wiping the bat, and staring at the wall in front of him.

"Want some ice cream?"

"No."

"Got a new record. Look. The Monkees. Wanna hear it?"

"No."

She sighed, shrugged, and left the room. The next day, Mom called her at school.

Malcolm was dead. Dead. Just like that.

And now she couldn't help but wonder, would it be like that for her too? One day she would be going about her life of blindness, and the next . . .

No. She thrust her legs straight out across the rock, then jolted to her feet. She wouldn't be like Malcolm. She couldn't. At least not yet. She would live first. Really live. And not even the encroaching darkness would stop her.

Behind her came the sound of footsteps on stone.

Paul watched her lying there, still against the thin white pillow. Her lips were dry, cracked. Her skin, colorless and waxy. They would come soon. A nurse, a doctor, someone. They would moisten her lips, touch her skin, check her vitals. And then they would go. And he would wait, here in the dim light, in the shadows, beside her. It seemed he had waited forever.

In the last hour, she had gotten no worse. She had gotten no better. The outlook was grim, they'd said. There wasn't much hope. But he wouldn't believe it. He couldn't. There was hope. There had to be. He wouldn't lose her now.

Please . . . Maddie.

He rose and stood over her. And did not weep. Some would say that tears showed he cared. But that wasn't true. Some things went deeper than tears. And his love for Maddie was one of them.

So he bent his head and would not cry. Even if he'd wanted to, he could not. There were no more tears left. Not anymore. He'd used them up, long ago, it seemed. And now nothing remained but the waiting. And the dimming hope. And the love that had bound him to her for so long. That love had carried them through the darkness before — those days when he thought he'd lose his mind. He'd shaken his fist at God then, wondered, cursed, doubted, paced. Lost faith. Then found it again. Now, he did none of those things. He only waited . . . and watched . . . and listened to her faulty breathing.

Lord, help us. Make her whole. Let me take her home.

A quiet prayer. Simple. All he could manage. All he needed to.

She stirred, just a little. She knew someone was here. He could sense it. And for now, it would have to be enough.

And so he waited. Just as he had so many years ago, as she sat there on the edge of the water in Pacific Grove . . .

Paul stuffed his hands into the pockets of his jeans and stared out the front window of his parents' house. Behind him, coffee percolated in the kitchen. News about the latest in the Watergate scandal chattered from the radio, followed, moments later, by the sultry voice of Gladys Knight and the Pips. The heady smell of frying bacon wafted toward him, but he didn't care. All that mattered was what was happening across the road, down the embankment, at the very edge of the ocean's waves. From where he stood, he could just make out Maddie's form, sitting huddled on the rocks. She sat there in her brown poncho, her arms tucked at her sides, her back hunched. For the longest time, she didn't move.

His throat tightened. He'd seen that pose before. It meant she was thinking, praying. It meant she was sad. A breeze off the bay lifted her hair and flung it about her. She didn't raise a hand to smooth it.

He should go out to her. Maybe. Or maybe not. It was hard to know at a time like this. Would she welcome him, or wish him away? He couldn't tell anymore. Just like he couldn't tell on New Year's Eve. Something had been there in her face last night. Just a flash. A moment. A look that spoke something different from the turn of her cheek. And now, he didn't know what to believe — that fleeting look, or the face that turned away.

The fog thinned, dissipated, and sunlight reflected off the surface of the bay. And still she didn't move.

Paul frowned. She shouldn't be out there like that. The light off the water was bad for her eyes. She should know that. It would speed the degradation of her vision. He glanced at the hall tree near the front door. A pair of sunglasses hung by a lanyard from a hook. His glasses. He took two steps toward them, then stopped. Maddie wouldn't want him hovering over her, babying her. She would want him to leave her alone.

He sighed and looked back out the window. There was something so lonely about her there. It tugged at him. Called to him. But he couldn't answer. He shouldn't. He ran his hand through his hair.

She was different lately. Sure, she was losing her sight, but it was more than that. More than impending blindness. That would have been enough, but it wasn't all. It was almost as if she was holding on so tightly to . . . to what? To herself maybe. It didn't make sense. None of it did. She was going back to Boston, even though she would be able to manage on her own for months more. That's what the doctor said anyway. He'd taken her to a dozen appointments with the ophthalmologist. And each time it was the same. Her vision continued to deteriorate. Wear sunglasses when she was out. Avoid strain. She'd repeated the instructions back to him after every appointment. Halfheartedly. Bitterly. Sometimes she'd heed them; sometimes not.

At first, friends prayed for her. Marisol, Candy, Kelli — they all gathered around and laid their hands on her. But they didn't do that anymore. And he was glad. Sometimes the burden of their expectations was as heavy as the coming blindness. But he still prayed. Silently. To himself. Yet God didn't answer his prayers any more than He did those of the others.

Maddie was still going blind.

Each day, every day, she saw a little bit less. She didn't tell him so, but he could tell. And the worst part was that there was nothing — absolutely nothing — he could do about it but sit and watch and wait. He hated it.

A finger poked into his shoulder. "Hey, whatcha doing?"

Paul turned.

Jenny stood behind him, coffee mug in one hand, dripping spoon in the other. She jabbed the spoon at him. "Coffee's ready."

"Mom will kill you if she finds coffee drips on her floor."

"So?"

"So."

Jenny stuck the spoon in her mouth, then pulled it out and licked it clean. "Satisfied?"

Paul shrugged.

"So, what are you doing?" She edged past him, looked out the window, and scowled.

"Thinking."

"Yeah? 'Bout what?"

"About how rude you were the other

night. What's gotten into you?"

Her scowl deepened. "I don't know what you're talking about."

Paul turned toward her and lifted his eyebrows. It was Pete who was supposed to object to Maddie. Solidarity in bachelorhood and all that. But Pete hadn't said a word. Hadn't teased him at all. It was Jenny who had dropped comments here and there. Jenny who hadn't warmed up to Maddie as he'd expected. What was wrong with her? But in his heart, he knew. They both did.

Jenny dropped the spoon back into the coffee and sighed. "Okay, you're right. It was rude. And I regret it, okay? She didn't deserve that. But someone's got to show you the truth."

"Maddie shows me the truth."

"Come on, Paul. You know as well as I do —"

He lifted his hand and cut her off. "Don't say it."

"You know what I mean."

Paul crossed his arms over his chest and lied. "No, I don't."

"Don't be dense."

Heat flushed Paul's face. "Why don't you like Maddie?"

Jenny glanced down, to the left. "I do."

"Sure."

"You know, Paul. You know what I think. And you know I love you. I don't want to see you get hurt, that's all. Not this time."

"Maddie won't hurt me."

She stepped closer, and her voice dropped to a whisper. "Good grief, you're as blind as she is."

"Mom and Dad accept Maddie. Why can't you?"

Jenny let out another long sigh. Her gaze bore through him. "You want me to say it aloud? All right, then. It's because they don't know about Samantha. Not like I do." Her voice hardened. "They think she was just some girl you dated for a few months in high school, and felt a little sad about after . . . after . . . you know. But I was there. I know the truth. And here I am supposed to watch it happen all over again and do nothing — say nothing?"

"All over again? What does that have to do with this? With Maddie?"

"Everything. And you know it."

Paul's stomach clenched. "I can't believe you said that."

"Why not?"

"This is nothing like Sam."

"Sam had leukemia. Maddie's going blind. But other than that . . ."

"You don't understand."

"Don't I? You've been praying she'll be healed, haven't you?"

A coldness settled in his gut.

"And what if she isn't healed? What if she just goes blind, and you can't fix it? What will you do then?" Jenny turned away so quickly that coffee sloshed onto her sleeve. "Great. Now look what you've made me do." She held her arm away from her side and stormed toward the kitchen.

Paul watched her, then spun back toward the window. *Stupid sister. What does she know?*

Too much.

Still, she's wrong.

Is she?

Of course.

Paul closed his eyes and pinched the bridge of his nose.

Sam . . . He had tried to forget. Tried to bury that pain. It had only been a few months, that year in high school. His junior year. But, wow, she was beautiful. Inside and out. She was everything to him. And then . . .

It was a long time ago.

"Not so long."

Long enough.

"You don't understand."

The last voice in his head sounded just

like his sister. He rubbed his temples. This wasn't about Samantha. It was about Maddie. And she wasn't dying, only going blind. And yet . . . He pressed his forehead into the window. And yet, he'd loved Samantha too.

They went miniature golfing on their first date. She wanted praline ice cream. He did too. They walked and laughed and kissed. Just once. Then they went on a second date. A third and a fourth. They went to the prom — her in a lilac dress, him in that ridiculous rented tux. And he started dreaming big, dreaming of marrying that beautiful girl.

But then things changed. Sam started to get tired. And pale, and weak. There was no more miniature golf, no more jogs along the beach. Nothing too taxing.

For a full week, she didn't tell him what was wrong, then came the dreaded *C*-word. Cancer. Leukemia. A big word for a guy in his junior year of high school. Samantha got sicker. Stopped going to school. Lost her hair. But Paul went over to her house every day after school anyway. He told his folks he was studying with friends. But he wasn't. He was with her. He thought he could make it better. Thought he could fix it, somehow. They talked, dreamed about what they'd do after she beat the cancer, planned for their

251

senior year, when everything would be back to normal. And when he was alone, all by himself in his room at night, then he would pray for Samantha.

Sam died anyway. On a rainy Saturday in January. Paul couldn't fix it. And God refused to.

He was sick for three weeks after that. Throwing up, shaky. Mom and Dad thought he had the flu. But Jen knew better. Samantha had been her friend too. Only Jen knew what they'd meant to each other. Just Jenny, his twin sister, who walked with him through the pain of losing the girl he'd loved. Grieved with him and stood beside him, holding his hand when he decided to go into medical research — because of Sam — and when he swore he'd never let himself get so close again. He'd never care that way again. He'd keep his distance, keep relationships casual. And he had. With Jenny's help. She protected him. Kept him safe; kept him smart.

Until Maddie.

"This is different." He said the words aloud, but they sounded weak, unconvincing, even to him. He said them again, louder this time.

"If you say so."

He glanced over his shoulder. Jenny stood

in the kitchen doorway. A huge wet spot darkened the fabric over her right sleeve.

He turned and faced her. "I do."

She shook her head. "You sure? Because you'd better be, Paul. You'd better be really, really sure."

"I am." But he wasn't. Not at all.

She nodded, slowly, seemingly unconvinced. "Well, the gang is getting together again at the beach tonight. Maybe you want to come this time?"

"Maddie might like that."

She dropped her chin. Her voice lowered to a mutter. "Samantha always did."

His eyes narrowed. "Jenny . . ."

She waved away his warning. "Okay. But Paul, think about it. Please."

He scowled at her.

She pressed a finger to her lips. "I won't say another word. Except —" She paused. "Be careful, Paul. That's all I'm saying. Be really, really careful."

He grabbed his sunglasses from the hall tree, then pushed open the front door. He strode out and let the screen door slam shut behind him. He crossed the street and hopped the short split-rail fence on the other side. He glanced back.

Jenny still stood there, watching him through the window. She wasn't going to let this go. Not yet. He knew her too well for that.

Then she stepped back. And her face became shrouded in shadow.

15

Something lingered there, over the water. Not uncertainty. Not doubt. Anger. At the black water that held her here. At the dull pain that scratched through her mind. Even at the dim light that illuminated the shore. A light she could see, and that made it unreal.

It's not fair. Why me? Where is God now when I need Him most?

Questions she refused to ask, refused to acknowledge. What was faith, anyway? The absence of doubt? The lack of fear? No. Even the faithful questioned. Even the holy had their doubts; the saints, their dark nights of the soul.

And she'd had hers as well. That night, when the rain came down in wicked sheets. And earlier when the storm brewed clouds of frozen ice. And earlier yet when the ocean swept the shore, the fire crackled and a stranger strummed songs of faith in the darkness.

But it hadn't started there. It started with Jenny.

"It's going to be cold tonight. Wanna borrow my coat?" Jenny's voice came from the bedroom doorway.

Maddie turned. "I've got my poncho. Thanks."

"You sure you want to come?"

Maddie picked up her brush and ran it through her hair. The curls sprang back up, refusing to lay tame. "Sounds like fun."

"Oh. All right."

Maddie squinted, wishing, just this once, that she could see the expression on Jenny's face. All her conversations with Paul's sister had been awkward, stilted. Polite, but stiff. And this one, so far, was the worst of them all. "Of course, if you don't want —"

"Don't be silly."

"Okay."

Maddie expected Jenny to leave then. But she didn't. Instead, she stepped inside the door and flopped down on the beanbag. "So what's up with you and Paul, anyway?"

"Up?"

"You know."

"We're friends. Have been for over three years."

"Just friends, huh? So you two never went out?"

A smile touched Maddie's lips. She set down the brush and settled cross-legged onto the bed. "Sure, we went out all the time. Just not like that."

"Why not?" Maddie heard the frown in Jenny's voice.

She shrugged. "Well, uh . . . I don't know. It just wasn't like that, that's all." *It should have been. It couldn't. I wish . . . Don't!*

For a long time, Jenny said nothing. Then she sat up in the beanbag. The beans shifted and rattled. "I guess it makes sense, then."

"What?"

"Why he never brought you around until now. Mom said she met you in Palo Alto, but Paul never brought you home. Makes sense, I guess."

Why did he? Now, I mean? Maddie lifted her chin. Did she dare ask? Should she? "Why's that?"

" 'Cause you're going blind."

Something cold and awful slithered through Maddie's gut.

Jenny's voice lowered, and words tumbled out like rocks kicked down a cliff. Fast, as if she was afraid she'd lose them if she waited too long. "Look, you've got to understand something — I've got nothing against you.

257

You seem like a great person. Really. But I love my brother. I don't want to see him hurt. Not again." Her tone became strained. "I know it's not your fault, but you need to know. Here's where he always brings things that are in trouble. Those baby mice he found under the rotten board in the garden. That pigeon with one foot and the bent-up wing. Samantha. Don't ask about her. And of course, that stray shepherd pup with the abscessed paw. I can't remember his name."

Maddie tried to sift through Jenny's words, but the attempt failed. "So, did he nurse them all back to health, then? That paw get all better?" That would make sense, Paul bringing her here because he wanted to fix her.

The beanbag shifted again. "Sport — that was his name. Sport." Jenny coughed. "Would have healed, I guess. Paul took him to the vet. Doc treated the foot, but it turned out that Sport had distemper."

Why was Jenny telling her this? What was behind those rushed words? "So? What happened?"

"Had to put him down. Nothing Paul could do."

Then Maddie understood. Her stomach dropped. *So I'm like a stray dog, am I? Incur-*

able disease and all. How could Jenny be so cruel?

The answer was obvious. Painfully so. Jenny was just protecting her twin, saving him from getting tangled up in another lost cause. Because that's what she was. She knew it. Jenny knew it. Only Paul seemed to have his doubts.

As if conjured by her thoughts, Paul popped his head through the doorway. "You girls coming?"

Jenny leaped up. "They're there already?"

"I see the fire going."

"Cool." Jenny rushed from the room. She glanced back only once.

Maddie couldn't see her expression, but she'd bet anything that it said, "Stay away from my brother." She should have hated Jenny for that look, but in her heart, Maddie agreed. She really did. If only he wasn't the best friend she'd ever had, ever would have . . .

Paul waited. "Better get a coat."

Maddie hesitated. "I know."

"You all right?"

"Sure." A lie. Always a lie. She hated it.

Maddie scooped her poncho from the back of a chair and strode toward the door.

Paul stopped her. "Here, let me." He took the poncho from her hand.

"I can do it."

He shrugged. "I know." But he helped her anyway. "Lisa'll be there. Short brunette with glasses. She's been Jenny's friend since kindergarten. And Joe. Good guy. Used to be a wild child, but that all changed in college. You'll see. And his sister, Jodi."

Maddie pulled away. "She's the blonde?"

Paul flung his arm around her shoulder. "How did you know?"

"Jenny told me."

He guided her toward the door, then slowed. "Hmm."

"Is she cute?" Maddie forced the question.

Paul took a moment before answering. "I guess so. I don't know."

"Yeah, sure."

"You can see for yourself." He paused and sighed. "I didn't mean it that way, Maddie. Now, let's go enjoy ourselves. We'll just roast some marshmallows. Joe'll play his guitar. We'll all sit around and gab. No big deal. You don't need to see like an eagle for that." As he spoke, he patted her arm and walked her toward the front door. "We'll see you later, Mom," he shouted toward the kitchen.

"Don't forget your coat, dear."

"Mo-om." He spoke the word in two syllables.

Maddie elbowed him. "See?"

"What?"

She shook her head and grabbed the door handle, then pulled open the door and stepped out. A cold wind slapped her face and reached chilly fingers down her neckline. But she refused to shiver. Refused to pull her poncho tighter. She wouldn't give him the satisfaction.

She took a deep breath and noted the smell of salt water and dying poinsettias. A car rumbled by. A horn beeped.

"There's Lisa." Paul pulled the door closed behind them.

Maddie squinted and looked across the road. She couldn't see anyone on the beach. She couldn't even see the fire. "Are they there?"

Paul's coat rustled as he adjusted it, then zipped it higher. "Come on. Hold my elbow. It's dark out here." He lifted his arm for her to grab.

"I can tell it's dark. I'll be okay."

"Come on, Maddie." He bumped his arm into her side. "Don't argue."

She glanced up at his face, but of course she couldn't see him. He was only the blur that had come to be "Paul." Just darkness and a wash of skin-colored features that couldn't be distinguished. She turned away.

She missed the sparkle in his eyes, the look of his smile. She used to love his eyes. It wasn't fair.

He bumped her again.

This time she took his elbow — lightly, tentatively — wishing she could have done anything but.

"You okay?"

"Fine." Another lie. The same one.

"You don't have to come."

Maddie's throat tightened. "You don't want me either." It came out as a whisper, a breath.

Paul moved closer. He was looking into her face. At least, she thought he was. "What are you talking about?"

She turned away. "Nothing."

For a moment, he didn't move. And she could tell that he almost said something, then changed his mind. Instead, he moved toward the steps. "Come on. Lisa's bringing the marshmallows." Paul modulated his steps to make it easy for her to follow. "We're making angels on horseback."

"What?

"S'mores. You know."

"Oh."

"You have made s'mores, haven't you?" Paul reached the end of the yard, pushed open the gate, and paused before crossing the road with her at his side. They stopped on the other side. "Well?"

"There are a lot of things I've never done."

He reached across his body and squeezed her hand. "There's the fire. Can you see it?"

"No." She dropped her hand.

"Here." He stepped back, took her by the shoulders, and shifted her a quarter turn left. "Now?"

She got the vague impression of an orange glow against a backdrop of black. "Yes. I see it now."

"Knew you would."

They started toward the fire, down a small embankment, across some rough stones, and then to the seaweed-strewn beach. As they got closer, she could hear the fire's crackle, and beyond, the gentle, insistent roar of the bay. She drew in the smell of the sea and allowed it to calm her. There was something vaster, stronger, about the great Pacific than the Atlantic where she had grown up. Even there, she had loved the ocean. But here, it wooed her with gentler tones.

Paul touched her hand again. "Are you coming?"

Only then did she realize that she had paused. She blinked. "Sorry."

"They're all here."

Maddie became aware of the rumble of voices and the strum of a guitar beyond them. The guitar stopped. "Hey, man, 'bout time you got here."

"That's Joe." He whispered the words in her ear.

She scowled. "Of course."

Paul raised his voice. "Great fire. Too big yet for marshmallows."

"Not for me."

Paul laughed. "I forgot. You like 'em burned." She could feel Paul give a mock shudder. "This here's Maddie, a friend from Stanford."

"Hey, Maddie." Joe's voice came closer, but she still couldn't catch a glimpse of him through the darkness. "That's my sis, Jodi, there, and her friend Lisa."

Maddie held still. Joe had motioned toward the girls, but she couldn't tell if they were standing or sitting. Her hand tightened on Paul's arm. Her breath came faster.

His voice was in her ear again, a soft whisper, barely breathed words. "To the left of the fire. Sitting."

Her fingers relaxed. She turned toward the left and smiled. "Hi, Jodi. Lisa."

"Hi there."

"Hello."

Two voices. One a warm alto, the other more nasally.

"Sit down. We've already put out blankets." That was the warm voice. "And Joe brought clams."

"Clams?" Maddie wrinkled her nose.

Paul scooted closer. "Sometimes Joe gets them from his dad's restaurant. They're good. You'll see."

Joe's voice came from somewhere ahead of her. "They're already cooking by the fire. Should be ready soon. You like clams, Maddie?"

She shrugged. "I've heard they're kind of rubbery."

He laughed. "Yeah, but you'll have to pretend to like them anyway, or I'll get my feelings hurt."

Maddie smiled as Paul guided her to a blanket in the sand. She sat and crossed her legs. She looked left, then right. Shadows, only shadows. And the shimmering glow of flame. It was bad enough trying to see in the daytime, but here on the shore, with nothing but darkness and fire, it was nearly impossible. Why had she ever thought it might be fun?

Footsteps came toward her.

"What kinda chocolate you like? Milk or

dark?" the nasally voice asked from above her.

"Dark, of course, for me."

The girl giggled. "I know, Paul. I remember."

He nudged Maddie with his elbow. "What about you, Maddie?"

"Milk chocolate, please." She paused. "I'm afraid of the dark."

For a moment, no one said anything. Then Paul chuckled.

And the girl giggled again. "Oh, a joke. I get it. That's cute. Afraid of the dark. Hee hee."

Now Maddie wished she hadn't said it. Her face warmed.

Paul leaned back beside her. "Sharp as a tack, you are, Jodi. Not much gets by you."

Jodi. The nasal voice is Jodi's. The blond one.

Silence followed in which Maddie suspected that Jodi was making a face at Paul. He laughed again. His relaxed laugh. She'd heard it a thousand times. But not with some blonde looking down at her from a face she couldn't see.

A bit of sand sprayed over Maddie's ankle as the girl turned and made her way to the far side of the fire.

Maddie kicked off her shoes and stretched

out her legs until sand dribbled between her toes. The fire was warm on her face; the air, brisk and salty.

Paul sat up again. "I didn't tell them." His voice was low, meant only for her.

"Tell them what?"

"About your sight."

"So? Why would you?"

The blanket moved as Paul shifted away from her. "In case, you know. Just in case you need help or something. They could watch out for you too."

Maddie clenched the blanket in two fists. "I don't need —"

"Hey, guys, listen to this." Joe's call cut off Maddie's response. He strummed a loud C chord. "Wrote it this week. Tell me what you think."

Maddie heard the shifting of blankets, the movement of sand, as the others sat in a circle around the fire.

"Go ahead, Joe." The warm voice. Lisa's.

"Play it." That one was Jenny's. So, she was here too. And sitting to the right, almost on the other side of the fire.

Joe modulated to a D, then plucked a mournful arpeggio. He repeated the sound and began to sing:

Jesus made the dead to rise.

He made the lame to walk.
He healed the man whose skin fell off.
And made the mute to talk.

Paul coughed. "Skin fell off. Well, that's a new one."

"Oh yeah!" Joe shouted, then followed with another "yeah" and a long, almost frantic interlude of strumming, interspersed with loud banging on the guitar's belly. Maddie cringed.

Jesus made the deaf to hear.
And set the prisoner free.
He healed the chick who bled and bled
And made the blind to see.

A chill scampered up Maddie's arm. They didn't know. Paul said they didn't know.

"And now He's changed me." He sang the line twice more, then plucked the arpeggio again in D.

And now He's healed me.
Jesus set me free.
And I can truly see.

There was a big flourish of sound, and then Joe started again. But Maddie wasn't listening. There was no way Joe could know how his song hurt her. No way he could be aware of the pain it caused. Jesus healed. The blind saw. But not her. Never her. And not Malcolm either.

Then the *why*'s came again. Why didn't Jesus heal her? Why couldn't her life go back to normal? Why did the darkness have to come? Faith had been easy last spring. Bible studies on Tuesday nights, church on Sundays. And the other days filled with classes and homework and work in the lab. Prayers consisted of frantic cries for help for exams and mercy for unstarted papers due tomorrow morning. And healing? Sure, she and her friends had prayed for healing. For someone's aunt's pneumonia. For a friend with the flu. For a cousin's appendix scare. But never for a girl going blind. And never for her. Until the summer. And then they'd prayed. Prayed and prayed. But nothing happened. The darkness just kept coming, growing, blocking out the light.

What was faith supposed to look like then? What did it mean to believe now? She didn't know, but she still prayed and smiled and pretended that nothing had changed. There was no freedom, no healing. Only pity. Not from God, but from Paul. The one thing she never wanted. She had become a project.

No, not a project. A stray dog named Sport.
She drew her knees up to her chest and wrapped her arms around them. *Stop it. Stop! Stop telling me that Jesus heals the blind.*

Abruptly, the song ended and was met by awkward silence. Paul cleared his throat. "I think it's even better than the last one."

"You think so?" Joe's voice moved upward as if he had stood. "What did it say to you? Did it speak?"

"Sure." Maddie could tell by the way Paul slurred the word that he was grinning. "It told me you're a Jesus freak."

Joe guffawed. "And proud of it."

Everyone laughed. Except Maddie.

"Play 'Kum Ba Yah.' " Jenny's voice came from a place closer to Paul than she'd been before.

Joe strummed a G chord, then the song started. The girls sang, Joe played, Paul hummed. He wouldn't sing. He never did. "Can't carry a tune in a bucket," he always said, which was one of the things she liked about him. But now she realized that his humming was on key. He probably would sing just fine, if he'd try it. Someday, maybe, she'd tell him so.

His shoulder brushed hers. Then he whispered, "Moon's bright on the water tonight.

Wanna go for a walk?"

"Won't Joe be offended?"

"Naw, he knows what I think of his music."

"What's that?"

"Not much."

"But he's your friend."

"So are you. Come on."

The song ended.

Maddie didn't move.

"Time for s'mores!" Joe's voice boomed across the campfire. "Coals are perfect. Even for Paul's standards."

She turned toward Paul. "I guess we're staying here."

He grunted. "I guess we are." He stood up. "Who wants marshmallows?"

"Sticks are in the back of the Bug." Lisa's voice came from a distance, as if she was already halfway up the embankment behind them.

"Bug?" Maddie envisioned a large beetle with sticks coming out its back.

"Her Volkswagen, she means." He hesitated. "She's coming back with them now. I'll get yours."

Maddie stood. "I can."

He put his hands on her shoulders and pressed her back down. "Sit. Relax. Enjoy yourself, would you?"

She listened to his footsteps leaving her, then turned her face toward the water. *I'm not a stray. I'm not . . . yet.*

A few minutes later, Paul squatted in front of her. "Here." He handed something toward her.

She reached out. Her fingers contacted something gooey, sticky. "What is it?"

"Your angel on horseback."

"You made it for me?"

"Of course."

She saw a quick movement, as if he flourished his hand in a grand gesture. She scowled. "But I didn't even tell you how I like it."

Paul gave an exaggerated sigh. "There's only one way to do it. Graham cracker, chocolate, the marshmallow toasted to a perfect brown so the insides are gooey but the outside isn't burned, and then another cracker. Press slightly so the marshmallow melts the chocolate. And, voilà! Perfect."

She didn't answer. And she didn't reach for the s'more either.

Paul straightened. "What's wrong with you tonight?"

Coldness seeped through her stomach and into her chest. She refused to look up. Refused to even try to see him. "I'm not your project, Paul."

He moved back. "What are you talking about?"

"Jenny told me about Sport."

"What's this, a lover's quarrel?" Joe's question sliced between them.

"No." "Yep."

She and Paul spoke at once. She glared up at him, even though it did no good.

"She doesn't like my s'more." Paul said the words like a joke, but they fell flat.

Joe snorted. "Impossible."

"Crazy, isn't it?" Paul grabbed her wrist. "We'll be right back. Keep the fire hot." He hauled her to her feet. "Come on. We're taking that walk. Now." He dragged her away from the fire. Five yards. Ten. Fifty. Until the sound of voices faded and the crack of fire and the crunch of graham crackers breaking in two. Only the voice of the water was left. The lapping of waves on the shore. And Paul beside her.

He stopped and turned her to face him. "Okay, so what's this all about? 'Cause it sure isn't about marshmallows and chocolate." His tone was low, hard, and furious.

Maddie crossed her arms over her chest. "You know I never wanted your pity."

"And I haven't given it."

"Haven't you?"

His hand slapped his thigh, or at least she

thought it did. "Why, because I made you a s'more? Get real, Mad."

"Yes, because you made me a s'more. And put on my coat. And made me hold your elbow. And brought me here, and . . . and . . . and . . ."

"Good grief, lighten up." He was so close she could smell the chocolate on his breath. Dark chocolate.

I'm afraid of the dark . . .

She shivered. "I can't. Remember, I'm going blind. As if you forgot."

He sighed. "Of course I'm not going to forget. Why would I?"

"Because . . ." Pain stabbed through her, and she couldn't finish the thought aloud. *Because . . . I want you to.*

"Maddie." He said her name softly. Too softly. The sound of it hurt.

She sniffed. "Don't you get it, Paul? I don't want to be Maddie the Blind Girl. Poor Maddie. The Maddie everyone has to look out for."

He touched her arm. "You aren't."

Tears welled in her eyes. "I am. And you know it."

He gripped her shoulders and squeezed. "Here's what I know. You're the one making yourself into Maddie the Blind Girl. You're the one who can't see past it."

"See? Ha ha." Even she could hear the bitterness in her voice.

Paul dropped his grip. "Yeah, but it's no joke. You're holding on so tightly that you're smothering yourself, drowning yourself in your fear. It's not the dark that you should be afraid of. It's yourself."

"I'm not afraid."

"Yeah, right."

"I am *not* afraid of going blind." She straightened her shoulders and flung out the lie as if only it could save her. He didn't know what it was like to go blind. He had no idea. Didn't he know that if she let go, if she let even one thing slip, she'd slip away herself? She couldn't trust today. She couldn't trust tomorrow. So how could he expect her to trust him?

Then Paul was there, his voice soft, his breath on her cheek. "Then what are you afraid of?"

She stepped back. *You!*

"Tell me the truth."

Pity? Yes. No. Darkness? Loss? Change. A change she couldn't control. A change she didn't understand. And he was part of that change. Only he didn't know it.

"You said it was your mom who was like this, but you know, it's you. You're the one who can't just get on with it and live. It's

275

not like you have cancer, Maddie. It's not like you're going to die."

"Like Sport?"

He backed away. "Sport?"

"The dog."

He laughed, bitter and full of pain. "No, not like Sport, Maddie. Like Samantha. All right?"

Breath escaped her in a deep whoosh. "Samantha? She . . ."

"Died. Yeah, Maddie." He took her arm and held it.

"I didn't know . . ."

His voice lowered until she barely recognized it. "So don't talk to me about pity."

She closed her eyes. "I'm not like her."

"No, you aren't. But one thing's the same."

And she knew what that was. They were both hopeless, both beyond cure. Both nothing but a source of pain and regret. "One thing?"

Suddenly, he was close again, so close that she was sure she could hear his heart beating.

She couldn't move. Didn't dare. *Paul* . . .

"One thing." He edged closer until his lips brushed her ear. "I loved her too." He turned on his heel and stomped away, leaving her there, bereft and trembling in the sand.

Love? Had he really said *love?* He couldn't mean it. He didn't understand.

For a moment, she could hear the sound of his boots sloshing in wet sand. And then the sound faded. The waves lapped. The breeze blew in from the ocean. And finally, Maddie turned and made her way back to the fire.

As she approached she could hear their voices. Lisa's. Joe's. And closer, to the side, Jenny's and Jodi's. A few steps more and their conversation became clear.

"They're just friends."

Maddie stopped.

"He's available, then?" That was Jodi, the blonde. "Groovy."

Maddie turned away. She stumbled toward the steps leading up the embankment. Her feet pounded into the stone, her fists balled tight beside her. She paused only once and glanced back. There, still, was the warm glow of fire. And someone beyond it. Two people. Paul maybe. And that Jodi. She was probably even cute, despite that nasally voice.

Maddie reached the top of the embankment and headed toward the street. Paul didn't follow. Why would he? Love? He couldn't have said that. Couldn't have meant it. If he had, he'd be beside her now. But he wasn't. He shouldn't be.

I don't care. I don't! They were only friends. Just like Jenny said. Just friends. And probably not even that anymore.

Somewhere to her right, a light flashed.

16

Memory was doubled edged, Paul knew. It healed and hurt. It cut and gave hope. It revealed failure and the footprints of God. Maddie knew that. And so did he. So, why must the night last for so long? Why did the minutes stretch when the light faded to black and cheap fluorescent bulbs sputtered and snapped? When the footsteps in the hall grew quiet, and the intercom no longer buzzed, and there was only the sound of the EKG beeping — steady, incessant beeping — to fill the dark hours of night? Why? Because of memory. Because of hope. Because tomorrow was built on the blocks of yesterday. Because he and Maddie had been here before.

And now, he was so close, so near her in the darkness. He could almost touch her, almost feel her breath mix with his.

Then she turned her face and groaned in a darkness that was more within her than without. The groan faded. The door swung open.

The nurse looked in. "Good night, then. I'm going home now." Her voice caught and she sighed. "I'll be back in the morning. By then" — her voice softened — "well, by then we should know."

Paul nodded. "Thank you. I'll keep watch."

The door closed, and Paul and Maddie were alone again. Alone in the darkness, alone with only memories to warm the night.

"Don't you see, Maddie?" He spoke aloud, but the words made no dent in the night, no sound in the silence. "I'm with you. You don't have to face the darkness alone. You never have."

This time, she didn't groan. But she didn't move her head toward him either.

"I was there that night on the beach too. You didn't know it. But I never left you alone . . ."

Paul watched her pull her poncho tighter, cross her arms in front of her, and hunch her shoulders in a way that made his chest ache and his throat turn dry.

Don't do it, Maddie.

But she did. She turned her back and

strode toward the embankment, away from him.

He wouldn't follow her. She didn't want him to, and he didn't need the aggravation. After all, it wasn't every day that a man declared his love, only to have his girl storm away from him in the dark. He shook his head and crossed his arms over his chest.

The things she said tonight were crazy. What did a dog have to do with anything? And why was her going blind somehow his fault? Doggone it, he'd done everything he could to show her he was there for her. He took time to hunt up advice on how to best lead a blind person. He sat in the library for, what, six hours? And on a Saturday night, no less. Looked up everything. The history of Stargardt's, advances in ophthalmology, even how to pick a good guide dog. And then he'd checked out a book on Helen Keller. Okay, so that may have been stupid, but he'd done his best. He'd tried. So why wasn't it good enough? Why had she walked away tonight? Right when he'd told her he loved her?

Because I walked away first.

The truth. It pierced him. But there was no way he could stand there any longer, with his soul laid bare, vulnerable. With the word *love* burning on his lips. He swore

281

he'd never let this happen again. But it happened anyway. And more. He'd cared for Samantha. He was crushed when he lost her. But he loved Maddie. Really loved her. And still he walked away.

The fire flared up, spitting sparks toward a black sky. Too black. Too dark. He gritted his teeth. Couldn't she tell how dark it was? Too dark for her to make her way alone, even the short distance back to the house. Ridiculous to go stomping off when she couldn't see half of where she was going. She should know better. He sighed. Maybe she did. Just not tonight. Tonight, he had lost his heart. And Maddie had lost her mind.

He dug his fists into his sides and glared after her. On the other side of the fire, Joe struck up another song, a dreary, folksy thing that clashed against the sound of the ocean's waves. Jenny picked up the song, perfectly pitched, but still grating. Maddie didn't even pause.

Paul gritted his teeth. He ought to just let her go. If she wanted to leave him, fine. If she wanted to go back to Boston, fine. If she was bent on going it alone, well, he ought to just let her. He dropped his arms to his sides and relaxed his jaw. He ought to, maybe. But he couldn't. He couldn't even look away.

If it were anyone but Maddie . . .

He took a step to follow, then stopped. If Maddie knew he was coming after her, she'd be furious, and the accusations would fly again. He took another step.

A hand touched his arm. He turned.

"Hey, Paul." Jodi smiled up at him with one hand behind her back.

"Hey."

She pulled her hand from behind her back to reveal a long stick with a marshmallow stuck on the end. She waved it toward him. "Make me a s'more?"

He frowned and glanced back up the bank toward Maddie. "What?"

"A s'more." She tapped his chest. "Joe says you're the best."

Paul looked down at her wide eyes and pouty lips. He blinked. "Oh, yeah, sure. I guess."

She thrust the stick toward him. "Jenny said you would. She said . . ."

But Paul wasn't listening. Instead, he was watching Maddie, halfway to the top of the embankment.

Jodi put her arm around his waist.

Just then, Maddie stopped and looked back.

Paul raised his hand, then dropped it. He

would catch her eye, if he could. But Maddie wouldn't be able to see him, not from this distance, not in this light. He could have called to her. But he didn't. He didn't dare.

She's going to cross the road. By herself. In the dark. Again. The thoughts came to him with a parade of images as if from some nightmare. Maddie running, a car racing. Brakes squealing. Except it wasn't a nightmare. It was a memory. Of a truck in the rain. A pizza parlor. Headlights. And that moment when he thought he was too late.

How could she do this to him again? How could she not remember the risk? He shoved the stick back at Jodi. "Maybe later."

"Paul?"

The stick dropped between them. He didn't pick it up. Instead, he dashed toward the embankment and bolted up it. She wasn't to the street. Not yet. But almost. A short way down the path. Up a couple steps. A curb, a streetlight, and a road where anything could happen.

He cut across a narrow strip of sand and jumped over a short fence. The streetlight cast a sallow glow onto Lisa's VW Bug and threw tiny shards of light onto Maddie as she reached the sidewalk. She paused on the edge of the road. He moved toward her. Close, so close. But she didn't hear him.

Didn't know he was there.

Good.

He snuck into the circle of the streetlight. She stood just beyond it.

Don't do it, Maddie. Don't be stupid. You can't see if anything's there.

She stepped out into the street. Without looking. Without trying. Without knowing if anyone was coming.

Someone was.

A light flashed. Paul whirled around.

A biker zoomed toward them. A light blared from a band around the man's head. He rocketed down the hill, wheels spinning, legs pumping.

Paul glanced back. Maddie had stopped in the middle of the lane, in the middle of the bike's path. Only she didn't know it.

He rushed out. Almost yelled to her, almost shouted her name. But instead, he threw himself into the bike's path and waved his arms beneath the brightness of the streetlight. Frantic. Hoping. Praying.

The bike swerved. A man cursed.

And Maddie was safe.

He glanced over his shoulder at her. She stood, shaking, in the dimness of the street. He nearly went to her, took her in his arms, but what would he say? How would he say it?

I love you. I'm here.

He stepped toward her, but she ran across the road away from him. Without seeing. Without realizing. Without ever knowing he was there.

A moment later, a door banged. And she was gone.

Paul tossed and turned. Then sat up and punched his pillow. He stared at the ceiling and listened to the numbers on the alarm clock flip from 4:59 to 5:00. He yanked on the covers, pushed them aside, balled them up, and pulled them back over him. He turned over again and shut his eyes.

But it was no good. Sleep wouldn't come. He'd been lying here for hours. And in all that time, he'd only figured out two things for sure. One was that he was mad. Mad at Maddie, at God, at Jenny and Jodi and Joe. Mad that Maddie was going blind and he couldn't fix it. Mad that God could, and didn't. Mad that Maddie had run off last night, and for the first time since he'd known her, he hadn't been able to make things right. And the second was that he loved her all the same.

He knew what he had to do. He had to tell her the truth. All of it. Even if she took it as pity. Even if he lost her friendship for good. Paul punched the pillow again and rolled onto his left side. He'd do it later this morning. As soon as she got up. He'd march into her room and . . . His eyes grew heavy. He'd tell her that he loved her. His mouth fell open. Loved her better than that mother of hers. Better than her friends. Better even than God. He loved her, and he'd take care of her and make everything all right. He would . . .

Finally, he fell asleep.

Paul slid lower in the hospital room chair. He had been an idiot back then. Full of grandiose dreams and silly proclamations. He thought he knew, thought he understood. But he hadn't understood a single thing. He hadn't known it wasn't the blindness that would hurt her, but him. A simple drive in the rain. A little too much speed. A deer in the circle of headlights. And here he was sitting beside her in the darkness of a hospital room, waiting for her to wake up and know he was there. If she ever would.

I'm sorry, Maddie. I never wanted to cause you pain.

Paul jolted awake. His gaze shot to the clock. 9:48. He sat up and ran his hand over his hair. It was standing on end, and he didn't care.

He'd been dreaming. Something good. Something important. He couldn't remember. Something about Maddie? He caught his breath. He was telling her that he loved her. This morning. Now.

He stood and threw on a T-shirt. She wouldn't care what he looked like. Wouldn't care if his hair looked like a porcupine or his feet were bare. He strode to the door and flung it open. He took two steps into the hall, paused, and turned back. Maddie might not care what he looked like, but she'd sure care if he had bad breath or if his pits stank. It wouldn't be good to declare his love — ask her to stay with him, marry him — with words that smelled like old garlic. He coughed and ducked into the bathroom. He brushed his teeth and slapped on some deodorant. There, he was ready now.

He walked back down the hall and tapped on Maddie's door. No one answered. He knocked again. Louder. Nothing. He turned the knob and pushed open the door. The bed was made, the closet empty, her suitcase gone.

He stood there, with his heart hammering and a thousand thoughts pounding in his head. Did she want him to take her back today? Already? Was she that upset? She had to be to pack up this early. He'd blown it. Worse than he thought.

He backed out of the room and strode down the hall to the kitchen. Jenny stood by the counter, stirring a cup of coffee. She picked up an empty mug and held it toward him. "Good to the last drop." She smiled. "Want some?"

"Where's Maddie?"

Jenny set down the empty mug and took a sip from her own before answering. "Gone already. Left about an hour ago."

Paul gripped the corner of the kitchen table. "She's gone? How could she be gone?"

Jenny took another sip. "She said to say good-bye and to tell you thanks."

"What?"

"Her roommate called early. Said Maddie's mom was coming."

"Today? She wasn't supposed to come until later this week."

Jenny huffed. "Well, I guess she didn't check her plans with you first, did she? So, what's the big deal?"

Paul pulled out a chair and sat down. "Maddie can't drive. Did Dad take her back? Or Mom?"

"Naw. Some girl came. Said the roommate

called her too. She was driving through from King City anyway. Going back to school, I guess." Jenny frowned. "Maddie seemed fine with it. Don't see why you aren't."

"What girl?"

"I don't know. She was wearing this psychedelic poncho. It was really cool."

"Marisol?"

Jenny shrugged. "I guess."

Paul rested his elbows on the table and put his head in his hands. Marisol. She'd gone back with Marisol. Now that was really stupid.

Jenny's mug clattered on the counter. "Oh, and Maddie said something else. She said you shouldn't worry. She'll be okay. And this was weird. She said, after all, she wasn't going to die."

Paul gritted his teeth. Of course she'd say that. After last night. "I'll go after her."

Jenny picked up her cup and whirled toward him. A bit of coffee spilled on the Formica table. "Why, Paul? She was perfectly fine when she left. She had to go back. So what? You aren't her guardian angel."

Paul lifted his head from his hands and stared at Jenny. "No. I'm not. I wish I were. Or if not that, at least the one who's there for her when she needs me. The one who takes her home. I could have done that much."

"Let it go."

"No."

Jenny shook her head. "Get smart, Paul."

Smart. Yes, he'd have to be smart. Paul blew out a long breath. "I'll have that coffee now." Jenny was probably right. He could talk to Maddie when he got back. Tell her what he wanted to say then, when he was better prepared. When they were alone. She wouldn't be leaving for Boston for a few days. He'd be able to convince her to stay. He still had time. He could still do what needed to be done, say what needed to be said. He could still ask her to be his wife.

Jenny handed him his mug. "It's probably better this way anyway."

He set down the mug without taking a drink. "Why?"

"Well, you know."

"Don't start."

"Really, Paul."

"Jen, I mean it."

"What are you two arguing about?" Dad sauntered through the kitchen door and made his way toward the coffeepot.

Paul frowned. "Nothing."

Jenny gave a phony smile. "Maddie."

Dad's eyebrows rose. "Ah, so you told him

what you did, did you?"

Paul made a fist and glared at Jenny. "What did you do?"

Jenny turned away. "I didn't do anything. This isn't my fault."

Dad crossed his arms. "You let her get away, didn't you?"

"I did not."

"Or was that Paul's fault?" He shot a glance toward Paul, then poured himself a cup of coffee, dropped in two sugar lumps, and stirred. "Of course, if my own son wasn't such a lazy, good-for-nothing bum . . ."

"Now that's not fair."

He shook his head. "Early bird gets the worm. Or the girl, in this case."

Paul groaned.

His father clucked his tongue. "Fine girl too. You don't let a girl like that get away."

But he had. Maybe he really was a good-for-nothing bum.

"Well, all's not lost yet. Phone's there on the wall." His dad motioned toward the mustard yellow telephone hanging over the counter.

Paul grimaced. The memory of Maddie's back as she scurried across the road flashed through his mind. "And what will I say?"

"You'll figure it out." Dad grinned and

lifted the mug to his lips. "Girl like that doesn't come along every day. 'Course she'll need some convincing."

"Dad?"

He laughed, took a step forward, and clapped Paul on the shoulder. "At least she isn't blond."

"Dad!"

He continued to chuckle as he made his way out of the kitchen. At the doorway, he paused and gazed back. "Jenny. Come out here. Give the boy some privacy."

Jenny shot Paul a single look, then stared down at the floor. "She might not even be home yet." She barely murmured the words.

"She will be."

"How do you know?"

"I've seen Marisol drive."

Jenny remained silent for a long moment. "You wouldn't have to call, you know. Just forget it."

"I can't, Jen."

"Why?"

"Just go, all right. I need to figure out some things."

Jenny nodded, then left the room.

Paul stood and walked to the telephone. He lifted it off the cradle and dialed Maddie's number. And then he listened as the phone rang and rang and rang.

The sky rolled and curved. The biplane shuddered. Wind teased Maddie's face and sent her scarf fluttering behind her. It nibbled her cheeks and sent cold chills scampering down her neck. But it couldn't penetrate the thick leather coat they'd made her wear or the silly leather cap that pressed over her head and buckled under her chin. The goggles she wore were too tight. They pushed into her cheekbones and made her eyes slant like a Siamese cat, so she wouldn't have been able to see much, even if her eyesight were perfect.

She glanced out over the biplane's bright red wing. The plane tipped left. Hundreds of feet below stretched the green forests of Half Moon Bay. At least that's what the voice in her ear said was there.

She adjusted her earphones and tucked a small paper bag beneath her thigh. "Just in case," the pilot had said. But Maddie wouldn't need it. She'd promised herself that she wouldn't. This was her first big adventure, before, before . . .

She ran her hand along the tight straps that held her in place in the plane's front seat, then she wrinkled her nose and tried to make out the front of the biplane. She couldn't, of course. There was just a splash of red, and beyond it, a sea of gray-blue sky that went on forever.

She could hear the gentle buzz of the engine and the pilot's voice droning in her ears. He'd kept up a steady monologue in the earphones, telling her what he could see and she could not. What she might have beheld if she'd only done this two years ago when she first heard that Stanford students got a special deal for biplane rides over the bay. But she'd put it off. Thought there would be a better time. For this, and for so many other things. She had been a fool.

But no longer. She couldn't wait anymore. She'd known it that night at the symphony. Knew that this day would come, and she'd have to take it. Quickly, quietly. Before her life was stolen. She'd known ever since her mother had found out and insisted she go back to Boston. Well, she wouldn't go yet.

She'd had the brochures for months. And lately, she'd made some phone calls, considered some plans. Checked out taxis and buses, hours and dates. She could still see well enough to make her way. At least from her peripheral vision. That's what she thought anyway when she left her apartment this morning with her fat duffel bag over one shoulder and her purse full of money on the other. She told herself she'd be all right. She could do this. And she could.

Yet the biplane ride wasn't all she'd thought it would be. It had seemed so glamorous in the brochure. And it was fun as they lifted off and soared into the sky. Wondrous as they headed into the clouds, with the upper wing shading her face and the engine gently rumbling in front of her. But it was bumpier than she had anticipated, though not as loud. Paul would have hated it. He'd told her plenty of times how he didn't like to fly, not even in regular airplanes where you could barely feel it.

"I'm not getting up in one of those tin cans," he'd say whenever she would tease him about coming with her to Boston someday to see the sights.

"It's a long drive." And then she would add, "But it's a short flight."

He growled and whispered, "Never. I'm telling you, never ever ever."

She could hardly imagine what he would

say if he saw her now. And he might be right. It was cold and her stomach didn't feel right. It twisted, writhed, and lodged in the middle of her throat.

But that wasn't the worst thing. The worst was that all this tipping and spinning didn't stop the fear. Or the regret. Those flew with her, like bees buzzing through her mind, stinging her soul. She thought to leave all that behind, replaced, at least for a time, by the thrill of being in flight. It hadn't worked.

The pilot grew silent. Then, in her mind, another voice replaced his. A man. A stranger. Just some guy in the parking lot. She'd only asked where the entrance was to the terminal. He'd told her it was right in front of her. And then he muttered those hateful words: "You blind or something?"

She'd answered only one word as she strode past him. "Almost." And she wondered if his face had turned red as she passed. It should have. Hers did.

Maddie squinted and looked down at the blur of dark green carpet below her. And then, the color changed.

"We're over the ocean now." The tinny voice spoke again through a hum of static. "Calm day out there today. Smooth as silk, and no white-tipped waves. Tide's in, though. You can see it against the cliffs.

Look." The plane dipped lower.

Maddie's stomach rose. She took a quick breath.

"See the spray?"

She tried to imagine it. Thick redwoods giving way to the vast blue-green of the water. Ocean spray breaking against the rocky cliffs. A highway winding through the hills toward the bay, and tiny cars making their way along it.

"We're heading north now. If we're lucky, we'll get a glimpse of the Golden Gate Bridge in the distance."

The Golden Gate. She'd love to see it. But she wouldn't. Never again. Still, she had this moment. Flying high above the world, the breeze caressing her face, the smell of cool ocean air, and that queer, queasy feeling in her gut.

It doesn't matter. None of this matters. She pushed away the thought. It did matter. It made things better. It had to. This was all she had.

"There, look directly north."

Maddie raised her hand to show that she'd heard him. The wind took her hand and pushed it back. She tucked in her arm again. The windshield in front of her protected her from the full blast of the wind's strength. Inside she was comfortable, safe.

Outside . . .

She shivered. *No, it's not like that.* She reached up and adjusted her goggles. She had to do these things. Had to try. *If I don't, I'll end up just like Malcolm.* That's what she told herself. And yet deep down, she knew she was like that hand pushed outside the windshield. A hand she dare not draw back.

God, I just want to live. I don't want to go blind. I don't want to go back.

She raised her hand again and let the air tear into it. Raised it, and let it be. One second, two. Ten.

"All right, then." The pilot's voice came again in her ear.

She pulled back her hand. The plane dipped. Rolled.

The pilot laughed. And for an instant, they were upside down, weightless.

Her stomach jumped to the top of her throat. And stayed.

The plane righted. The pilot jabbered.

Maddie grabbed the paper bag and did what she promised herself she wouldn't do.

Paul had barely stepped into Maddie's apartment after driving home from his parents' house in Monterey when it happened. Kelli opened the door and a moment later, Isabelle plunged across the room, flew

299

at him with her fist raised, a paper crumpled in her fingers.

"Zis is all your fault!" She shoved the paper into his chest.

He took it and frowned.

"You pushed her on. Treated Madison like nothing was wrong. Made her think . . . made her believe . . ." She sputtered to a halt, took a shuddering breath, then turned aside. "I knew it. You could not be trusted."

Kelli shut the door behind him. "It's all right, Mrs. Foster. She'll come back."

Paul pulled off his coat and tossed it onto the couch. "What are you talking about? Where's Maddie? And what's this?" He held up the paper.

Mrs. Foster whirled back toward him. "As if you do not know." She grabbed her hip with one hand and jabbed her finger at him with the other. "You know very well where she is. And you better get her back here right this moment." Her finger pointed to the floor, then back at him. "Do you hear me, young man?"

Paul glanced at Kelli. "What's going on here?"

Her face was pale. She chewed her lower lip as she met his gaze. "She's gone, Paul."

"Gone?"

"Right after Marisol dropped her off, I

think. Before I got back from the store."

"But . . ."

"Read the letter."

"What letter?"

Kelli pointed to the paper in his hand.

Paul looked at it as if it had suddenly become poisonous. He glanced at Mrs. Foster. She stood there, her jaw tight, her chest heaving, her toe tapping furiously into the red shag carpet. He unfolded the paper and read.

Mom,

I'm sorry you've taken a trip out here for nothing. I know it's expensive. I would have told you to cancel your flight, but you came early, before I had the chance.

So now you're here and you've found out that I'm not. And I won't be back. Not for a long time anyway.

You have to understand, Mom. I can't come home with you to Boston. At least not now. I've got things I have to do. Things I want to do, before it's too late.

I know you aren't happy about this. I know you wouldn't have given your blessing. But I'm an adult now. I have to live my own life. Really live it. Not like Malcolm.

Paul heard Mrs. Foster's quick intake of

breath, like a sob, but stifled. He looked up. Her eyes were watery now, but her jaw was just as firm. And he saw it. The fear. And the slight tremble of her lips. And he knew her for what she was — a mother who was afraid. His grip loosened and he continued to read.

Don't worry, Mom. I'll be fine. I'll call you in Boston when I get back. But in the meantime, know that I'm safe and busy. Please, don't look for me. And don't bug Kelli. She didn't know anything about this. No one did.

I love you, Maddie

Paul read it through it again. It was her writing, her voice. But it was unbelievable all the same. Where had she gone? What was she doing? And why hadn't she waited for him? The thought stuck in his chest and twisted like a knife. He would have gone with her, would have helped her with anything she wanted to do. Did she know that? Didn't she realize? He paused. Maybe she had. And that's why . . . He shut off the thought, lowered the paper, and turned toward Kelli. "You didn't know?"

Kelli grimaced and shook her head. "I told you she's been acting funny. But who would have thought? Who would have even dreamed . . ." She shrugged. "And they call me the flighty one."

Mrs. Foster paced in front of the couch. Her shoes made a strange swooshing sound against the shag. "Do not pester the girl when it is you who is to blame. Movies, and symphonies, and who knows what all."

Kelli laid her hand on his shoulder. "Don't worry, Paul. God will help us."

Mrs. Foster straightened and pierced him with a fierce gaze. "He had better."

Kelli stepped away. "It's not Paul's fault."

Paul crinkled the paper in his hand and dropped it on the table. Mrs. Foster was right. It was his fault. Maddie had run away. Not from her mother, but from him. And he needed to find a way to bring her back.

Mrs. Foster stopped pacing and pressed her fists into her forehead. "There has to be some clue. Some way to find her."

Kelli plopped down on a beanbag chair in the corner. "But she said not to look for her. Shouldn't we do what she says?"

Mrs. Foster gave Kelli a piercing stare. "Do not be stupid, girl. Of course we will search for her. And bring her home. I cannot leave her out there" — she waved her hand in the air — "who knows where, wandering about blind. Anything could happen." Her voice dropped, and again Paul could hear the dread in it. "Anything at all."

Kelli stood. Her voice cracked. "There are some things in her room."

Paul moved forward. "What?"

"Papers, brochures. Hidden away."

"Gah!" Mrs. Foster turned and walked around the couch. "Why did you not say something before?"

Kelli flushed. "I think we would do better to pray about it. Would you like to join hands?"

Mrs. Foster paused and looked back at Kelli. Her lips pursed. She spun back around and hurried toward Maddie's room.

Paul followed.

Mrs. Foster flung open Maddie's door and went inside.

He reached the doorway.

She glanced back at him. "You wait outside, Mr. Tilden. It isn't proper —"

He stepped in and strode to Maddie's desk.

"Mr. Tilden!"

He opened one drawer after the next. Then he called out over his shoulder, "Hey, Kelli, where did you see them?"

Kelli came in and motioned toward the bed. "In a box under there. Saw it one day when I was looking for my slippers."

Paul rushed to the bed, knelt down, and flipped up the brown bedspread. Then he peeked underneath. There, near the headboard, was a small cardboard box. He pulled it out and opened it. Inside, in a neat pile, were a stack of slim brochures and a skinny pad of paper with numbers indented on the first page.

Above him, Mrs. Foster drew in a sharp breath.

He picked up the pad and tilted it toward the light. "She must have taken the page she wrote on, but I can still make out some of the numbers." He took out the brochures.

"Give those to me." Mrs. Foster snatched them out of his hand and riffled through them. With each brochure, her breathing became heavier, more labored. "Lord, help us." The brochures dropped.

Paul picked them up again. A dozen pictures flashed in front of him. A guy in a canoe, an old railroad, a biplane, a sailboat, a cabin in the woods, a race car, and a photo of Half Dome. He stood.

Mrs. Foster pressed her hand over her mouth, blurring her words. "You do not think . . . She would not dare . . ."

He placed the pad of paper on top of the brochures and walked toward the phone. If he knew Maddie, she would dare. All of this and more.

He took a pencil out of her desk and sketched lightly over the paper. The numbers came into clearer focus. He picked up the phone and dialed the first one.

"Rigo's Taxi Company. Roxy speaking. How can I help you?"

Taxi. Paul mouthed the word to Kelli and Mrs. Foster before asking Roxy if they'd had a pickup that morning at Maddie's address.

"Let me check, sir."

Paul waited. He switched the phone from his right to left ear, only then realizing how tightly he'd been holding it.

"Yes, here we are, sir. We picked a woman up from that address at 9:56."

Paul glanced at his watch. Six hours ago. Why hadn't he come back sooner?

"Do you know where she was going? Where she was dropped off?"

Another pause met his question. Then finally the woman spoke. "Is there a problem, sir?"

He rubbed his forehead and sighed. "No, not exactly."

Before he could say another word, Mrs. Foster strode over and grabbed the receiver from his hand. She glared at him, then spoke into the phone. "Hello, who is this with whom I am speaking?" She waited for half a breath before continuing. "Yes, there is a *problème*. The girl your driver picked up has a serious medical condition. She left this morning without telling anyone and could be in danger. Now, I am sure your company would not like to be held in any way liable . . ." She twisted the spiraled phone cord around her finger. "You can? *Oui*. You will do it, then." She dropped the cord then put her hand over the mouthpiece and spoke to Paul. "The woman is radioing her driver. We should have an answer shortly. You cannot allow people like that to —" She broke off and uncovered the mouthpiece. *"Oui?"*

Paul could hear the buzz of words coming from the other end of the line.

Mrs. Foster tapped her fingernails on the desk. "That is all he knew?" Another pause. *"Merci."* She hung up. Her hands shook as she gripped the edge of the desk and drew in a long breath. "The child is *fou*. Crazy." She rubbed her temples. "What am I to do?" She turned toward Paul and Kelli. "It is worse than I expected."

Paul stepped forward. His heart beat faster. "Where is she?"

"The driver took her to an airstrip and left her there."

Kelli gasped. "That's it?"

"Oui."

Paul glanced at the pile of brochures beneath the pad of paper. "Then she could be anywhere. Anywhere at all."

And that's when he knew he had lost her.

18

Something was wrong. Maddie could feel it in the mist that swirled through her mind, in the eddies of pain that whirled in her body and made shadows against the canvas of her dreams.

Yes, she had been dreaming. Of dark water, shaped by fear. And of flying. No, that was real. The water was the dream. Or was it? And did she dream still?

She did. For there was the sound of water lapping. Or was it just her breath, steady and harsh in her ears? Beyond, a low beeping. And a sound like rubber soles against cold tile.

But they faded and came no more. They'd left her alone, here in this watery dream. Here, where confusion mingled with memory. Where it beckoned her back to a place she didn't want to go.

Paul . . .

But he wasn't here. Not here on the

water's edge.

Paul . . .

If she could only hear his voice calling her, just one more time.

Paul . . .

It was too late. She knew that. She remembered it. Just like then. When she'd been a fool, and so much more. She was crazy then — crazy to cram life into a few weeks' respite, crazy to forget, to bury the pain in her heart. Everything reminded her of Paul.

She was alone. Now. Then.

Alone.

Maddie flung her arms over her head and shrieked at the top of her lungs. Her shoulders slammed left, then right. Her seat dropped away and she was flying, free — the wind in her face, screams in her ears, and the rattle of the Giant Dipper all around her.

She laughed as the roller coaster hiccuped over a bump and then curled into a tight spiral. She'd been meaning, for years, to get down to the Santa Cruz Beach Boardwalk to ride its historic wooden roller coaster. Too bad it had to be in winter, when they were only open on weekends. But at least she was here, riding the coaster Paul had told her about. He said it was like skydiving in an earthquake. And it was. She loved it.

If only he could see her now. The car plummeted down another hill and then jarred right. She grabbed for the safety bar and grinned. This was the fifth time she'd ridden the roller coaster today. And she planned to ride it five more times before the day was out.

The car turned a final corner, then ground to a halt. The safety bar rose. Maddie placed her hands carefully on either side of the car's opening and felt her way out. She counted steps until she reached the narrow hallway that led out to the boardwalk. She knew the way. Down the ramp, around the corner, and back in line. She reached out and touched the wall. It was rough, and the paint was peeling.

Someone pushed past her. She stumbled and hit her elbow against the railing. She paused and rubbed it. Then she started again. A few steps more and she was outside in open air. Sound burst around her. Shouts from above as another car made its way along the tracks overhead. The cry of sea gulls. A baby wailing. The pounding of small feet, and a mother's voice calling, "Johnny, you get back here right this minute." The squeak of wheels. A stroller? Or maybe a wheelchair. And the smell of cotton candy

311

and popcorn, drowning the scent of the sea.

Maddie turned the corner, counted ten steps, then three more, and reached for the railing she knew was there. The line was short today. She tapped the railing as she edged her way along the building and to the opening that would lead to the line inside.

Ah yes, here it was. She smiled as another car rattled overhead. This was the best thing she'd done yet. Better than that trip around the track in the passenger seat of a race car, better than her hike along the clearly marked trails in the redwoods, better even than building a sandcastle earlier that day out on the beach by the water. On a roller coaster, it was just as fun to be nearly blind. Seeing didn't matter. It didn't matter at all.

Maddie pushed through the turnstile and found the end of the line. She could just glimpse the bright red shirt of the person in front of her. If she stayed right behind him, she would be able to tell when the line moved. She touched her fingertips to the wall. And waited. And waited.

Two days ago she'd almost decided to go up in a hot air balloon, but after the airplane incident, she decided to forego that adventure. Now, she was glad. This trip to the boardwalk was going much better. Her cheap motel was just down the street, and she could easily find her way from the motel to the boardwalk's entrance. And once inside, the boardwalk was wide and uncluttered, the steps down to the beach plainly marked, and the sounds crisp and clear to guide her. And sometimes, when she was at the highest peak of the Giant Dipper, when she was just about to take the big plunge, she could almost imagine that she wasn't going blind after all.

A hand tapped her shoulder. She jumped, then turned.

"You gonna go or what?"

Maddie squinted at the owner of the gravelly voice. A woman, she thought. One who had smoked away the sweetness of her voice and was left only with the deep rattle.

"Well?"

Maddie frowned. "What?" She turned back around. The splash of red was still in front of her. The person hadn't moved even an inch.

"Come on." The rough voice shot from behind her again. The woman huffed and stomped past her.

"Hey!" Maddie reached out and touched the person in front of her. The red fabric shuddered, then fell to the ground. She gasped.

"Don't tell me you were waiting for that

coat to sprout legs and walk?" The voice
was in front of her now, and moving away.

Maddie's stomach dropped. There was no
line before her. Only a red coat someone
had stuffed between the wall and the hand
rail, where it puffed out and made her
think . . . She bit her lip and hurried
forward until she saw another color. Yellow
this time. She turned her head left and
right, catching the image in her peripheral
vision until she was sure it was actually a
person. And, if she guessed right, it was the
woman who had been behind her.

The woman grunted. "I ain't giving up
my place. You don't go when you should,
you lose it. That's how it is."

That's how it is. Maddie swallowed and
turned away. *I hate this. I hate going blind.*
Even the roller coaster couldn't rattle away
the pain.

She silenced the thought. It would do no
good to wallow. She knew that. Malcolm
had wallowed. And look where it had gotten
him.

For a moment, Maddie saw Paul clearly
in her mind, his eyes glittering with mis-
chief, his lips quirked in a teasing smile.
Her throat tightened.

*He would have come with me, if I'd asked
him.*

But she couldn't ask. She wouldn't. Not after that night at the bonfire. It wasn't fair to him. It wasn't fair to her. Soon, though, she'd have to go back, she'd have to face him. And she'd hear that tone in his voice. The one that said she was being foolish, stupid. The one that said that things had changed, their friendship was over. He didn't really love her after all.

But she didn't have to go back yet. Didn't have to face it. To face him. There was one more thing she had to do.

Maddie turned her face toward the opening in the wall above her. She breathed in the salt air. No, she wasn't done yet. Tomorrow she would head out for her last adventure. And then . . .

The yellow in front of her moved, and she moved with it. The line split, and she made her way to the gateway for the last car. The track rattled. Cars roared. A squeal, a hiss, and she knew the cars had stopped before her.

She listened for the clatter of people entering the cars. It came, and she followed. Hands carefully on the edges of the opening. Step forward. Turn, sit, pull down the safety bar. A whistle. And the car jolted forward and plunged into total darkness. Faster, faster.

But this time, Maddie didn't laugh. She didn't shriek. She didn't even smile.

This time, all she thought about was Paul and how he ought to be with her. How he never would be. Never again. It shouldn't have been this way.

Would it have been different if I weren't going blind? Would we have ever been more than friends?

It was the strangest thing Paul had ever seen. Isabelle Foster, with her head in her hands, weeping. She sat there on the couch, dabbing her eyes with a tissue and sniffing. And apparently, there was nothing Paul could do to make it stop.

Mrs. Foster had stayed angry for three days. Blamed him for everything from taking Maddie away to her going blind. And then she started to cry. And she hadn't quit.

And still Paul came by Maddie's apartment every lunchtime and every day after work. Even though it had done no good. No good at all. He picked up the phone. Again. This would be the third time he'd called the hot air balloon company. The first day that Maddie disappeared, he'd called all the numbers in Maddie's brochures. Only the biplane pilot had heard of her, but the man couldn't tell him where she'd gone.

He did, however, seem quite incensed that Maddie had not told him she got motion sickness.

Paul smiled. She was gutsy, that Maddie. Biplane rides, and kayaking, and who knew what else. It took quite a woman to do all that alone. But he'd always known that. It was one of the things he loved about her. And one of the things that drove him crazy, especially lately. He sat back in his chair and dialed the number.

It made sense now why Maddie had gotten so angry. It wasn't in her nature to be dependent or needy. And yet the encroaching blindness forced it on her, and he had too, in a way.

The phone rang and rang.

Maybe, if it were up to him, he might just let her have her adventures and not attempt to stop her and bring her home. He might just hang up this phone and not try to find her. But Mrs. Foster had described, in excruciating detail, every single thing that could possibly go wrong. The hundreds of ways Maddie could be hurt, lost, killed. So he called the numbers on the brochures. Again and again and again. Sure, he was afraid for Maddie too. But like she told him, she could take care of herself. He just wished she would have let him come with her. Maybe she would have, if it weren't for that night on the beach when he told her he loved her and then walked away.

Someone picked up on the other end of the line. "Hello. Riding the sky in Pete's balloons. How can I help you?"

Paul recognized the man's voice. He cleared his throat. "Hello, I was wondering if you've had a customer named Maddie, or Madison —"

The man cut him off. "She's not here. Not yesterday, not the day before, not today."

"Sorry to bother you."

Mrs. Foster dabbed her nose again, then stood and walked to the window.

The man's tone sharpened. "I've got your number. I'll call you if she shows up, all right? I'll tell her that her daddy's looking for her."

Paul grimaced. "I'm not her father."

"Could have fooled me." The man hung up.

Mrs. Foster turned from the window. "She is not there." It wasn't a question.

Paul sighed. "No." He put the phone back on the cradle, then picked it up again.

Kelli walked in from the kitchen, carrying a cup of tea. Steam flowed from the cup as she brought it to Mrs. Foster. "Two sugars, plus cream."

Mrs. Foster took it, then leaned forward and gripped the windowsill with one hand. Her voice lowered to a pained whisper. "This is my fault." It was the first time she'd said that, the first time she'd taken any blame.

Kelli laid a hand on the woman's arm. "Mrs. Foster."

She let go of the windowsill and shook her head. "*Non.* I cannot deny it. I drove her to this. I should have told her . . ." Her breath caught. "I should have told her the truth."

"The truth?" Paul replaced the phone without dialing another number. "And what's that?"

Mrs. Foster swallowed, then motioned toward the phone. "Call the racetrack again."

"I did."

She sighed and pinched the bridge of her nose. "The white water rafting company?"

"Closed for winter."

"Maybe there are more brochures in her room."

"What truth were you talking about?"

"Maybe she has hidden some in her dresser."

"I've checked."

Mrs. Foster set her cup on the sill, drew

herself up straight, and turned toward Paul. "Check again, *monsieur.*"

He raised his eyebrows.

"S'il vous plaît. Please."

He pushed the old brochures to one side and stood. "Look, Maddie clearly doesn't want to be found. Why not just let her be? She'll come back soon enough."

Mrs. Foster stiffened. "You do not know anything about this."

"I know Maddie."

"Do you?"

"Yes."

Her eyes narrowed. "And do you know what it is like to go blind?"

He looked away and sat back down. "Of course not."

She left the sill and came toward him, stopping only when she was inches from his chair. "Then I will tell you this. I let my son be. And now I do not have a son. I will not allow the same mistake to be made again."

"But Maddie said . . ."

"Maddie does not know —" She broke off and turned away.

He waited, but she said no more. Finally, Paul spoke again. "Know what, Mrs. Foster?"

After a moment, she answered. But not to him. To the wall, to the air, to some unseen person that only she knew. "Madison does not know anything. Nothing at all." She turned back and looked him in the eye. "Check again, please. We must find her."

Paul nodded, got up, and went down the hall to Maddie's room. He flicked on the light. It was strange that Mrs. Foster didn't look for herself. She didn't make the calls herself either. It was as if she couldn't. As if to do so would cause damage in ways no one could see. He stepped into Maddie's room and shut the door behind him. There was something odd about that woman. Something more than Maddie's blindness that made her afraid.

He crossed the room and opened Maddie's dresser drawer. He riffled through her sweatshirts, then her perfectly folded T-shirts. Her favorite was missing. The ugly one with the daisy on the front. A few others were gone as well. He rested his fingers on the top shirt. It was green and pretty. He remembered the last time she wore that one. They were going to have pizza and see the latest Bond movie. He rubbed the fabric between his fingers. He would have kissed her that night. Except that's when she first realized she was going blind. That's when everything changed.

Paul picked up the shirt, sat on the floor,

and lifted the soft cloth to his face. It still smelled of perfume. He sighed. Things should have been different. He should have been different, made his move sooner. He should have seen what he had before it was too late. If he would have, would it have made a difference? Would he be with her now instead of here trying to find her? Would she have kissed him back?

He tossed the shirt back into the drawer and slammed it shut. No wonder Mrs. Foster didn't want to do this. It was too much like what loved ones did after a funeral. Go through the dead person's clothes, closets, drawers. Touch things, and remember. He shook himself and stood.

Maddie wasn't dead. She was fine. And she'd be back. He knew she would. He pulled out another drawer and checked her sweaters, socks, and bell bottoms. Nothing.

He strode over and pulled out the drawer of her desk. Inside were only pencils and a stack of lined paper. He picked up the paper and paused. There beneath it lay the little blue bookmark he'd given her when she'd gotten her first B in physics. He set the papers on the desktop and smiled. The bookmark had been a sympathy gift. Poor Miss-All-A's had gotten a B minus. He took the bookmark and read it. "God is with you in your time of darkness." No wonder she had hid it beneath the papers. It had been a joke at the time. But now . . .

He frowned and ran his thumb over the smooth surface. The words stood out in bright yellow against a background of green and blue. A waterfall splashed through the center of the picture. He squinted and read the tiny inscription at the bottom. *Bridal Veil Falls in Spring.*

Paul gripped it tighter, then slowly turned toward the picture on the far wall. Yosemite. In winter.

He knew where she had gone.

19

Maddie pressed her hand against the cabin's window and closed her eyes. It was cold outside but not too cold. Not yet. She opened her eyes. The light was still bright enough as it filtered through the window and into the tiny cabin she'd rented for the weekend. She touched the rough curtains. The night was far enough off. If she left now, she could make it. She could do it. And then tomorrow, maybe she'd go home. Or not.

Perhaps she'd stay a day more, or two, here in Curry Village at the eastern end of Yosemite Valley. After all, what did she have to lose? There was nothing to hurry back for. Nothing, except more loss. And now she was here for this final venture. And maybe this, somehow, someway, would fill that black void of fear in her soul. Maybe this would do what all her other adventures had yet failed to accomplish — to make her forget, for at least a moment. Maybe this one would heal her heart.

Only God can do that . . .

Hush!

She didn't want to think about God, about her questions, or her doubts. Not here, not on the very edge of her last quest.

She moved her fingers until her skin squeaked against the glass. Somewhere out there water tipped down Yosemite's Vernal Falls. It fell and froze into a million droplets of ice. And when the sun came out, you could see the reflection of dozens of rainbows as the water-turned-snow piled at the bottom of the falls. It was a sight to behold. A sight like no other. At least that's what the guide had said that morning as she snowshoed with a group of strangers across the valley. He'd told them but not taken them there. Instead, he stopped partway along the path. Turned around and led them back, with no more than a passing comment about what lay beyond that spot on the trail.

And so she'd seen nothing, heard nothing but the roar of the Merced River as it traveled beneath a wooden bridge and vanished somewhere beyond the trees. She could hear the river still, gurgling against the rocks, calling her to follow its song and trace it back to the falls from which it came.

She remembered the way. She'd counted the steps. Paid close attention to the turns and dips in the trail. She could find it again. If she wanted.

And she did. It was why she came all this way. Why she chose Curry Village. Why she bought the picture that hung back in her apartment in Palo Alto. She couldn't go back — wouldn't — until she'd stood at the bottom of those falls and felt the frozen mist brush her face and seen at least the shadows of the water as it fell.

Maddie inched forward until she felt the coolness of the windowpane against her forehead. There was still time. A chance to do one more thing. To prove that she could. To pretend that she was normal and everything was as it ought to be. She could answer the call of the water, before it was too late. She could fulfill this one final dream.

And then . . .

She moved away from the window, pulled on her gloves and her hat, zipped up her new goose down coat, and laced up her boots. After that, she opened her door and stepped outside.

Snow fell from the sky. Wispy flakes landed on her lashes, brushing her cheeks with cold. She held out her palm and caught the bits of ice in her gloved hand. It was only a light snow. Nothing much. A storm was predicted to roll in by morning. But morning was a long time away. And besides, sometimes you just had to take a chance, grab the last bits of light — of life — when you could. And she could. Now. Before the storm. Now, when the afternoon sun still glowed through the clouds and cast rainbows of color from waterfalls she couldn't see.

She stomped her boots on the sidewalk outside her cabin, then reached for the snowshoes resting against the side of the wall. She squatted down and put them on. They were awkward things. Made her legs feel ten pounds heavier and twenty pounds more unwieldy. Rented and cheap. But they worked. And they would allow her to do this last thing she'd always dreamed of.

She rose, closed her eyes one more time, and envisioned the path in front of her. Thirty steps, and she'd turn left, then head to the roped walkway. Two hundred and five steps later, she'd turn out into the field to the path that would eventually lead to the base of Vernal Falls. She'd find it from there. It would be simple to follow a path through the rocks and trees.

Maddie smiled and tightened her snowshoes. She pulled down her hat, put up her hood, and started counting. One step. Two. The air was crisp, invigorating. Seventeen. Eighteen. What would Paul say if he could see her now? What would her mother say? She grimaced. Mom would probably have a hissy fit. It was best that she didn't know. Good thing Maddie hadn't waited to tell her.

A truck rumbled down the road behind her. And farther away, from the direction of the ice skating rink, voices mixed with loud laughter. Someone shouted. Another called back. She couldn't distinguish the words, but she could tell they were moving away from her. A door slammed. Something creaked.

Thirty. She turned left. Her snowshoes sank deeper into the snow. She kept walking and counting. The angle of the light told her to adjust her path to the east. She did. The snow underfoot grew harder. It seemed thicker than this morning. It was harder to lift her feet and move on to the next step. But she tramped on. Slowly. Doggedly. Until her breath came in quick puffs.

She could distinguish dark patches in the white of the snow — rocks or fallen branches. She had drifted too far north again. The snow was too soft here, but she trudged on. In a moment, the snow thinned. She grinned and took a swig of water from the bottle slung around her shoulder.

Her feet had found their way back to the well-trodden path now. She picked up her pace. The sky must be getting cloudy, for it was darker than it should be at this time of day. She should still have a few hours of daylight. But it seemed too dim, too gray.

Somewhere to her left, she heard the thump of snow falling from a branch and the call of a blue jay, followed by the far-off answer of another. The path narrowed. Trees pressed in on either side. She remembered this part. They had turned around not too far ahead. So, if she just kept going, she'd reach the bottom of the falls in about half an hour, maybe more.

She walked faster. It was too bad Malcolm couldn't be with her now. He would have loved Yosemite but hated the cold. A sad smile brushed her lips. They'd always talked about hiking Half Dome someday. In the summer, of course. One spring they'd even made plans. Wrote for brochures on where to stay. Studied the little dotted lines on the maps that told them where the trails curved into the mountains. Planned meals, bought a cheap tent from the army surplus store. Maddie still had that tent, somewhere, back in her closet in Boston. Malcolm's tent, which they never once used.

Her arm brushed a branch on her right. Snow slid onto her shoulder. She moved left.

I wish you were here, Malcolm. I wish you hadn't . . . I wish Mom hadn't . . .

She pushed the thought away and settled instead for an earlier memory, a better one. She was scampering after Malcolm as he hiked along the cliffs at Moshup Beach. Her with her short, little-girl legs, and him with his long, teenage ones. Pebbles skittered from beneath her feet.

Malcolm paused, turned around, and cocked his head toward her. "Hurry up, short stuff." His voice seemed to echo over the rocks. "You can see all the way across the world from up here."

So she scrambled after him and caught up. And she could see across the world. Way out across the water. Forever.

Malcolm put his arm around her shoulders and grinned down at her. "You're all right, short stuff. And don't let anyone tell you different."

Their mother's voice came then, shouting from down at the shore. Demanding they come back right that instant. Quoting rules about not climbing on the cliffs — rules they didn't care about — and calling out dire warnings against the dangers of a fall.

Well, they didn't fall. They climbed back down, sweaty and happy, and ran along the beach until Mom's voice faded into the background.

Maddie paused and sighed. No, they didn't fall. Not that day, anyway. The fall would come later. Much later. But it was best not to dwell on that now.

She slogged forward in Yosemite's snow for another twenty steps, then stopped. It was colder than it had been and darker. She took another step. Her foot sank deep into the snow. She pulled it out and tried again, more to the right this time. But the snow was still too soft, too powdery. She frowned. She ought to be at the bottom of the falls by now. But she wasn't. She turned a slow circle. The path wasn't where she thought it would be. She backed up and moved toward a patch of light between the trees.

Her foot slipped. The ground dropped away. She caught herself and moved back. That wasn't the path. It was a gully.

She turned around again and moved forward. A pine branch scratched her face and tipped back her hood. She righted it, then swung her arm out to her left. Her sleeve swooshed against the soft needles of the pine. She turned right and reached out. Her hand sank into three inches of snow. A boulder, covered in white. She turned again. Another tree. Left. Three steps. Her foot hit something hard in the snow. She tipped forward. And fell.

Her back jarred. Her gloves buried in the cold. Wetness seeped through the fabric at her knees. Her hands moved forward until they hit something solid, something dark. A fallen tree trunk. And beside it, another rock.

Maddie pulled herself to her feet and shivered. The path was gone. Her arms shook. She stumbled forward. The boulder again. And back. Trees. Nothing but trees.

The snow drifted between them now in fat clumps. Faster, thicker. She held her breath and listened. No sound of falling water, no distant rumble of cars or voices. Nothing but silence and dropping snow.

She sank to the ground and pressed her back against the boulder.

I'm not lost. I can't be lost. Oh, God . . . no.

And then night fell. And the storm with it.

A deathly chill soaked into Maddie's feet, up her legs. Through her elbows, to her arms. It seeped into her bones, her mind, froze along the narrow place where her breath met bare skin. But that was then. It was not cold now. Not here in this darkness, in this strange room where silence oppressed and was broken only by the odd beeping that came from somewhere beyond the blackness. Yet, she still felt it. Tendrils of ice. Creeping higher. Tightening. Choking.

That's not now.

But it was. She was cold. So, so cold.

I'm going to die.

The sound of beeping slowed. Her breath slowed. She couldn't feel her toes anymore. Or her feet. They were gone now. It was all gone. Except the cold. The ice. The snow like a blanket wrapped around her. And growing tighter.

And then she was there again. In the woods of Yosemite. Back to that time when the darkness came, the snow fell, and there was nothing that could lead her back to the warmth and light. She'd dug a little hole in the snow, made walls of ice on either side of her. Then she pressed her back against the fat boulder and hoped the branches above would shield her from the falling snow. They almost did.

She huddled there, in the cold and darkness. And waited.

The numbness came. And the lethargy.

She had to sleep, but she couldn't. The bed was too hard. A window was open. She should close it. No. Wait. This wasn't her room. It was . . . She was . . . She couldn't remember. Why was it so cold?

I'm lost in the storm.

No. There was no storm.

Then why was it so cold, so wet? And that sound. Like the howling of wind through the trees. The fake fur around the edges of her coat tickled her cheek. She opened her eyes but saw nothing, not even the shadows. The snow around her turned to ice. And still more fell. It hit the branches above and dropped in chunks around her. She pulled her knees tighter against her chest, but it was no use. The cold still seeped into every inch of her being, still sent shivers up her arms and spine.

The storm wasn't supposed to come until morning.

Maybe it was morning. Maybe her sight had failed her altogether. But no, it couldn't be morning yet. It was still the night. Dark. Black. Freezing.

Branches creaked and groaned overhead. Her feet numbed.

No one will find me. No one knows I'm here.

Her throat closed. She gasped in a stinging breath. It hurt, like a razor slicing down her sternum. She took another breath. It went down like shards of glass.

God, help me. Save me . . .

Now she prayed, humbled. Now she gasped for help. No questions. No whispers of how God had betrayed her. The wind, the cold, the ice had stripped that all away, leaving only this: *God, help me now . . .*

Maddie's head fell forward onto her knees. And suddenly she could see again. But the images were strange, distorted, like pictures reflected on the surface of water. Pictures formed in the delirium of a mind half frozen and growing colder. It wasn't real. But it was. As real as memory. She went there now, following the shadowy images, driven by the cold, by the wind, to a time she'd almost forgotten.

The picture gelled and came to life. And she saw him.

Malcolm's face. His hair sticking out, all on end. Stains on his shirt, wrinkled as if he'd slept in it all night. And the green duffel thrown on the bed beside him.

Outside, it was raining.

"You can't go to Sunday school like that." That was her voice. Younger then. Much younger. "And we're already late."

"I'm not going."

"You have to."

He put his hand behind him, touched the bed, and sat down on it. "There is no God. So, what's the point of Sunday school?"

Maddie scowled. "That's stupid talk."

Malcolm pulled off his shirt. Strange red lines coursed up his arms. "Look at me, Mads." He laughed. "Look and see. At least you can. I can't see you at all."

She scuffed her sock-clad feet along the floor and turned away.

"If there was a God, would I be blind? What kind of God would take away a man's sight? Take away everything that mattered to him?"

"Mom says you're doing well, learning to get around with your stick and all. And you'll get a dog, she said, next month."

"I don't want a dog."

"You could name him R.B.I. You know, Runners Batted In. Baseball." She smiled.

"That's Runs Batted In. And the dogs come with names already."

"Oh." Her smile fell away.

For a moment, Malcolm said nothing. He just twisted his shirt in his hands and slapped it against the side of the bed.

She folded her hands and rocked back and forth on her heels. "Come on. Hurry up. You've got to comb your hair."

He turned his face in her direction, as if

he were looking at her, though she knew he wasn't. "What will it take, Mads, for you to see the truth?"

"What truth?"

"That I'm not going to Sunday school anymore. Or church. Or choir practice. Or Bible study. Or anything at all that has to do with a God who left me like this." He jabbed a finger toward his eyes.

"God still loves you."

"Why? Because the Bible tells me so?" He tossed his shirt toward a basket in the corner. And missed. "That's a children's song. I'm all grown up now. I've given up on fairy tales."

"I haven't."

"You will. Someday, something will happen to you, and you'll realize that God either doesn't exist or He doesn't care. And you'll be right where I am, wondering why you've wasted your time with prayer."

The pictures in her mind faded and were replaced by another. The same bed, still rumpled. The same duffel bag, now lying on the floor in the closet. The same shirt, washed and folded, waiting to be put away. But no Malcolm. He was gone. Forever.

"I am sorry, Madison." Her mother's voice, behind her.

"But . . ."

"Come out of there. Come on."

She turned around and saw the redness of her mother's eyes, the blotchiness of her cheeks, the shimmer of tears as they spilled down pale skin.

"Mama?" She flew into her mother's arms and buried her face in the soft silk of her shirt. They held each other. And wept together for Malcolm.

The image faded . . . died . . . and she was back again in the cold, in the trees, in Yosemite. The wind was howling now. The blue jays long gone. There was no silk shirt to cry into. No arms to hold her. Maybe Malcolm was right . . .

No. It wasn't God's fault that she was out here in the darkness, freezing in the snow. It wasn't Him who drove her here, beyond the reach of reason. It was . . . what was it? Fear, maybe. Of the darkness. Of the blindness. Of the unknown days to come.

She'd run from the unknown, out here in the woods of Yosemite. She'd tried to out fly it in a biplane, lose it on the curves and dips of a wooden roller coaster, bury it in the sands of Santa Cruz. But it had found her. Fear and the unknown and the chill of wind-driven ice.

She couldn't feel her legs anymore. Or her hands. She laid her head in her arms and closed her eyes.

No, Malcolm. You were wrong. I still believe . . .

A sound came, like a branch breaking. And in it, she heard the voice of an angel.

20

"Maddie! Maddie, no! Stop!" Paul tilted closer, would have shaken her if he dared. The beep of the EKG had slowed, become unsteady. The nurse would rush in any minute.

"Maddie!" Paul glanced toward the door. No nurse. No anybody. He wouldn't go out and find someone. He didn't dare leave her. Slow, so slow, was her heartbeat. He moved to the other side of the bed and back. Why wouldn't she listen, why wouldn't she hear?

Her breath became shallower still. It hissed from her lips.

"Maddie!"

She groaned.

"Maddie."

He turned away and prayed.

Her heartbeat steadied. He sensed it before he heard the change in the EKG. Her breathing deepened but still rattled.

He sunk back into the chair. He wasn't

tired, though it was the dead of night. He had no need to sleep, no desire to do anything but watch and wait and call her from her darkness.

Because, just now, he almost lost her. Almost. So close. And it wasn't the first time.

They crunched through the snow, Paul and some park ranger named Sandy. What kind of mother named her boy Sandy? Why couldn't it have been Dirk, or Sven, or even Bob — some manly name that gave him confidence? But no, he was out here, in the cold, in the dark, with Sandy.

Their flashlights splashed pathetic little circles of light onto the snow-filled path and reflected off a million falling shards of ice before them. The air was white; the ground white. The sky, somewhere far off in the darkness.

"This way." Sandy called out to him from somewhere ahead. How he knew the way, Paul didn't know. He could see nothing but snow. It looked the same here as it had back where they'd started.

"See those trees?" Sandy flashed his light toward a crooked red fir, surrounded by a bunch of miniature ones. "We're getting close to the trailhead again. You see anything?"

Paul pulled his hood further down over his forehead. His puffy down coat made him look like the Pillsbury Doughboy and sound like the swoosh of tearing paper every time his arm passed his side. Thick gloves made it difficult to manage the flashlight. He gripped it with two hands and pointed it west. Nothing. Just like the last time they'd passed here. Nothing but snow and trees and darkness.

Sandy stomped back down the trail toward him. "You sure she'd have come this way?"

Paul nodded. "I think so."

Sandy flicked the light up the trail. "Not an easy path if your sight's not perfect."

Not an easy path even if it was. Not in this storm, anyway. But he had to try.

He'd been so sure when he'd arrived late that afternoon. They'd given him her room number, told him when she checked in and when she would check out. It seemed so easy. Go to her cabin, knock on the door, talk some sense into her, and bring her back to the lodge to talk to her mother. Then they'd all go home. No problems. No worries.

Except she wasn't there.

He knocked for five minutes until his

knuckles were red and throbbing. He peeked through the window, paced on the porch. Knocked some more. Peeked. Paced. Until the sky grew dark and snow began falling in thick sheets. That's when he knew she wasn't coming back.

Her mother had gone back and forth from the lodge a dozen times. Finally, she brought Sandy.

He'd never forget the look in that woman's eyes as she stared out into the night with her face whiter even than the snow, her hands clutched so tightly that her fingernails had broken through the skin on her knuckles. When he and Sandy left, she was twisting the end of that ridiculous, flimsy scarf she'd tied around her neck. Just twisting it and twisting it and twisting it. And muttering something about Malcolm.

So he and Sandy had grabbed giant flashlights and a first aid kit, and set out for the bottom of Vernal Falls. He'd been so sure that was where she'd have gone. With that picture in her room and the number of times she'd told him, "Someday, Paul, I'm gonna snowshoe my way all the way to the bottom of those falls, and I'm going to see the water turn to snow right before my eyes. Someday."

And he'd say, "But not today." Then she'd

stick out her tongue at him and laugh.

But would she really be that foolish, now that her sight was failing? To set out alone, into the woods, with a storm coming in? His Maddie? Had she really lost her mind?

"You'd be surprised what crazy things people do up here," Sandy had said.

But Paul didn't want to believe it. "Maddie isn't crazy. She's just . . ."

"What?"

"Going blind."

Sandy had walked a lot faster after that. But that was over two hours ago. Two excruciatingly long hours. They'd been to the bottom of Vernal Falls and back. They'd called and shouted, yelled and whistled. But there was no answer. Once, Paul thought he'd seen snowshoe prints. Sandy wasn't so sure. "Not with the snow falling this heavily," he'd said.

But Paul insisted they try again. Back up the path, watching for spots where Maddie could have gotten confused, wandered off, and . . . He didn't want to think any further. The woods weren't safe beyond the trails. Anything could happen, especially to a woman who could hardly see where she was going in the daylight, let alone the night.

So here they were, trudging through the soggy underbrush, dipping back and forth to the trail, then fanning out away from it again. Searching, always searching, with their weakening flashlights and their ever-diminishing shouts.

And still, nothing.

Paul had never prayed so hard in all his life. Funny how he railed at God for not curing Maddie's blindness, for letting her have that stupid Stargardt's disease in the first place. He had stomped and fumed. But when he needed God — when there was no other hope — back he came, heart in hand, pleading for mercy. He supposed God was used to that sort of thing.

Help me find her now. Show me the way . . .

His flashlight made a fuzzy ray of light, hitting off the snow in the air and bouncing back to illuminate nothing. Flickers and shadows and nothing that made sense. He was wet now and cold. His nose was running, droplets freezing on his upper lip. Still, he flashed the light. A group of trees to his left, a boulder on his right. A little way ahead, thick branches heavy with snow. It all looked the same, felt the same, was the same. How could he ever find Maddie in this?

He pulled aside a branch. It shivered and cracked. Snow thudded to the ground and covered his boots in a blanket of white. The flashlight dimmed, sputtered.

It was no use.

"Paul!"

He jumped.

"Here." Sandy's voice echoed eerily through the snow.

He turned toward Sandy's light. His heart hammered. "You found her?"

"Look." He flashed his light toward the trees.

"What is it?"

"A gully."

A gully? His shoulders slumped. Why should he care about a gully?

"There's a low spot, just here." Sandy's light circled a spot on the edge of the darkness that Paul assumed was the gully. "Looks like a bunch of snow was knocked down. See?" His voice deepened. "Almost as if . . ."

As if someone had been there and almost fallen in. Paul rushed to Sandy's side.

Sandy's light was moving carefully, methodically, searching the bottom of the narrow gully. "I don't see anything."

Neither did Paul. Nothing but a little slash of light against the white nothingness.

"I'm going down." Sandy stomped the snow with his boot, then began to sidestep down into the gully. "You keep going up the trail. Meet back here in ten minutes. And don't stray. I don't want to be looking for two of you."

Paul frowned. Up the trail? He'd been that way already. Maddie wasn't there. She wasn't anywhere. Maybe he'd been wrong.

Sandy reached the bottom of the gully. A moment later, his light disappeared behind an outcropping of rock.

Paul flashed his light down the embankment. It showed it him nothing. And then, it dimmed. Again. He shook it. The light wavered and grew shallower. He backed away from the gully's edge. The snow thickened until he couldn't see beyond it. Couldn't see if the dying light contacted tree or stone or only the unending whiteness.

He turned and stumbled forward. His foot hit a hard place in the snow. He tipped forward, spun left, then righted himself. He strained to see through the shadows and snow, but it was all a confused mess. Nothing made sense. Nothing told him where Maddie might be, where she could have gone. In this light, he couldn't tell anything at all.

And then he knew. This was how she felt, how she lived. And not just in the snow, but every day. All day. She was confused, blinded, able to see only small bits when she needed to see more. Needed to see everything.

Oh, Maddie, I'm so sorry . . .

It came to him here, in this darkness: desperation — why she didn't want to be treated like a blind person, why she pushed and scraped and held on to every bit of sight she could. Why she had come here, and why she shouldn't have.

"Maddie! Where are you?" He shouted the words, heard them muffle and fall in the dropping snow. And still, he shouted again.

But he couldn't find her, not like this. Not with this storm, with this light.

He slogged two steps forward, then paused. "Maddie!"

No answer.

He glanced down at his flashlight. Then, he flicked it off. Darkness fell around him. Cold, and complete.

I'm blind now too, Maddie. Just like you. I'm out here in the snow, in the storm. I can't see where I'm going. I'm lost. Alone. Afraid.

Just like you.

Where did you go, Maddie? Where are you in all the blackness?

He took another step forward. Then two. He could feel the tilt and layout of the ground beneath his feet. He could sense how it curved left, how it hardened, just slightly, when he supposed he was on the trail. But the ground still sloped away. When he had been able to see the trail, he kept on it, his eyes guiding him along the narrow path. But now his feet wanted to take him another way, veering to the left, away from the trail, away from the path he'd taken before. He walked on, so slowly, feeling his way step by step, one hand in front of him, the other out to his side.

He touched the needles of a low-hanging branch. And then something fat and tall. His hand sunk deeper. A boulder, probably, covered in snow. He turned right, and fell. Flat on his face. Snow flew up his nose, stung his eyes. He choked on it and spat out a mouthful. Then he sat up and reached back, his arm swinging through the darkness, his hand moving, searching for what had tripped him. He found it and moved closer, patting his hand along the rough, thick trunk. A fallen tree, almost covered now by the snow. He gripped a branch that stuck straight up and hauled himself to his feet.

This sort of thing explained the bruise he'd seen on Maddie's forehead, the scratch on her cheek, the tentative way she walked through doorways and down steps. How easy it was to trip and fall when you couldn't see clearly the ground in front of you. How often had she walked into a half-closed door, fallen over something as simple as a short bench, made her way down a flight of stairs, only to find at the bottom there was one more than she'd anticipated? He'd seen her do that before. Seen her body jar and tip forward as she fought to regain her balance. He wanted to help, but she'd been so confident, so determined. She wanted to live her life, despite the blindness. Problem was, she didn't know how.

Paul brushed the snow from his pant legs and coat. His hand swished loudly against the fabric. Then he heard it. Faint and almost indistinguishable. A sound like a groan. A human sound.

He grabbed for the light in his pocket. Turned it on. The sound didn't come again, but he knew he'd heard it. Somewhere to his left. He lifted the light in that direction and swung it in a wide circle.

A flash of yellow.

He stopped the light. Yellow, and those silly, bright purple gloves.

She was there, maybe thirty feet away, huddled in a hole in the snow, unmoving. "Maddie!" He ran toward her, his feet too slow, too heavy in the snow.

She didn't move, didn't look up.

He knelt beside her and brushed the snow from her hood, her shoulders. Her eyes were closed, her arms clutched tightly around her legs. Light shimmered off her coat as he gathered her in his arms.

"Maddie?" He drew her close.

She was ice cold.

Maddie awoke with pain screaming through her feet, a bare bulb glaring in her eyes. The light hurt. Her toes throbbed. But she wasn't awake. Not in this time, anyway. There was no light, no bulb. But the pain was real. Except it didn't come from her feet. Not now. But there was a voice. Both then and now. A voice like an angel.

Paul?

He can't be here. That's what she thought then.

But he was. He found her. Could he find her again? Here too? In this gray place between light and water?

She reached through the grayness, searching again for that splitting pain, for the garish bulb, for anything that would take her away from this in-between place, back into the folds of memory.

And then, she was there again.

■ ■ ■ ■

"Hold still, Maddie."

"Paul?" Bits and pieces of the room swam before her vision, dipped in and out of the darkness at the center. She tipped up her head and could make out some posters on the far wall — charts, maybe, or drawings. And something orange, like a chair in the corner. And on the opposite wall, dark green splotches, curtains closed over windows shut tight. And above her, the bare bulb against a too-white ceiling. "Where am I?" She tried to sit up.

An arm, strong and familiar, slid beneath her shoulders, supporting her. She relaxed into it. Her coat was gone, her gloves removed, her hair plastered to the sides of her face in thick wads. She touched the worn blanket that covered her. It smelled of antiseptic and damp dog. Pain shot up her legs from her feet. She looked down at them. Two shadowy figures stood there, one burly in bright yellow, another slim and shaking. "Mom?"

Another voice answered. A man, his voice deep to match his brawny frame. "No frostbite in the toes, as far as I can see. So you won't lose any." He touched the top of her foot. Exquisite pain radiated from the point of contact. "Just a little deadening." He stopped touching her. "You probably feel like that's quite enough, though."

She opened her eyes wide and tried to make out her feet far below. "It feels like they're on fire."

"That's good." He paused, and she wondered if he was smiling. "Despite how it feels. These warm towels will do the trick and have you back up on these toes in no time." His head turned — she could tell by the shift in his voice. "Mrs. Foster, can you hand me the hot water again?"

The pain decreased slightly. The sounds of splashing water filled the room. A swoosh, a plunk, and the rapid rattle of drops hitting the water's surface. Then the agony came again.

"Be still, Madison." She could hear the strain in her mother's voice, the tightness that indicated fear or anger. She didn't know which.

The pain dulled again.

And she wondered what had happened, what she was doing here, and why that man was putting hot towels on her aching feet. It was all so strange, so surreal. She would have thought it a dream, if not for the pain.

"Good thing you have people who care

about you, miss." The man spoke again as he dipped the towel and reapplied it to her feet. "It would have been a rough night out there."

Then Maddie remembered. The blinding snow, the awful cold, and the darkness that hemmed her in, caught her, and held her in stormy arms. She fought to clear her mind. She was lost, but someone found her. An angel. No. Paul. She leaned into him. "How did you find me?"

He squeezed her shoulders. "It was the picture in your room that gave you away. And a good thing too."

She nodded and closed her eyes. "I always loved that picture." A strange lethargy stole over her again. Comfort. Warmth. Then a voice, sharp with emotion, shattered the stillness.

"She will be okay now?"

The man at her feet answered. "I'm just a park ranger, but I've treated feet that looked a lot worse than this. She'll be fine. In time." His voice rose as he patted her leg. "In the meantime, young lady, there will be no more hiking alone for you. Especially not with a storm coming in."

"It wasn't supposed to be in until morning." Her words sounded slow, slurred.

He laughed. "That's what you get for

trusting the weatherman."

Her mother cut in again. "Storm or no storm, there will no more hiking for Madison."

A chill, colder than the snow, clutched her chest. "Mom!"

"No, you are coming home to Boston. I cannot — I will not — let you risk yourself again."

"I'm okay."

For a moment, her mom said nothing. Then her voice softened, broke. "I cannot lose you. Not like . . ."

Malcolm.

The name buzzed between them, unspoken.

Her mom sniffed. "No, it is time you came home. It is time you learned how to live with the blindness."

Blindness. She hated the word.

"This will never happen again. Never. Never. Never!" Her mother's tone took on a hysterical edge. "Do you hear me?"

Paul squeezed her arm.

Maddie slid lower on the cot and opened her eyes. The bulb seemed to swing above her, but it couldn't be moving. Not here. It was her head that was swimming, silent denial that made her vision waver. She clenched her jaw and forced one word through tight lips. "No."

"No arguing. You do not know —"

"But . . ."

Paul's voice tickled her ear, his tone quiet, compelling. "Maddie, you could have died out there."

Died? His words echoed through her mind and silenced her. *Died?* Like Malcolm. Her body trembled. Resistance melted. She'd been a fool — as crazy as Malcolm, maybe more. No wonder her mother's voice had risen to an octave that could peel paint.

The pain in her feet receded to a dull ache. She reached up and gripped Paul's hand in hers. Squeezed its warmth, as if by doing so she could take some of his strength into herself to sustain her for the months, the years to come. "Oh, Paul . . ."

He raised her hand and kissed it, his lips soft, yet firm, tingling against her still-cold skin. So gentle. Startling. Full. The ache in her feet moved to her chest.

She looked toward him, wanting to see him, to know what his eyes would tell her. "Paul . . ." She spoke his name. Then he broke her heart.

"You have to go, Maddie."

Pain exploded in her chest. "Go?"

"Your mother's right. You have to go back to Boston."

Her vision darkened.

And his voice came again. Far away. So far, though he stood right next to her. "We can't." He shuddered. "I can't." He placed her hand gently on her lap. "We can't pretend anymore that this isn't happening."

This. The blindness. He was talking about the blindness. And he was right. But, oh, how his words hurt her. "It's just that . . ."

"Shh . . ." He touched a finger to her lips. "I know."

"How can you?"

His thumb stroked her cheek. "It's just that you don't want to go blind."

He did know. Did understand. A little, anyway. Tears pooled in her eyes.

A strange sound came from the bottom of the bed. A sniff. A quiet sob. Was Mom crying? Weeping for eyes that were failing fast, that had almost killed her? That would have, if not for Paul? Weeping for the end of a life that could have been?

She turned her face toward the wall and gave in to the pain.

Maddie held Paul's hands as the intercom above her screeched and the voice announced, "Final boarding call for Flight 762 to Boston. Final boarding call."

"I'll call," he said.

"Don't write," she answered.

A smile came into his voice. "I might. If you do."

And she would, in the big, loopy letters of the nearly blind. She squeezed his hands tighter. "Thank you, for everything." Stupid words, silly. Words that meant nothing, and everything. There was so much she wanted to say, to tell him. For a moment, she imagined herself standing on tiptoe, her hand moving to his shoulder, him leaning close, her whispering in his ear, "I just want you to know — I love you." But she didn't do it. Then in her mind, she put a hand behind his head, touched the short, soft curls of his hair, and kissed him. But she didn't do that either. Instead, she just stood there like a fool, with tears clogging her throat and his hands held in hers.

"You'd better go."

"I know."

"I'll miss you."

"I'll miss you too." It was all she could say. The best she could do. It would be wrong to tell him more.

She let go of his hands and turned toward the boarding ramp that led onto the plane.

"Come, Madison, it is time to go."

Maddie walked down the dim ramp, then stopped halfway and turned back. Paul was still there. She knew it, though she couldn't see him well enough to even wave good-bye. But she waved anyway.

Waved and waved, until her mother took her arm and led her away.

21

Spring was fading to the first blush of the summer of 1974. Maddie knew that by the warmth in the air, but no longer by the angle of sunlight through the window. She knew it from the laughter of children playing hopscotch on the sidewalk outside and the jingle of the ice cream cart as it passed.

But those sounds diminished now, covered by the melody of a record playing behind her. It was a simple song. It shouldn't have made her cry. She'd heard Frankie Valli singing about his lost love a hundred times since her mother had brought home the pre-release record. Such a simple song. Sweet. About a boy missing his childhood friend. About how his eyes once adored her. *His eyes* . . .

She closed hers and turned away.

Her mother had only put the 45 onto the record player to give her some background noise. She was supposed to be tuning out the music and listening instead for the little clues that would tell her where she was in the room. On the far side, her mother had placed an egg timer and set it. It was ticking now. She was to focus in on the ticking and find the timer.

She'd done it four times before — each a little faster, a little surer.

But then her mom had turned on the record player, put on the record, and placed the needle. And the music had come, obscuring the sound of ticking, and filling her ears with memories of Paul.

Her eyes had adored him, before she lost her sight. And like a million miles away, he couldn't see that she loved him. And now, it was too late. For her eyes, for her heart. And the song just made it all the worse.

My eyes adored you, Paul . . .
Tick. Tick. Tick.
But we, too, went our separate ways . . .
Tick. Tick.
You are the love I left behind . . .
Tick.

And she was there, the timer in her hand, the needle thumping against the inside of the record.

"Acceptable." Her mother took the timer. "But slow. Try it again."

Maddie sighed.

Her mother touched her shoulder. "With these this time." She pushed something flat and long into Maddie's hand.

Maddie gripped the thing and looked down. A pair of strange glasses lay in her fingers. She didn't wear glasses. "Mom?"

"Put them on."

The needle continued to thunk against the inside circle of the record.

"What are they?"

"Occluders, of course."

Maddie threw aside the glasses that would completely block her sight. "Aren't I blind enough already? I don't need those."

Her mother retrieved the glasses from where they'd fallen on the couch and again pressed them into Maddie's hand. "You have to learn how to get around without any sight at all."

Maddie's jaw hardened. "That's stupid."

Her mom said something that Maddie didn't catch, though she did hear the name of her brother in it. She moved closer. "Malcolm thought this was stupid, didn't he? Did you force these horrible glasses on him too?"

For a moment, her mother didn't say a word, and then she took the glasses from Maddie's hand. "*C'est bien.* If you want to be like Malcolm, then fine." Her mother's voice was tight, strained, as if she pushed the words out between lips drawn too taut.

Maddie reached for her mother's arm, her hands, and found them and the glasses in them. She took the occluders back.

Her mother stepped closer. Her voice softened. "I am doing this for your own sake, Madison. The darkness starts at the center, but it always spreads. You may not keep your peripheral vision. Malcolm did not, nor your grandmama before him. Malcolm did not use the occluders. Perhaps if he had . . ."

Mom was right. Maddie knew it, and that made her angrier still.

"Put them on, and do it again."

She put them on. But she still didn't like it. She was sick of these lessons. Sick of banging into walls and low tables. They'd already practiced folding money into different shapes for the different denominations, boiling an egg and making toast without help, feeling the size and edges of coins to distinguish dimes from nickels from quarters. And now, it was this drill. Moving toward a sound and finding it without falling or running into something. Well, she wasn't getting it. Maybe she never would.

But in one way, these lessons helped. They made the blindness less frightening. In another, they didn't help at all, because they did nothing for the ache in her heart. Nothing had — not all her adventures, not her rescue, not her months here with Mom.

Problem was, it wasn't that long ago that she'd been racing around a racquetball court smashing a little blue ball. Now, she was smashing into furniture. Not long ago when she was zooming around slower students as she biked to class. Now, there was no zooming at all. And no class. There was only the darkness, the lessons, and that awful Frankie Valli song reminding her of how much it all hurt.

Her shins already throbbed from banging twice into the coffee table and once into a chair on her previous trips across the room. Her head ached from trying to focus. And now, her chest hurt from holding back tears, gulping back sorrow. She relaxed her hands, rubbed her forehead, and removed the occluders. "Let's just stop."

"One more time, with the glasses, *s'il vous plaît*."

Maddie jumped. She had thought her mother was across the room already, but she was standing right next to her. Maddie hated that — hated not knowing where people were, if they were looking at her, if they were about to speak. The thoughtful people would touch her arm, say their names. But most weren't thoughtful. Most didn't know how to be. But it wasn't as if it mattered. She was hardly with people anymore. Mostly, she was just alone.

"With the occluders, Madison."

Maddie's hand tightened on the glasses, but she didn't put them on. "Okay. But I hate these." She knew she sounded petty and childish, but she didn't care. Everything was awful about going blind — the glasses, the shadowed images she couldn't make out, the bruises, the clumsiness of her feet, the doubts. And especially these endless lessons that were supposed to make her feel more competent but instead highlighted everything she'd lost.

Her mother lifted the occluders, set them on Maddie's nose, and hooked them behind her ears.

The fuzzy images at the edge of Maddie's vision vanished. The distinctions between light and dark became only black. She took a step forward.

Sharp footsteps indicated that her mother was moving away, to the other side of the room. Then the ticking came again.

Maddie took three steps forward. And ran into the chair. Again. And cursed.

"Watch your language, Madison."

She gripped the chair back in her hands and squeezed tight. She raised her head toward the place where she imagined her mother stood. "Why did you give this to me? This awful, horrible, nightmare of a disease?"

It was unfair to blame her mother, but Maddie couldn't help it. She'd been this way ever since she'd come to Boston — surly, rude, unreasonable. She'd left the sane, normal Maddie on the boarding ramp in San Francisco and hadn't been able to find her since.

Her mother made a quiet, choking sound. "If I could have spared you this . . ."

Maddie waved in the direction of her mother's voice. "I know, I know. I'm sorry."

"But we will beat it. We will."

Maddie's jaw tightened. "Come on, Mom, you know there's no cure."

"That is not what I mean. You will learn to get around. With your stick, by using your other senses. I shall get you a dog. And you will see."

Maddie grimaced. "Poor choice of words, Mom."

"I will make this all right for you." Her mother paused. "I must."

Maddie licked her lips. "I'm sorry I said it was your fault."

Mom didn't answer. The timer dinged.

"I'll try again. Across the room. One more time. You reset the timer." She heard footsteps, a clacking, then the ticking began again.

"I'm putting on the record."

"No!" Maddie cleared her throat. "I mean, can we put on a different song? Please?"

"If you wish."

More footsteps, then a scratching, a click, a squeak, and the voice of Perry Como filled the room.

Maddie breathed a sigh. Perry Como she could easily ignore. Slowly, carefully, she made her way across the room, focusing on the ticking, making a picture in her mind of where she knew the furniture to be. *Step around the coffee table. Move left. Hear the grandfather clock against the wall. Pass the window. A car is going by outside. Another step, then angle right. The ticking is louder. Forward, right, forward. Reach. There!* And she had it again.

Relief surged through her. Maybe she *could* do this. Maybe she *could* learn. "Perhaps if I get good enough, I can get my own place."

"No!" The vehemence of her mother's tone surprised her.

"Not now, of course. But someday —"

"No."

"But you said —"

"Let's go for a walk."

"What?"

"Outside."

Maddie touched her occluders.

"Keep them on. You need to practice listening to traffic. I have your cane."

Maddie groaned. Of course her mother had her cane, and her Braille books, and her clock that announced the time. She had everything. Everything that Maddie would have liked to forget in Palo Alto. But by the time she'd returned to her apartment after the Yosemite fiasco, everything was packed and shipped back to Boston. All the new implements of blindness were here waiting to greet her and welcome her. To her mother, it was a sign of thoughtfulness; to Maddie, a gift of pain.

She heard the snap of the cane being straightened and put together. A long, white cane with a bright red tip, fitted specifically to her height. Her mother had been so careful, but Maddie didn't care. To her, it wasn't a tool, but a symbol and a screaming declaration to the world that she was less than a woman, less than what she should have been. Could have been.

"I don't want to go out with that thing."

"Do not be silly."

"People will look at me funny."

"Well, that will not matter, because you will not know."

"I will too."

"Madison."

Maddie knew that tone. Ever since she was a toddler and had gotten into her mother's music sheets, it meant she was being naughty, selfish. And maybe she was. But to go out with that awful cane . . .

Wasn't it bad enough that she had no friends here? She never went out. Never did anything fun, just for enjoyment. All she did was practice being blind. They went to church and right back home. Sometimes her mother took her to the grocery store and once even to the symphony. She grimaced. She still didn't like the symphony, even though it was one of the only nonpractical things she'd done since arriving in Boston almost four months ago.

At first, some of her old high school friends had come by to say hello. They sat on the couch, exchanged a few awkward words. Promises were made that they'd "get together soon," but nothing ever came of them. Except once. Christy had invited her to a movie, and Maddie had gone, just to get out, just to hear the sounds and special effects. But it was terrible. And she couldn't see paying two dollars to just sit through a soundtrack, wondering what she was missing on the screen.

"Come on, cherie."

Maddie put out a hand and walked toward the door, the stupid occluders stealing from her even the little perception of light around the door frame. She edged forward. This was ridiculous. It shouldn't take five minutes just to get to the door. She scowled and dropped her hand. The door should be right in front of her anyway. It had to be.

"I'm coming." She picked up her pace. And ran straight into the window. Pain splintered across her forehead, radiated up her nose. She stumbled backward into the couch. Her head throbbed. She tipped and fell over the couch's arm, into the velvety plushness. *I hate this! I hate it, I hate it, I hate it . . .*

Her hands balled up and her throat tightened. She leaped from the couch.

"Try again, Madison."

"No!"

Maddie fought back the tears, swallowed them, and instead put her fist through the wall.

Paul swirled the liquid in the Erlenmeyer flask. He sucked up exactly one milliliter of diluted sodium hydroxide in his glass pipette and dripped it into the solution. Nothing. No sudden cloudiness. No rise in temperature. The liquid stayed exactly the same. Clear. Cool. Unchanged. He must have done something wrong.

He set the flask aside and picked up his notebook. Ten milliliters of distilled water, then he added the powdered compound John had made. He stirred, heated, cooled, and then added three drops of scopolamine. Just three, and no more. And he'd been careful, oh so careful, not to lose any of the scopolamine and especially not to touch his eyes after he touched the bottle. If he got even the tiniest bit into his eyes, he'd be wearing dark glasses for days, as the scopolamine would make his pupils dilate and refuse to narrow. Last, he added the sodium hydroxide. And it should have worked. The mixture should have become cloudy, warm. Unless . . . He looked at the paper that John had given him, then compared it with his notes.

He groaned. He'd added the wrong

amount of the compound. It should have been three hundred milligrams, not thirty. No wonder nothing had happened.

He sighed and poured the mixture into the chemical waste bin. He'd have to do it again. And this time, do it right. He carefully measured out the distilled water, then poured it into a clean flask. Next, he took the beaker that held John's concoction. *Three hundred. Not thirty. Focus!*

But it was no use. He needed a break. Some coffee maybe, with lots of sugar and cream. He adjusted the protective glasses over his eyes and undid the top button of his lab coat. As he did, the letter in his pocket crackled.

Someone tapped on the door frame behind him. He turned to see a man with spiky black hair and scuffed, black biker boots sticking from beneath his lab coat.

"Hey, dude." John snapped his fingers and pointed at the beaker on the counter. "You done with that sample yet?"

"I'll need another hour."

"You okay, man?" John stretched out his arms to reveal two tattooed snakes curling around his wrists.

Paul shook his head. Then he lied. "Sure. Just working too hard lately. You know how it is."

John shrugged. "Kathy said it was girl troubles."

Paul forced a laugh. "Girl troubles? Who, me?"

"I told her she was full of it. Paul Tilden, having a problem with a woman?" He snorted. "I've known you too long to believe that."

"Then get out of here and let me work, will ya?"

John tapped his hand against the door frame again. "I'm booked for the spectrometer this afternoon."

Paul waved him away. "I know. I'll get you what we need before then."

"Cool." John backed out of the doorway and sauntered down the hall. For a full thirty seconds, Paul could hear the clump of John's boots before the sound faded and stopped altogether.

Paul peeled off his thin latex gloves, strode over, and shut the door. Then he grabbed his notebook and walked to the desk in the corner. He tossed his notebook on the desk's surface, then pulled out the chair and sat down.

Again, the letter in his coat pocket crackled. This time, he pulled it out. He'd found it in his mail this morning. So eagerly he ripped open the envelope, flattened the paper, and devoured her words. But they'd turned bitter in his stomach. Bitter, and hard to swallow. And still, he flattened out the pages and reread the big, loopy letters, written in black ink:

Dear Paul,

Thank you for your letter. The words were big enough for me to read. Except my mother saw them. I don't know if she knew the letter was from you, but she didn't seem to like it. I could tell by the way she paced around the room and made all those growly sounds in the back of her throat. Please keep writing to me, though. It's nice to hear from you. I . . .

The next word was crossed out so thoroughly Paul couldn't make it out. The letter started up again with a new paragraph.

Not that I don't have friends here, you know. Lots of girls from my old high school have come by, and it's been good to renew old friendships. I even went to a movie not too long ago. It had been playing for a while, so we knew it would be pretty good. Of course, I couldn't see much, but it was fun to listen to the dialogue and all the music and sound effects. Funny how I never noticed the music in the background until I couldn't see the screen so well anymore. Anyway, the movie was Blazing Saddles with Gene Wilder and Madeline Kahn. She did a great job. All that passion in her voice. I bet she'll get the Academy Award this year.

Paul skimmed the next section where Maddie summed up the movie's plot, then went on to talk more about her friends, their names, and all the exciting, fun things she was doing. He stopped at the last paragraph and read on from there to the end.

So, you see, you don't have to worry about me. I'm doing fine. I'm learning all kinds of new skills and can practically go out for a walk all by myself now. I guess going blind isn't that bad after all.

Write back soon.

Love, Maddie

Paul scanned the letter one more time, then wrinkled it up and threw it in the trash. Maddie may not mind going blind, but he sure hated it. None of this would have happened except for the blindness. The blindness that God didn't heal. That blasted blindness that took her from him just when he realized what he had. What he almost had, that is.

Paul groaned and stormed back to his flasks and beakers. He pushed the flask to the back of the counter and grabbed the vial of scopolamine hydrobromide. The liquid shimmered as he set it on the shelf above him. His hand shook. His stomach growled.

I really need a break.

He pulled off his lab glasses and rubbed his eyes. Too late he realized his mistake.

22

Dear Maddie,
You won't believe what I've done. At work, I got scopolamine in my eyes, and now my pupils are dilated like big quarters. I've got to wear sunglasses around all day, and of course it's been raining, so people look at me funny when I go out. The guys at work all think it's a big joke. They've started calling me Ray, for Ray Charles.

Maddie smiled at the huge letters Paul had used, then turned the page over to the back side. There, too, big, black words covered the paper. Bold enough for her to read without help.

Every time I walk by his lab, Tony (you remember Tony, short guy with

the 'fro) well, Tony calls out, "Yeah, baby," in the most awful imitation of Ray Charles you ever heard. Then he starts singing "Baby, Let Me Hold Your Hand," which wouldn't be so bad except that he's the worst singer ever. And besides that, I made the mistake of telling him what happened to me the other day. Somebody really did hold my hand. Well, close enough anyway.

Maddie sat on the chair and turned up the lamp by the table. Daylight faded from the window as twilight turned the sky a dull gray. She adjusted the shade until the light spilled over Paul's large letters. Then she turned to the second page.

Now, that's a story you'll appreciate. I was crossing Embarcadero, right where the fish market is, and I feel this hand on my arm. I look down and there's this little old lady — and she's helping me across the street! I'm not kidding. A real, honest-to-goodness little old lady. She pats my arm and tells me what a fine young man I am and it's too bad about my eyesight. I couldn't bear to tell her I could see just fine to cross the street.

 So then I find my halibut. It takes forever because the place is so crowded, and I get in line to wait. And wait. And wait. I'm almost to the counter at last when this guy in a fancy suit and tie walks up and stops a couple feet away from me. He stares at me for the longest time, and I can tell he doesn't think I can see him. Then just as it's about my turn, this dude slips, ever so quietly, into line right in front of me. Well, lucky for him the man behind the counter said something before I could. I had visions of shoving the dude to the ground and stuffing those glasses right up his nose. And the halibut with them. Not very Christian, I know. But still . . .

On the third page, there was a change in the writing, as if Paul had paused and come back to the letter later. The writing grew smaller. She widened her eyes and moved closer to the light. She tipped the page this way and that, until the letters became clearer.

Anyway, all that's to say I guess I'm

getting a clue what you've been going through. I bet you get this kind of stuff all the time. No wonder you said the things you did on the beach that day. I've been at this for three days, and it's already getting mighty old.

So how do you do it, Maddie? Stay faithful, I mean. Still believe, and hope, and trust God when He doesn't heal you? How do you keep a thankful heart when someone cuts in front of you in line, when some old gal you don't know wants to help you cross the street?

Maddie paused and glanced toward her cane sitting against the umbrella stand by the door. How did she stay faithful? How did she trust? She didn't. At least it didn't seem that way. She doubted and wondered and asked a thousand *why*'s in the silence of her heart. But she still believed. The snow taught her that. Jesus was real. And He was God. He saved her. She knew that, but somehow it still wasn't enough.

God, how do I trust in the darkness? How do I learn to walk where I can't see? How do I live a life of blindness when everything I wanted is lost with my sight? God, are you out there? Do you see . . . even me?

She didn't know. Not the answers to her questions. Not the future of her faith. Not the reason she was going blind when there was a God in heaven who was supposed to love her. Once, it seemed, everything was so clear. Believe in Jesus. Obey. Go to church. Be happy. But that formula didn't work anymore. Not in this darkness. Not in this doubt. Would God find her even here? Even in these shadows of pain and loss? And if He did, what could He tell her that would make a difference, any difference at all?

Maddie sighed and shook her head. Leave it to Paul to uncover wounds she had tried to ignore. Nothing got by him. She had filled her letter to him with fluff and lies. He had responded with depth and truth. And she'd always thought him the shallow one. She had been wrong. Very, very wrong. She sniffed and continued reading.

I miss you, Maddie girl. I wish you were here. But I understand now why you can't be. I'll try to call this week. Maybe Friday. I called last week, but your mom said you weren't there. I don't think she likes me.

Maddie frowned and turned the paper over to the last side.

I could be wrong, but I don't think people usually slam the phone down like that when they like the person on the other end. My ear is still ringing.

So I'll talk to you soon. But talk loudly because now I look blind, but I'm really deaf. Ha ha.

Love, Paul

P.S. Kelli got pink cowboy boots and a matching pink cowboy hat through mail order last week. She's calling everybody "y'all" and answering the phone with "howdy." You've got to hurry up, learn what you need to, and get back here before it's too late. She's driving us all crazy.

Maddie chuckled. The sound faded as she heard heels clicking on the tile floor in the kitchen. She folded the letter and slipped it into her pocket. She'd read it again later. Alone.

"Mom?" It had to be her mother, in those new high-heeled leather boots she'd bought from Saks last week. "Do you need me to help with dinner?"

"Have you practiced your Braille today?"

Maddie didn't answer.

"Madison?"

"Yes, Mother."

"Practice your Braille."

"I don't want to." She said the words too low for her mother to hear her.

"Did you hear me?"

She raised her voice. "Yes." Of course she heard. She always heard. She moved toward her Braille book on the coffee table. Her fingers brushed the surface.

The phone rang.

She jumped. Maybe it was Paul. She hurried toward the kitchen. *Around the chair, avoid the table, watch out for the step up.* She had practiced long enough to get there quickly. But not fast enough. She'd just made it through the kitchen doorway when the ringing stopped.

Her mother's voice turned sweet. *"Allô?"*

Maddie sunk back and rested her shoulder against the wall. She touched a seam in the gold flowered wallpaper and waited.

"No. I am sorry." The sweetness fled from her mother's tone. *"Oui. Certainement."* She paused.

Maddie picked at the seam. A bit of wallpaper paste stuck on her finger.

"*Non.* I told you. She is not here."

She straightened and dropped her hand. "Mom? Who is it?"

Her mother slammed down the phone.

Maddie stepped toward her. "Who was that?" She jabbed her finger at the wall where the telephone hung.

Her mother blocked the phone with her body. "Nobody. It was a wrong number."

Maddie bristled. "It was Paul, wasn't it? He said he was going to call."

"He said?"

"In his letter."

"What letter?"

"The one he wrote me."

"Give it to me." She flung out her hand.

Maddie put her palm over her pocket and pressed the letter into her side. "I will not."

Her mother came toward her. "*Oui.* You will."

She stood her ground. "It *was* Paul. You told him I wasn't here. How dare you?"

Her mother snapped her fingers and pointed at Maddie's pocket. "I want to see that letter, Madison. *Immédiatement.*"

She stepped back. "No."

"I am doing this for your own good. You must trust me."

"Trust you?" Something inside Maddie snapped at those words. She'd heard them before. But at that time they had been spoken quietly, painfully, whispered outside Malcolm's door. *"Trust me . . . For your own good . . ."* And then Malcolm died.

Maddie straightened to her full height and faced her mother. "You said that about Malcolm too."

"How do you know?"

"I heard you, Mother. That day, before . . . before . . ."

"You do not know what you are talking about."

Heat surged up Maddie's chest, her neck, her face, and burst from her lips in a loud accusation. "You smothered him. Took everything from him. You said you were helping him, but you didn't help. Didn't help at all. And now you want me to trust you? I don't think so. Not after what happened to Malcolm."

"I did the only thing I could." Her voice lowered, trembled with heat. "But it was too late."

Maddie's voice grew louder, drowning her mother's words. "What did you do for Malcolm that was for his own good?"

She caught a glimpse of her mother from the edge of her vision. The image was fuzzy, distorted, but she knew that look all the same. The lips pressed tight, the cheeks pale, and that aggravating tick that would jump in her mother's cheek, only when she was especially angry. Well, she was angry now. Angry enough so Maddie could see that tick even with her poor vision. "Whatever it was, it was wrong. And now you want to do the same thing to me."

"You do not understand. You never did."

"I understand enough to know it was your fault."

"Yes, it was."

Maddie stopped. She had expected denial, defense. But her mother's words were soft, defeated. Sad. "You admit it?"

Her mother moved closer. "*Oui.* I admit that I sent that witch away, and I should have done it sooner. If I had . . ." She paused, as if the next words refused to come. She took a shuddering breath. It hissed through her lips into the silence between them.

"Who are you talking about?"

"Patricia. You remember Patricia, *n'est-ce pas?*"

"His girlfriend?"

"If you could call her that."

"You stopped her from seeing him?" Just like with Paul. Just like . . . A chill washed over Maddie's skin. Her breath wouldn't come right. It choked in the back of her throat, gasped, and turned sour. "But . . ."

"I did what I had to do. Only I did not do it in time."

"You took everything."

"Not everything. Not enough anyway."

And suddenly it all became clear. "You killed him. You, with your worry, your overprotective ways, your fear of this stupid thing called Stargardt's. You couldn't just let him live his life and be happy." Her eyes narrowed. "Wasn't it bad enough that he couldn't play ball anymore? Wasn't it hard enough that he had to come back here to live — had to give up everything he wanted, dreamed of, hoped for? You had to take Patricia too?"

"*Oui.*" Her mother's tone was flat, defeated.

"You killed my brother."

Her mother looked away. "I did not."

Maddie's cheeks flushed with the heat of her fury, the fire of her fear. She glared at her mother, unseeing, uncaring, and spat words through lips now taut. "How? How can you say that?"

For a moment, her mother didn't answer. But Maddie could tell that something had changed. In her stance, her demeanor, in the air that crackled between them. "I have failed you too, have I not? Even though I have tried so much."

Maddie jutted out her jaw, refusing to back down. Not this time. "How can you say you didn't kill him?"

"The truth? *Oui,* perhaps it is time." Her mother muttered the words. She stepped forward and lifted Maddie's chin toward her. Gentle. Unexpected. She leaned over and spoke in her ear.

"Because, Madison, your brother is not dead."

23

Paul dropped the phone onto the receiver and ran his hand through his hair. A few choice words about Mrs. Foster skittered through his mind. Maddie had been there. He knew it. For some reason Mrs. Foster was blocking his calls. He didn't know why, but it had to stop. He had to do something.

Yet, what could he do? Call again, and again, and again, until he finally got to Maddie? And then what? What could he possibly say that would make any difference at all? How could he help her, make things right? He wasn't a doctor. He couldn't restore her sight. He was just some guy she used to play racquetball with. Just some guy . . .

He slammed his fist into the table, but that didn't help. It only made his hand throb. He shook out his fingers, then crossed to the far side of the room. There on the bookshelf lay a novel she'd given him. *The Hobbit.* She said he would love it. He'd never even read it. And beside that was half of a broken racquetball, a scrawled phone number of someone named Sherry, and a photo taken last year.

He stared at the picture. It was a head shot of him and Maddie snapped by a friend after a particularly intense game of racquetball. He and Maddie wore matching white headbands. She was holding up her racquet and making a face. He stood with his forehead glistening with sweat and the bright blue racquetball in his hand. Maddie hated that picture. He loved it. And not just because he'd won that game by a mere two points. There was something else about it. Something in the way she looked at the camera with her bottom lip out but a grin in her eyes.

Paul touched his fingers to the frame, then turned and walked away. He wandered into the kitchen, opened the fridge, and pulled out a can of Mountain Dew. That would keep him up half the night. Just what he needed. He peeled back the aluminum tab and tossed the bit of metal toward the trash can in the corner. It clinked on the floor. He left it there and took a long swig of the yellow soda. It burned at the back of his throat and made his eyes water. He took another drink.

Paul glanced back at the phone. What was he going to do? Let her go? Now that their relationship was hard — almost impossible — would he just let it end?

No.

Because there was something in that stupid letter she'd sent to him. Something that wasn't in the words she wrote, but perhaps in the ones she crossed out. He'd thrown that thing away, but he couldn't so easily erase it from his mind. He'd thought on it, pondered it, and finally understood. The whole thing was a lie. A bright, cheery, put-on-a-happy-face lie. And there was only one reason Maddie would do that to him. Because she didn't want him to worry. Because she didn't want to hurt him. Because she cared. And maybe, just maybe, she might love him too. He couldn't be sure. But one thing he was certain of — somehow he was going to find out.

He sucked down the rest of the soda, crushed the can in one hand, then threw it at the trash. This time, he made it.

I've got to do something.

He grabbed his next letter to her from the table, opened the pages, and glanced at the last one. *I hope I'll have talked to you by the time you get this,* it read. He picked up a pen and scratched out that last line. Then he scrawled a P.S. *I called Friday. Your mom said you weren't there. I don't believe her. Call me.* He wrote his phone number bigger, blacker than the rest, even though she knew it already. Even though she could probably see it just fine at the normal, large size. He underlined it twice, then folded up the letter again.

Now he just had to get it to Kelli. He yanked his coat from the back of the chair and stormed out of the house. Twenty minutes later, he stood outside Maddie's old apartment, banging on the door. No one answered. He rang the bell. He thumped on the door again. This time, it swung open. But it wasn't Kelli who was inside. It was Ryan.

Ryan flipped a lock of his hippie hair behind one ear. "Hey, dude, what's up?" Paul pushed past him into the room. "Where's Kelli?" His gaze darted around the room. He noted the bowl of potato chips on the coffee table, the Bibles lying on the couch and chair, and a half-full package of Oreos tipped up against a lamp. "She here?"

"Store."

"Humph." Paul paced across the room, then turned back and grabbed a cookie from the bag. "They should put twice the stuffing in these." He twisted off the chocolate top and licked the white filling.

Ryan picked up the cookies and set them beside the chips. "What are you doing here, man? You coming for the Bible study?"

"When's Kelli going to be back?" He reached for the chips.

"You two aren't dating, are you?" Ryan picked up the chips and moved them farther from Paul's hand.

Paul glared at him. "No. Of course not."

"Then what's up?"

"Nothing." Paul crunched on a chip and turned his back to Ryan. He wasn't going to tell that guy a thing. And he wasn't going to stay for any Bible study. Not tonight. He used to come every Tuesday, and then on Fridays, but not anymore. Now he just needed to get this letter to Kelli, and then he'd be out of here. Kelli could get the letter to Maddie.

He'd tried to write to Maddie directly, using some P.O. box number, soon after she'd gone to Boston. But Maddie hadn't gotten that letter. Or the next one he sent. She seemed to get the mail sent by Kelli, though. Those went through just fine. He smashed the chip in his hand.

"Dude!"

"Sorry." He bent over and picked the crumbs off the chair.

Maddie got his letters now, and he got the ones Maddie sent to Kelli for him. But he'd had enough. Maybe it was time to stop the games and —

"What's eating you, man?" Ryan's question cut through his thoughts.

Paul turned. "What?"

"You want a root beer or something?"

Root beer. Ryan's solution for everything. No problem was so big that a root beer couldn't fix it. "No. Thanks."

Ryan put down the chip bowl and motioned toward it. "Have as much as you want. There's plenty." He paused. "You sure you're okay?"

Paul looked directly at the guy for the first time in a long time. He noticed the stubble on his chin, the way his eyebrows crept together, leaving only a centimeter gap between them. He never liked Ryan, but maybe that was unfair. Sure, the guy was a dork, but that wasn't his fault. He was a good guy, an honest guy. He deserved an honest answer. "No, I'm not okay."

Ryan pulled a furry pink pillow from the chair closest to Paul. "Come on, sit down. Kelli'll be back soon."

Paul sat and rubbed his hand over his forehead. "Thanks."

"So, what's up?"

"Maddie."

Ryan nodded. "Kelli said her mother's being a real . . ." He cleared his throat. "Well, you know. I won't say it here, right before Bible study and all. But we both know what I mean."

Paul smiled. "Yeah, we do."

"So?"

"So, I don't know what to do."

Ryan picked up a chip and tossed it into his mouth. "Why do anything?" A bit of chip popped from his mouth and stuck on the table.

"Huh?"

"Well, Maddie's gone. You're here." Ryan shrugged and sat in the chair opposite him. "And if you don't mind me saying, you've never struck me as one who's in for the long haul."

Paul bristled, then sighed. Ryan was right. Everyone knew it. "This is different."

"Why?"

Paul sat back, kicked out his legs, and looked at Ryan for a long moment. Finally, he answered. "Because I love her."

Ryan rested his elbows on his knees. "Yeah? Well, you aren't the only one."

Paul sucked in his breath. "What? You?"

Ryan laughed. "Me? Don't be stupid."

"Then . . ."

"I was talking about God, of course." He rolled his eyes. "You know, God?" He pointed toward the ceiling. "The Guy upstairs. The Lord of the universe. The Big Kahuna. The Maker of heaven and earth."

"Yeah, I know who He is." Paul's jaw tightened as he recalled why he didn't like Ryan.

"And don't forget Jesus." He picked up a Bible, wiggled it, and tossed it into Paul's lap. "The dude who died on the Cross to save her. That guy."

"Get to the point."

Ryan heaved a huge sigh. "The point is that Jesus loves your girl more than you do. You don't gotta worry. He's taking care of her."

Paul crossed his arms. "A lot of good *that's* doing."

Ryan glared at him. His eyes narrowed to slits. "It is a lot of good. You don't know the half of it."

Paul sat up. "What do you know?"

Ryan raised his hands in a sign of surrender. "I don't know nothin'." He stood and held his hand out toward Paul. "Just what I've seen these last years."

Paul took his hand as Ryan pulled him to his feet. "And what's that?"

"Two people God loves. Too stupid to

know what's right in front of them."

They stood together for a moment, then Ryan clapped him on the shoulder. "Don't worry, man. It'll be all right. You just need to trust Jesus and do your part."

"What's my part?"

"I dunno. But it ain't His part. Leave His part to Him. You do that, and I'm betting you'll know what your part is too." He squeezed Paul's arm. "I'll pray for you, dude. You just gotta trust."

Trust. That wasn't something he did well. Not since . . . well, not since Samantha. Paul pulled loose from Ryan's grip and headed toward the door. He opened it and nearly ran over Kelli. "Hey!" He ducked away before the brim of her pink cowboy hat could jab him in the chin.

She stopped. "Hey. What are you doing here?"

"I need Maddie's address. Her *street* address."

"Sure." She threw him a strange look, maneuvered around him, and dropped her grocery bag onto the coffee table. "Who's been eating the chips?"

"Him." Paul and Ryan answered together.

Kelli chuckled as she entered the kitchen. A drawer opened. Then came the sound of a pen scribbling on paper. A moment later,

Kelli returned and handed him the paper. "It's about time." It was all she said before she marched to the table and began to unpack the grocery bag.

Paul glanced down at the note, shoved it into his pocket, and left. He took the steps two at a time, all the while Ryan's words pounding in his head. *"You just gotta trust . . . God loves her more . . . Do your part, not His."* Senseless words, stupid. No. Paul was stupid. He stopped at the bottom of the steps and looked back up. Stupid to let her go. To believe that if he couldn't fix everything, then he shouldn't try anything. Stupid to believe he was alone in loving her. Ryan had it right. Maybe God did love Maddie more than he did. But could he believe that, in spite of her blindness, in spite of all that had happened? In spite of unanswered prayer? Did he believe it? And if so, what would it mean?

He turned and strode toward his car. The paper crinkled in his pocket. He opened the car door and slipped inside. *"Do your part . . ."* He opened his hand. There his keys glimmered in the light. He flipped to the ignition key. *I don't make the car run. I only turn the key. I press the gas pedal. But I don't make it go.*

What if . . . what if . . . What if he could

just love Maddie and let God take care of the rest? What if he didn't have to save her, didn't have to make everything okay? Didn't have to heal her blindness or make the dark spot in her vision go away? Didn't have to pretend it didn't matter? Didn't have to have all the answers? He could just be there for her, with her. What if that was enough?

He could do that.

He turned the key and the car's engine started.

This isn't like Samantha at all. It was what his time with Sam should have been. Could have been. Just being together. Happy with the time they had. Grateful. Because God loved Samantha more too. Even when Sam died . . .

Paul gripped the steering wheel in tight hands. *I know what to do.* He glanced through the windshield at the sky. *I will . . .*

He pulled out the paper from his pocked and peered again at the address. Maddie's address. Boston. A tingling of fear shimmered through him. No, he wouldn't turn back. Not now. He knew what he had to do. His part. Only his part.

I just have to let God love her first. He jammed the car into reverse. *Even if that love includes blindness. Even if she is never healed. Even . . .*

■ ■ ■ ■

Paul stared at the pale, shriveled woman in the hospital bed before him. Her breathing was shallow still, harsh. A song came to his mind. An old song, a favorite from years past: "Just Remember I Love You." It would be all right. It was then, and it would be now. All right.

He only needed to let God love her first . . . even here as she lay dying in a hospital bed. Even when God could heal her. And still didn't. Not yet anyway. Not yet.

He leaned forward and began to sing.

Maddie was almost there. Almost to the place where she could remember what happened then and what was happening now. Why she was in this cold place beside the water. What she was waiting for. And why the pain in her chest wouldn't end.

The black water was receding. She could almost see past it. It ate at the shore of her memory. Steady, cold, relentless. But beyond, there was a light. Dim, but real. A constant beeping. And a presence.

Something else was there too. A mist, and with it a melody. Soft, chanting. Calm, with gentle words. A familiar song. A favorite. From so, so long ago. It drew her. Called to her. Took her back . . .

Not dead. Maddie backed away from her mother until her elbow knocked into the kitchen wall. How could Malcolm still be alive, after, after . . . ?

Her mother turned.

Maddie waited.

From the corner came the steady gurgle and pop of coffee percolating. The faucet dripped. The clock ticked. The aroma of Folgers filled the room. And her mother's words, bright as beads, still hung between them.

"Malcolm isn't dead?"

Her mother moved closer until her hand rested on Maddie's arm. "No. He is not."

Maddie tried to see into her mother's face, tried to determine the expression, but she couldn't make it out. All she could see was a glint of light, as if her mother's eyes were wet with tears unshed. "But . . ."

"But he may as well be."

So soft, so sad was the admission that Maddie barely heard it. And yet it stopped her angry response, halted her accusations, silenced all but the cold whisper of fear. "I don't understand."

"I know."

"You lied to me. All these years."

"It has not been that long."

Maddie moved around her mother, then walked forward with her hand held out until she touched the vinyl back of a kitchen chair. "How could you keep this from me?"

"I wanted to protect you." Her mother's tone was muted, as if she spoke with her back turned. "I wanted you to be able to move on. To put it behind you."

"Malcolm is my brother."

"And he is my *son*."

The pain in the final word took Maddie's breath away. "And you wanted to protect me. From Malcolm?"

"No." Her mother paused, and the silence came again. This time, heavy with words unspoken, questions unasked. Finally, her mother answered. "From what he has become."

Maddie frowned and pulled out the chair, the legs squealing against the linoleum floor. "What? Blind?"

"*Oui,* blind. But not just in sight. You do not understand, Madison. You do not know."

Maddie took a long, deep breath. "Then tell me. Everything. I want you to tell me all of it."

402

"Madison . . ."

"Everything, Mom. You owe me that much."

Her mother's heels clicked on the floor as she walked to the far side of the kitchen table and pulled out a chair. Vinyl squeaked as she sat. "Are you certain?"

"Yes."

"You know some of it already."

Maddie nodded. "Malcolm started losing his sight."

"Just like you."

"You made him come home."

"I invited him. *Oui.*"

"Just like me?"

Her mother sighed. "Do not make this harder. He wanted to come home. There was nothing left for him anywhere else."

"So he came back, and you taught him how to be a blind person."

"*Non.* I told you that already."

"No?"

The vinyl squeaked again. "Why do you think I give you canes and Braille books for Christmas? Why have I taken so much time off of work to help you? Why do we practice every day? Occluders. Music. Trips across the room. Across the road. Across the city. Listening. Learning. Training your other senses to do what your eyes cannot."

Because you're mean. Cruel. She couldn't speak the words aloud, because for the first time, she suspected they weren't true. A chill raced through Maddie. "I don't know. Why?"

"Because I did not for Malcolm. And I lost him. I do not wish to lose you too. And . . ."

"And?"

"And because I love you."

The words sounded odd in Maddie's ears. They rang there, speaking truth and untruth. Revealing, hiding. There had to be more. "And you didn't love Malcolm?"

Pain welled in her mother's voice. "Do not say that. Do not *ever* say that. I loved your brother very much."

"But?"

Breath hissed through her mother's lips. "But I failed him. I did not save him." A movement came then, as if her mother had waved her hand in the air. Then she spoke quietly, as if each word hurt to say it. "You do not remember. How could you? You had school and tennis and basketball and music lessons."

"I hated those."

"I know."

Maddie rested her elbows on the table and tucked her hands under her chin. "So did

Malcolm."

"I know that as well. I had hoped music could help him. Help you both."

"It didn't."

"It seems not. But I had to try. Out of love, Madison."

"What happened with Malcolm?"

Her mother paused, and Maddie wondered if she would say more. If she would tell the secret that she'd kept hidden for years.

"Mom?"

"Patricia."

"Who?"

"You said you remembered Patricia?"

"The girl?"

"Oui."

"What about her?"

"You want to know why I hung up the phone just now, why I said you were not here, why I told you not to write to him or call?" Her mother's voice lost its gentle edge. "It is because of Patricia."

Maddie waited.

After a moment, her mother started again. This time her tone was sharp, bitter. "Malcolm, oh, how he was taken with Patricia. She did not care if he was going blind. She loved him anyway. She understood. She cared." Her mother blew out a quick breath.

"Cared enough to bring him drugs. DLS, SDL, LDS."

"LSD?"

Her mother's nails tapped the table. "*Oui.* That was it. And marijuana and I do not know what else."

"You knew this at the time?"

"I suspected, and I did nothing to stop it. I felt sorry for him. Thought maybe it did not matter. But it did."

"What happened to Patricia?"

"It took her less than two months to tire of the blind boy. To become weary of leading him around, of never being told how pretty she was, of doing the things a companion of a blind man must. *Oui.* The novelty wore off, and she left him. You know the rest."

"He was hit by a car."

"One day, high on something, he walked out into the street, and . . ."

Maddie heard a gulp, as if her mother was swallowing a sob. "Then what? He isn't dead."

Her mother sniffed. "I did not want you to know."

"Why?"

"He does not know you. He does not know anybody."

"Where is he?"

"In a home where they treat people with head injuries."

"Will he get better?"

"They say he will not."

"I want to see him.

"No." Her mother's tone turned fierce. "There is no point in that. Nothing good can come —"

"I need to see him."

"I will help you. Everything will be fine. You do not need to see him. It is too . . . too painful. Trust me." Her mother reached over and gripped Maddie's hand in her own.

Maddie could feel her mother trembling, could sense the tears streaming down her mother's cheeks. She reached up and touched the wetness. "You don't need to protect me anymore."

"But . . ."

Words bubbled up from Maddie's soul, words long suppressed, long hidden beneath misunderstanding and fear. "You couldn't save him, Mom. And you can't save me either."

"But . . ." Her mother choked on the words. Her tone fell to a whisper. "But it is all I know how to do."

Softness filled Maddie. Understanding, and yes, even pity. Not for herself, but for her mother. All these years, Maddie had thought she was just being overprotective, controlling, but now she saw that it wasn't that. Fear and love and guilt and sorrow were all mixed together to create a mishmash of emotion that spilled out into actions that hurt more than healed. That oppressed when they were meant to free. It couldn't go on. Not any longer. She didn't need her mother to save her. Yes, now she understood. She squeezed her mother's hand. "It's okay, Mom. I already have a Savior."

Maddie put her arms around her mother and embraced her in a way that seemed new and strange. Her cheek pressed against her mother's shoulder, tears now filling her own eyes. "Just be my mom, all right? That's all I want."

"Oh, *cherie*." A sob broke from her mother's lips. Then she spoke words that were a balm to Maddie's heart. Words Maddie had never before heard her mother utter. At least, not to her.

"I'm so sorry, Maddie. So sorry . . ."

24

It was coming for her. A darkness and a light. A gull over the water. A song. A memory. A voice that made her ache with longing. With a hope that she'd thought long dead.

I must cross this water.

But she did not. Instead, she stood by the water. Silent. Cold. Unmoving. She waited for a moment that would not come. At least not here. Not on this black shore.

I must get back. I must wake up. Now.

But the water remained. The darkness. The light. The gull. The song with a voice from yesterday.

She was so close. So near the light she had once known. It was right there. Just beyond the water.

"Cross it."

I cannot.

"Why not?"

I am afraid . . . I am afraid to die.

"Come . . . Don't be afraid." The words beckoned her. Soft and shimmering. Steady and warm. Bright across the waves.

She took a step forward. Water brushed her toes. Another step. Wetness crept up her ankles. Another. She shivered and paused.

I want to go home. I want to be free. Oh God, help me cross this water.

And then, the memory came.

It was not a house or a hospital but some strange mutation of the two. It had thin, light curtains on the windows and brightly colored pictures on the walls. But the floors were covered with tiles of scuffed linoleum that reflected the artificial light of a dozen long fluorescent bulbs. And they reeked of that sharp institution-antiseptic smell meant to cover odors far less appealing. Handrails lined the halls, and metal doors, painted white, all in a row, held numbers large enough for even Maddie to see. And the heat. It blew from registers in the floor, making the air seem sticky, heavy.

Maddie slowed her steps down the hallway, trying to walk more softly so her feet wouldn't make noise on the tile. Beside her, her mother didn't seem concerned about the sound of her steps.

"Just up here, Madison."

Maddie stretched her cane out a little farther and tapped it on the wall to her left. Though she could vaguely see the wall, she was supposed to practice negotiating the hallway with only her white cane. She was told it would be good practice in an unfamiliar place. But instead, she just felt foolish while attempting not to make the cane's tip tap too harshly. But the sound echoed down the hall all the same, mixing with the confusion of noise and light — her soft footsteps and her mother's heeled ones, and beyond, a muddle of conversation and cries, a television in one of the rooms ahead, the slosh of a mop, the voice of Marlin Perkins announcing the beginning of *Mutual of Omaha's Wild Kingdom*. Maddie drifted left. Her arm brushed the railing.

"Not so near the wall, please, Madison."

"Yes, Mother."

Her mother slowed. "We do not have to do this."

"I do."

Her mother sighed.

She's right. I can still turn back. Maddie squelched the thought. She was here now. And so was Malcolm. Somewhere. He was alive, and that was all that mattered.

Her mother touched her arm, and Maddie stopped. The hallway had widened on

411

the right. She turned. There was a desk of some sort, or a counter, with a person behind it.

"Malcolm Foster, *s'il vous plaît*. Is he in his room?"

A rustle of papers answered her, followed by a pert voice that seemed to belong to a very young nurse. "He's in the common room now. Just down the hall." There was movement, as if the woman had pointed in the right direction.

Maddie tried for a closer look and got the impression of very large eyes in a brown face, framed with dark hair.

The voice of Marlin Perkins grew louder. Then came the hair-raising screech of some kind of bird.

The woman behind the counter stood and shouted. "Turn that down please, Marcy."

Wild Kingdom grew louder yet.

The woman groaned. "She just loves the animals." She moved around the desk. "Her husband should have never brought her her own black-and-white." Her voice rose. "Marcy!" She turned to Maddie. "I'll be right back." Hurried, hushed footsteps moved away from them. There was a jabber of voices, and then Marlin's voice returned to a normal volume. A moment later, the woman was again beside them. "Now, you were asking about Malcolm?"

Maddie's mother answered. "How is he today?"

"He brushed his own teeth this morning. Julie only had to put the toothpaste on for him." She moved back to the other side of the counter.

Her mother tapped her fingers on the low counter. "I have brought his sister to see him."

"Oh?" The woman's tone conveyed her doubt about the wisdom of bringing Maddie to see Malcolm. "She's to see him?"

Maddie shivered.

"Oui. To *see* him. Now, he is in the common room, is he not?"

"Oh, um, yes." The woman stuttered, then stalled. She cleared her throat. "The big room on the left. But you mustn't expect —"

"We know."

The woman said nothing, but Maddie imagined that she nodded. Then came the rustle of papers being stacked. "Therapy isn't until four."

"Merci."

Maddie's mother touched her arm, and Maddie moved down the hallway. From a room to her left, the voice of James Brown crooned, accompanied by the mellow notes of a saxophone. Maddie paused. "Malcolm?" Her brother loved James Brown.

"It is not him, Madison. Come."

Maddie moved past another room from which came sounds of a dull, rhythmic chanting, and another room that smelled of stale perfume. "We should have brought something for him. Flowers. Ones that smell nice."

"They do not allow flowers."

"No flowers?"

"Not here. No nuts or candy either. Nothing they can choke on."

Maddie shook her head. How could Malcolm be in this awful place with no fresh flowers, no chocolate, no light and cool air?

"They are very good to him. When he first came, he could not even lift his hand to his own mouth. But most days he can feed himself now. Sometimes he can put on a pair of slippers." Her mother's tone grew softer. "One day he put on a pink pair of bunny slippers that belonged to that Marcy girl. There is a picture in his room." Maddie could hear the sad smile in her mother's voice as she slowed. "We are here."

Maddie stepped through a doorway into a larger, square room. There seemed to be tables scattered throughout and a television in the corner with a long couch along one wall. Maddie turned her head, attempting to get a glimpse of the scene through her peripheral vision. Blurred figures sat at the tables. Two on the couch. Three in wheelchairs. Which was Malcolm? Some jabbered words that meant nothing. One sang "Happy Birthday" in a strange monotone that grew loud and soft by turns.

Her mother's hand brushed her arm. "He is over there by the window. He always likes to sit by the light."

"Can he . . . ?"

"No, he cannot see it, but the nurses tell me he knows. I do not know how he can tell. The warmth of it, maybe. So they sit him in the light."

A lump formed in Maddie's throat. She folded up her cane and tucked it against her side.

Her mother touched her hand. "I will take that." She removed the cane from Maddie's grip. "Come. Hold my elbow."

Maddie did and, for once, was grateful for the guidance.

Her mother led her through the maze of chairs and people, tables and couches, until she stopped before a figure in a wheelchair by the window. Maddie could see little of him, but enough to know he looked nothing like her brother. This man was gaunt, emaciated, his shoulders hunched, his hair black and ragged.

Her mother touched the man's hand. "Malcolm? Malcolm, *cheri,* it is your mother."

The man in the chair didn't move.

"I have brought your sister." She paused. "I have brought Maddie to see you."

Still, there was no response. Not a movement, not a grunt, not, as far as Maddie could tell, even a flickering of the eye.

Her mother sighed. "I suspected as much. He will not know you."

The tightness grew in Maddie's chest. Her breath shuddered. "It's okay, Mom. I hardly know him either."

Her mother sniffed and backed away.

Maddie knelt before Malcolm's chair and placed her hand on his knee. She strained to see him. The sunken eyes. The sharp cheeks. The hollow darkness. It was too strange, too different. But somewhere there had to be the brother she had once known, had once seen with clear eyes. The quick smile. The laughter, the quirk of a brow. They were gone now. She reached up and touched his face. Felt it. So different. He seemed cold, even though it was warm, too warm, in the room. "Hi, Malcolm." Her voice caught.

A sound came from him then, something like "Maaaaaa." It was not a word, just a noise, but at least it was something.

Maddie put her hand back on his knee. Seconds ticked by. She could hear them passing from the clock on the wall, steady through the hum of voices from those at the tables and the drone of some game show from the television.

"Oh, Malcolm, I'm sorry I didn't come sooner." She wanted to say more, so much more, but words wouldn't come. They stuck in her throat, refusing to be voiced. She wanted to tell him she was sorry she hadn't been here for him, sorry about what happened, sorry she could do nothing to help him now. Tell him she missed him — the pictures of waterfalls he used to draw for her, the ghost stories he'd tell her with a flashlight under the sheets at night when they were kids, the way he used to call her "Mads" and cuff her gently on the chin. And she wanted to share a funny story and hear him laugh, tell him about her adventure in Yosemite, how she'd almost seen the falls they'd always talked about.

But instead, she just knelt there, gripping his knee, her eyes full of tears, as the minutes ticked by and the program on the television turned to a margarine commercial about not fooling Mother Nature.

Eventually, her mother tapped her shoulder. "We should go, Madison."

She didn't look up. "Not yet, please." The words were barely a whisper.

"I've brought you a chair."

Only then did Maddie notice that her knees were aching, her back tense. "Thank you." She lifted her hand and felt the cold metal of a folding chair. She rose and sat, her fingers moving to rest now on her brother's arm.

"I will be down the hall, speaking with the therapist." Then her mother was gone. Maddie could tell by the sudden absence in the air beside her.

She leaned closer to Malcolm. He hadn't moved in all this time. Hadn't shifted, lifted a hand, or even moved his head as the light from the window changed. Nothing. He was so different, so very, very different. And yet . . . She reached up and smoothed his hair. "You need a haircut."

He didn't answer, of course.

Maddie parted his hair with her fingers and pushed it back in the style he used to wear.

"Maaaaaaa."

"That's right, Mal. I'm here. Finally." Her voice trembled. She wiped her nose and dashed the tears from her cheeks. She cleared her throat and steadied her voice, if only a little. "Do you remember that story you used to tell me of the little dog named Pierre? You said he was named that because he always peed in the air."

Maddie forced a smile. "There was a guy in my chemistry class last year named Pierre. I waited all semester to see if he'd live up to his name, but he didn't."

Still, Malcolm didn't move, didn't even seem to know she was there.

She closed her eyes and rested her forehead on his arm. Pain sliced through her chest and sorrow laced with regret. "Oh, Malcolm, life just doesn't turn out the way we think it should, does it?" She rubbed her nose again. "You're in this place, trying to learn something as simple as how to put a spoon in your own mouth. This isn't the life you would have wanted. It seems so wrong, so unfair. And yet, here you are. And here I am. We can't pick our lives, can we?" She pressed her cheek against him. "We get what we get, and then what? You're stuck here, and I'm . . . I'm . . ."

Malcolm twitched.

Maddie looked up and tilted her head until she could almost see him.

But Malcolm still faced forward, his head

unmoving, his eyes unseeing.

"I got Stargardt's too, Mal. I'm going blind, just like you did. Did you know? Mom probably didn't tell you. She says you don't understand much of what people say to you. Not anymore. But I wanted you to know anyway. Because of all the people in the world, you know what it's like." She rubbed his arm.

He didn't respond.

But she kept on anyway, pouring out words that had been bottled up for too long. Questions, doubts, pain, and fears. Whispered in a hushed voice that only he could hear, if he would, if he could. And maybe that's why she spoke at all, because he probably didn't hear and couldn't judge her. And because he was her brother, and she loved him. She always had.

"I thought you were dead. Thought I'd be too. But you're here, this shadow of who you once were. In a chair, in a light you can't see but only feel. I don't understand any of it. How did this happen? How could it — to you?" Then she voiced the question that had haunted her ever since she'd found out the truth about Malcolm. "Wasn't being blind bad enough?" She stopped and swallowed her words. They weren't helping. Nothing would. Nothing could explain this . . . except . . .

She raised her head until the light fell full on her face. She opened her eyes wide, allowing the circle of darkness at the center of her vision to mix with the blurred image of her brother. The blind spot was larger now than it had been even a month ago. And her peripheral vision was fading. Blindness. She'd blamed everything on it. Her fears. Her doubts. Her failures. And she'd blamed God for that blindness, saying He'd betrayed her.

But maybe she'd been wrong.

She placed her hand over Malcolm's and tightened her fingers. It was not blindness that had done this to him. Blindness hadn't made him take drugs, lose hope, walk out into the street that day. Not blindness, but the fear of it. The same fear that had driven her into a biplane, a roller coaster, a snow drift.

"I've been afraid, Malcolm. So afraid." She held his hand between hers. "But fear isn't going to help me, is it? It didn't help you." She rubbed her thumb along the back of his hand. "And neither will running away. But that's all I've been doing. And it hasn't turned out so well for me either. I thought I was being brave, but I was only being scared. Scared that if I didn't fight, I wouldn't have any life once I went blind. But I didn't know, didn't understand. It could have been me in that chair, Mal. Just like you."

Maddie thought back over the last few months, the last year. Over all her actions since that night when the screen disappeared in the middle of 007's theme song. Ever since then, she'd been fighting. Fighting going blind. Thinking people were feeling sorry for her. Caring more about what she was losing than what she still had. Unable to believe that God was in the darkness, that His love was greater than the blindness. So she grasped and clung, accused and hung on, when all she had to do was walk forward, face her fears, and believe that God loved her enough to take her through even this, even the places where she couldn't see past the shadows. God hadn't betrayed her. Fear had. It had cajoled and seduced, painted pictures without hope. Pictures she had allowed herself to believe. If only she had fought the fear instead of the blindness.

She moved back in her chair until Malcolm was nothing but a blur and a shadow before her. Fear had driven him too — to this place. Chased him through the darkness until he lost much more than just the light.

She'd almost let it happen to her too.

She tilted her head. "We can't run anymore, can we, Mal? This life is the only one we've got. Yours in this place, mine in the growing darkness. What would you tell me if you could, brother? What advice would you give?"

She closed her eyes until a vision of her brother as he once was filled her mind. His hands on his hips, his shoulders broad, his mouth laughing. The sun glinting off the red highlights in his hair. *There's probably a hundred things you would change, if you could go back . . . If you could face blindness again, this time without the drugs, without the fear, without that last walk out into the street. What would you say to me, now that I face the same darkness?*

Maddie tilted forward and rested her cheek against his chest. She could hear his heart beating, could feel his warmth against her skin. And there, she could almost hear her answer. Steady, beating, quiet words whispered in the dark. *"Live, Mads. Live and love and be happy. Trust that God loves you. Don't be afraid. There are worse things than the darkness."*

Maddie opened her eyes and moved back.

"Fear is worse than darkness. I won't be afraid anymore."

Malcolm moved his hand on top of hers. Then he squeezed.

25

Maddie sat with her Braille Bible on her lap and ran her fingers lightly over the bumps on the page. The Bible was huge, even though this volume contained only the four gospels. The other volumes sat on a shelf behind her. She was reading about the man born blind in the gospel of John, but the bumps were still hard to distinguish. She needed more practice. If she hadn't known this story so well, she would not be able to make it out. She rubbed her fingers over the words again.

"And his disciples asked him, saying, 'Master, who did sin, this man, or his parents, that he was born blind?'" Maddie touched the bumps on the next page.

"Jesus answered, 'Neither hath this man sinned, nor his parents: but that the works of God should be made manifest in him.'"

She loved this story. Mostly because it was funny, but also because it was deep. It reminded her that God wastes nothing. Even blindness. She turned her face toward the morning sun slanting through the living room window.

From the kitchen, the phone rang, and her mother answered it. She dropped her fingers down on the page and continued reading.

"I am the light of the world . . ."

A minute passed, then two before she heard her mother's shoes clicking again on the kitchen floor. Her mother spoke from the doorway. "Telephone for you, Madison. It is that boy from California."

Maddie set the book aside. *Paul?* "You told him I was here?"

"I do not believe this is wise for you. But, *oui,* I told him you were here."

Maddie leaped up and wove her way into the kitchen, avoiding the end table and the chair that was not quite pushed in around the Formica table. She picked up the receiver on the counter. "Hello?"

"How's it going, mountain climber?"

"It *is* you! No more hiking in the dark for me."

"Promise?"

"Promise." She paused. "Hey, you sound really clear. We must have gotten a great connection."

"Um, yeah." He hesitated. "Only the best for you, of course."

"Ha ha. So what's up?"

"You tell me. Your mom says things have been pretty exciting around there. They must be because this is the first time she hasn't told me you weren't at home."

"I know. I'm sorry about that." Maddie twisted the phone cord around her finger. "Did she tell you I've seen my brother?"

"The one who isn't dead?"

"She *did* tell you. Well, it's changed everything. I've been really stupid, but not anymore." She knew she was chattering, but she couldn't help it. "It's time I live, Paul. Just live with . . . with whatever sight I have, be it little or none."

"I'm glad because —"

"My life was bought with a price. A high price. And it's enough. I won't be afraid anymore."

"Good because —"

"I'm practicing my Braille, I'm using my cane, and I've even played a little basketball. Next thing you know, I'll be going on a date."

"A date?" His voice turned sharp. "With who?"

She switched the phone to her other ear. "Well, yeah, that's still a problem. Seems

427

I'm no better at getting a date now than before I started losing my sight. So that date thing might have to wait."

"I'll get you a date."

She laughed. "Sure you will. Just call up one of your many friends here in Boston, right?"

"I'm serious. I'll get you a date."

Maddie leaned her shoulder against the wall. "For when, next year?"

"Tonight. Seven o'clock. You be ready."

"I get it, a blind date. Ha ha."

"That's right. Be ready."

"You aren't serious."

"I told you I was."

Maddie frowned. This had gone on long enough. "Okay, enough joking around. Long distance is expensive, remember?"

"Will you be ready? It'll be a fancy date, so wear your best dress."

"Paul!"

"Promise me."

"You *are* serious."

"I am."

"Okay, but who do you know in Boston?"

"You leave the details to me. I have my connections."

"Just as long as he doesn't have bad breath."

"He won't."

"Or B.O."

"I'll make sure."

"And I don't want to go to the movies. I've decided I hate the movies."

"That's all right, because the next Bond flick doesn't come out until December."

"How do you know these things?"

"I know everything. Now you'd better go get ready. You have a date."

"But you and I haven't talked in ages."

"I'll call you tomorrow. You can tell me all about your date."

"This better be a good one."

"Trust me."

"I do."

For a moment Paul was silent, then he hung up. Maddie listened to the dial tone for a full thirty seconds before she returned the receiver to its cradle. She giggled. A date. She shook her head. Paul was crazy. The whole thing was crazy. But maybe crazy was all right. Yesterday she would have refused outright. But today, things were different. She was different. She was going to live, take some chances, enjoy the gifts given to her. And thank God for them. Even a blind date. Even a pity date.

She scowled and shushed her thoughts. She didn't care about pity anymore. It would be nice to go out. The first date of her new life of trust in God, of facing the darkness without fear. Besides, Paul would find someone not too awful. Someone he trusted. Someone he thought she would like. And that would be good enough for her.

Maddie stepped toward the kitchen door and called to her mother. "Mom, get out the ironing board, I'm going out tonight."

Her mother's voice came from just beside her. "With whom?"

Maddie jumped. "I don't know."

"What?"

"It's a blind date." She grinned. "Kind of apropos, don't you think?"

Her mother threw her hands toward the ceiling. "Have you gone mad?"

Maddie laughed and hugged her arms around herself. "You know, I think I have."

Maddie pulled the tiny brush out of the black tube and held it up. Mascara. *What was I thinking?* She moved it back and forth until it came to a spot in her vision where she could glimpse it. *If I weren't already blind, this would finish the job.* She brought it closer to her lashes. *Don't poke your eye. Don't poke your eye.* The end of the brush jabbed into her eyebrow. *Great.*

"Madison, are you ready yet?" Her mother's voice came from somewhere out in the hallway.

Maddie turned toward her bedroom door and raised her voice to a near shout. "Almost."

"Good, because it is seven . . . oh!" A flash of yellow in the doorway indicated her mother had come.

Maddie frowned. "What's wrong?"

"You look like — what do you call it? — a clown."

Maddie groaned. "Too much blush?"

"Blush, *oui*. And lipstick. And what is that black glob on your eyebrow?"

"I hope he's late."

"Tomorrow we will practice. We will count strokes and learn how to put on just the right amount." Her mother's footsteps came toward her. "But for now, you must let me help you."

Maddie put down the mascara brush. "Please. When Paul said a blind date, I don't think he meant that the guy would be blind."

Her mother chuckled. "We cannot hope for so much. So we must fix it unless you wish to frighten the boy away."

Maddie grimaced. "Thanks a lot, Mom. Don't get any ideas."

"Do not tempt me. You remember that I

do not approve of this dating."

"I know you don't."

"You can get hurt."

"I know."

"But I cannot be your savior." She paused. "Too much."

Maddie smiled. "You can be my makeup savior, all right?"

Her mother harrumphed.

Maddie didn't move while her mother rubbed her cheeks, her lips, and re-applied the rouge and lipstick. She strained to keep her eyes half open as her mom worked the mascara and eye shadow.

Her mother tapped her chin. "There, you are *très belle.*" She smoothed the collar on Maddie's dress. "Your stockings have no runs?"

Maddie stretched out her legs.

"They are good. Stand up."

Maddie did.

Her mother sniffed. "Ah, when did you turn into such a lovely young woman? I only hope your date will appreciate you."

"I'm sure he will, Mom." She said it, though still, she wasn't so certain. A stranger. A pity date. She licked her lips.

"No, no! You must not do that." He mother tapped her cheek. "You may press them together, but you must not lick."

Maddie bowed her head.

"Look up. Shoulders back." She touched Maddie's shoulder. "You are a beautiful woman going on a date with a handsome man. You will hold your head high."

Maddie reached out until her hand brushed her mother's arm. "Have you seen him? Do you know who it is?"

"Why do you ask that?"

"You said —"

"There is the doorbell. He is here."

Maddie heard it too.

"You wait a few moments, then come. I will answer. It is proper."

Maddie nodded and listened to the sound of her mother's footsteps, steady, measured, heading toward the door. The front door opened.

"You have come." Maddie could hear the resignation in her mother's words. Maddie grabbed her small purse and hurried out of her bedroom.

"She will think you could not find her another date."

Maddie reached the front room and faced the door. Her hands shook. She tried to steady them. "Who is it?"

Her mother turned. "Have you not guessed? It is that boy from California."

Maddie's breath stopped. "Paul?" She

barely breathed the word.

He was coming toward her. And she knew. It *was* him. Impossible. Wonderful. True.

"I never planned it to be anyone else, Maddie." His voice. Calm and confident. Filled with . . . with . . . with something she'd not heard in it before. "You have to know that. I always intended it to be me."

"But how?"

"I brought you roses." He touched her hand and lifted it toward him. "They aren't the best-looking ones, but they smell heavenly." The paper crinkled as he placed them in her arms.

"What color are they?"

He paused before answering. "They're red, of course."

Red? He couldn't mean . . . he didn't . . .

"Smell them."

She did. And he was right. They smelled exquisite. "They're beautiful."

He moved closer. "So are you."

She smiled and blushed. "I can't believe it's you."

"Are you disappointed?" He blew gently in her face. "See, no bad breath. And no B.O. Check for yourself."

She stepped even closer, stood on tiptoes, and breathed in. "Cologne!"

He had worn cologne.

■ ■ ■ ■

Footsteps came. Soft-heeled shoes on the hard tiled floor. They paused outside the hospital room door. Seconds drew out into minutes. The door shuddered. And then the footsteps moved on.

Paul moved closer to Maddie. He could hear her breathing rattle, sense the struggle for each breath.

The footsteps came again. Two sets. Then the door opened.

Paul stood and stepped back.

And they came. The nurse and a young doctor. So young. Younger, it seemed, than Paul had ever been. They glanced toward him. The nurse paused by Maddie's IV. She checked the level of the liquid, stared at the EKG, then gently — so gently — brushed a bit of hair from Maddie's forehead.

The doctor watched her. For a moment, he looked again toward the corner where Paul was standing. He opened his mouth, but words seemed to fail him, and he turned again without speaking.

And Paul understood. Everything had already been said. There was nothing more. Nothing except checking and waiting and hoping.

The doctor reached for the stethoscope around his neck, put it to his ears, then inched forward and pressed the silver disk onto Maddie's chest. For twenty long seconds he listened, then let out a long sigh and removed the stethoscope from his ears. He looked at the nurse and muttered some words.

Paul made out only one: "Soon."

The nurse nodded. "I know."

Paul moved back to the bed. Maddie's skin looked sallow, pale, in the weak glow of the fluorescent lights, so different from the warm flush of candlelight.

But still, she was beautiful. Now, in the cold flicker of fluorescence, with change coming soon. And then, all those years ago, when he gazed at her across a candlelit table.

Change was coming then too. Change, on the wings of a prayer.

Then, and now.

It was almost here.

She was beautiful, breathtaking. His Maddie, sitting there across the linen-covered table in one of the most exclusive French restaurants in the city. She was wearing her hair differently these days, a little longer and pulled back at the sides. The candle between them flickered and sent shadows dancing over the white linen.

"I've never eaten here."

"I picked this table special."

They spoke at the same time, then laughed.

Maddie sat back. "How did you get reservations here, anyway? I've heard they're booked months in advance."

"Your mom pulled some strings."

"She was in on this?"

"I twisted her arm."

And he had. Twisted with both threats and promises, right after he'd shouted into the phone, "I think Maddie cares about me!" and she'd hissed back, "Of course she does, *fou*." Paul's heart had soared at that and continued to soar as he told her that he was taking Maddie out, no matter what Isabelle said. He promised that no, he wouldn't hurt her, or lead her on, or — and this was strange — bring her something called DLS. Then her mother had hemmed and hawed and finally said, "I know of a good restaurant."

"You must have twisted pretty hard."

"Hard enough." Paul leaned forward. "She tells me this place is a little better than pizza."

Maddie grinned. The light shimmered off

her eyes. "You wouldn't like the pizza in Boston anyway. New York style, you know."

He gave a mock sigh. "Is nothing sacred? Not even pizza?"

She chuckled. "Now, are you going to tell me why this table is special?"

"Because it's by the window."

"So?"

"And you can see the city lights, almost all the way down to the water."

She frowned. "You know I can't see them."

He rested his elbows on the table. "Ah, but you can imagine can't you?"

She smiled. "Yes, I can."

"They're bright and sparkling. Like diamonds on black velvet."

"You've used that simile before."

"I was hoping you'd remember."

"Of course I remember."

"But there are more lights this time. Thousands of them. And they reflect off those earrings you're wearing. Kinda dangly, aren't they?"

She pointed her index finger at him. "Hey, if you're looking at my earrings, you're not looking at the lights."

He sat back. "You caught me."

She looked down and fiddled with the napkin on her lap. "Stop it, you're making me blush."

"I know."

She touched her hand to her cheek. "What else do you see out that window?"

He chuckled. "Well, you can look down the hill, across the lights, and almost see the water." His gaze never left her face. "A flock of herons are flying there."

"You can't see any herons."

"Don't interrupt."

She turned her face toward the window. "Tell me, then."

"And the moon is glinting off their wings. There's a sailboat in the harbor with a pure white sail. And there's a man on the dock wearing a black suit and . . . Wait, no, he's doing pantomime."

"Don't tell me — he's pretending to be in a box?"

"No, silly, he's pointing to his heart, then handing it to the woman standing opposite him."

"Is there a man with a music box and a monkey?"

He folded his hands. "There is!"

"And the monkey's wearing a yellow hat."

He laughed. "Of course."

She turned back toward him. "Oh, Paul, I've missed you."

He studied her face. The soft turn of her cheek, the curl of hair that had escaped to rest on her jaw line, the sweep of her lashes as she looked down again and played with the napkin on her lap. "I've missed you too, Maddie. More than you know."

"It's a long way from California to Boston."

"Too long."

"You flew?"

"Some fears just need to be left behind."

Her chin shot up. "How did you know?"

"I know everything, of course."

Her eyes narrowed. "Okay, smarty-pants, so what are we ordering?"

Paul gulped and opened his menu. He looked over it. Maybe he didn't know everything. It was in French. All in French. "Uh, how about this." He pointed. "Foy grass chad."

She giggled. "You know that's liver?"

He shuddered. "I hate liver." He moved his finger down the menu. "How about this one then?" He tried to say the word.

"Medallions."

"What?"

"You know, from a bull."

"Ew." He wrinkled his nose. Maybe this French restaurant idea wasn't such a good one. It was supposed to be quiet and romantic. A place where he could . . . He sighed. How did the conversation turn to bulls?

"Don't they have something, you know, nor-mal?"

She made a face. "Like a hamburger?"

He grinned. "That would be nice."

"I can ask."

"Don't you dare."

Maddie raised her hand.

The waiter noticed.

"Now you've done it."

"Monsieur, Mademoiselle." The waiter stepped up to the table with a bottle in his hand. *"Vin?"*

Paul sucked in a breath. "Uh. . . ."

Maddie smirked. "No wine, thank you."

"Monsieur?"

"No."

"Your order, then?"

Maddie plucked the menu from Paul's hand. "We'll have the *Thon rôti et glace de poivron* and the *porcelet.*" She paused. "And your *escargot.*"

"Oui, mademoiselle." The waiter threw a look at Paul, then snatched up the menus and returned to the far side of the restaurant.

Paul watched him go, then returned his gaze to Maddie. Her cheeks were pink now, and she wore that half-smile that made his heart beat faster. "I hope you didn't get me anything nasty."

"I ordered you snails."

He groaned.

She giggled. "Don't worry; they're just like clams."

He reached out and laid his hand on hers.

This time, she didn't pull back, didn't turn away. Instead, she turned her hand over and laced her fingers through his.

26

Paul guided Maddie into the ice cream shop. He had to have something to get the taste of those awful snails out of his mouth. Maddie had thought it was so funny when he chewed and chewed and chewed those rubbery things. Truth was, they didn't taste like much besides garlic. And that garlic was still hanging on.

He rubbed his tongue over his teeth. He'd promised her good breath. And if his plans were to work, he was going to need it. He stepped toward the counter.

Maddie moved closer to him, her hand still tucked against his side.

He loved the feel of her hand there, so warm, so . . . right. Tonight he would know. For sure. Tonight would change everything.

"What's this place called again?"

He glanced down at her. "Steve's. Opened last year."

"How do you know so much about Boston?"

"I've got my sources." He moved to the front of the line.

The man behind the counter tapped a flat spoon at him. "What can I get you?"

"Vanilla, please, with Oreo."

Maddie squeezed his arm. "Vanilla? That's kinda boring, isn't it?"

He covered her hand with his. "Trust me."

She smiled. "You said that before."

"And did I let you down?"

"Not yet."

He nodded and picked up the ice cream cup. He only needed her to trust him one more time. Just once more tonight.

He held his breath and touched the box in his pocket.

Maddie would never forget this night. She knew that even before they found the path that wound beside the Charles River, even before she tossed her empty ice cream cup away, even before Paul took her hand in his and held it in a way that meant something more than just friendship.

They walked beside the water. Tall lights shone on the path and danced on the surface of the river. Somewhere up ahead a man played a violin. A boy skated by. Some bird squawked as it passed. Far away, someone laughed.

And still, Paul held her hand and walked close beside her.

"I've always loved walking by the Charles. This was my favorite place to come when I was a kid."

"Not the park?"

"No, here by the Charles in the evening, with the lights glowing and dew just forming on the grass. There was something magical about it then."

"And now?" His voice was gentle.

"Now, it's perfect."

He moved closer. "Except there's no monkey to give a dime to."

"Not tonight."

They turned to cross a bridge.

Paul stopped at the top. "There's our monkey, Maddie. Toss in a dime."

"What?"

He pulled out a coin from his pocket and pressed it into her hand. "Make a wish, Maddie. And I'll pray it comes true."

She closed her eyes and tossed the coin into the water. She listened for the soft plunk far down below her. "Did you hear it?"

Paul drew her close. "No. But I don't need to."

"Are you looking at me again?"

"Of course."

She smiled.

"And what did you wish for?"

"I'll never tell."

"Your sight?"

She turned to face him. "No." And she hadn't. She had wished for more, much, much more.

He squeezed her hand. "You've changed your hair."

"You noticed. Do you like it?"

"Yes." He reached out and touched a strand. "What else has changed since you've been gone?"

"Everything. Nothing."

"Tell me."

So she told him everything — all about her lessons, her time with Malcolm, the work God had done in her heart to banish her fears. "It doesn't mean I like going blind, though. But I can live with it."

"We can live with it."

"We?"

She looked up at him, longing to see him, to read the truth in his eyes. To know what he intended by this date. Instead, all she smelled was his cologne.

He stepped nearer until she could feel his breath on her cheek. "I have something else for you, Maddie."

The breeze caught a tendril of her hair and blew it to the corner of her mouth. He brushed it back. Then he took something from his pocket and placed it into her hand. A small box, soft and velvet.

Her heart thudded.

His finger was on her chin, lifting it. His hand behind her back, pulling her close. So close. His head bent. Her eyes closed.

And then she knew nothing but the wonder of Paul's kiss.

In the hospital, Maddie woke up.

27

Maddie opened her eyes and saw nothing. Only the blackness, the same blackness that had been her companion for so many long years. But she could tell, at least, that it wasn't night. Not anymore.

A woman's voice, soft and calm, came from somewhere on her right. "Doctor, she's awake."

Paper rustled. A pen clicked. Something beeped. Something else hummed, low and steady. Then a man's voice spoke from just beside her. "Good morning, Mrs. Tilden."

It had come, then. The morning after the long night. Maddie tried to move her mouth, but something stopped it.

Gentle fingers removed something sticky from her cheek, something hard from her lips. Maddie swallowed. "I was dreaming." Was that her voice, so dry, so rough, like sandpaper over stone?

The woman came nearer. "What were you

dreaming about?"

Maddie turned her face toward the voice. "Heaven."

A hand patted her arm. "Then just give us a minute, and you can keep dreaming." The nurse removed her hand. "This is Doctor Nelson. He's been attending you."

A different hand touched her now. Larger, but just as gentle.

"Where am I? What's happening?"

"You're in the hospital. You're very sick. You remember that?"

She turned away. Yes, she did remember. That beep was her heartbeat, and the hum was from fluorescent lights above her. But sick? No. She wasn't sick. She was dying. And she had been afraid. That's why the water had come — the shadows and strange darkness. But she wasn't afraid anymore. The voice had come. That voice calling her back. Calling her to remember. She had remembered. And that was enough.

The doctor tapped her arm. "You should know, Mrs. Tilden, that we won't be able to operate."

Maddie nodded. "I know."

The nurse made a sound. Her voice lowered to a whisper. "How can she know that?"

Maddie smiled. "It's okay . . ." The EKG

stuttered. Maddie took a ragged breath. And coughed.

The blankets moved, then something cold touched her chest. No one spoke. And then the cold disk left her, and the doctor turned away. "It's time to make the call." He spoke not to her but to another.

Maddie closed her eyes. Breathing hurt. Everything hurt. She turned her head. And there, for just a moment, she thought she smelled it. Faint and musky. An aroma she hadn't smelled in a long, long time.

The scent of his cologne.

Paul rose and came near her. So near that surely Maddie would sense him, know he was here, that he had been for all this time. Her eyes remained closed. Minutes inched by. The doctor and nurse had left some time ago. They hadn't returned. So Paul waited.

No more memories came. No more visions of a time long past. Those were gone now. She needed them no longer. He listened to the sound of her slow, shallow breathing, watched the tiny bit of color fade from her face.

And still, she didn't look toward him, didn't say a word. She just lay there, awake, with her eyes closed.

Maybe she was waiting too.

The door creaked open, but it wasn't the nurse who entered. Nor the doctor. It was a woman, young and tall. Breathtaking in her beauty. She came closer, and Paul couldn't take his gaze from her face. She was a vision, beautiful, vibrant . . . and blond. The woman sniffed and wiped a tear from her cheek. Then she hurried to the far side of the hospital bed.

Paul reached toward her, but she didn't even look his way. She had eyes only for Maddie, tears only for the woman who lay in the bed. She leaned over Maddie and tried to smile, but instead more tears came. She took Maddie's hand. "I'm here, Mom. I've come."

Warmth flowed through Paul. And joy. He hadn't seen their daughter since she was five years old. She'd grown into such a beautiful young woman.

Maddie opened her eyes and lifted her daughter's hand toward her lips. "I can't hang on anymore, Mandy. My heart . . . it's too weak."

Mandy kissed her mother's cheek. "I know, Mom. It's okay. You can't fight congestive heart failure forever." Her voice lowered to a scant whisper. "I've prayed and asked God to send Daddy to take you home."

Paul smiled.

Maddie touched her daughter's cheek. "He's been dead twenty-five years . . . since the car accident." For the first time, Maddie turned her head toward him, toward the empty chair beside her. "But today, I thought . . . I thought I smelled his cologne." A racking cough tore through her chest.

Paul moved closer. There was no fear in her face now. No holding back. Only trust. And love. And joy. He extended his hand toward her. It was time. Finally. To take her home.

"Come, Maddie. Everything's ready." He touched her.

For the first time in over thirty years, Maddie saw clearly, unhindered, into the face of the man she loved. Paul was there beside her, his silhouette backlit by incredible light.

Joy suffused her. Wonder. Beauty. Pleasure without pain. She smiled into his face. "You came for me."

Paul grinned. "He sent me."

She rose and placed her hand in his. "Is it everything we dreamed?"

He laughed, full and without restraint. "It is. Wait till you see it, Maddie. Wait till you see Him. He's waiting for you."

Maddie stood and followed Paul into the light.

Behind her, the steady, flat ring of the EKG filled the room.

EPILOGUE

You can't tell me it never happened. You can't tell me it was a dream. Because I was there. I saw her hand reach toward him. I heard his voice. I saw their love.

Now, I stand here by her grave, and I weep. But these are not tears of despair. They are notes in the symphony of peace. They are tones of hope. Theirs and mine.

I've brought flowers today — red roses — to lay on her grave. They aren't pretty ones, but they smell heavenly.

I lay them on her headstone and touch it, knowing she's not here.

Then I step back and hold out my hand to my daughter, Pauline. She's five years old now, with her grandpa's blue-green eyes and her grandma's crooked smile.

She takes my hand. "Grandma's in heaven now, isn't she, Mommy?"

I smile. "She's seeing Jesus." Mom always told me God would heal her blindness. In the end, He did.

So you see, I'm not crazy, and I'm not a romantic. I'm just a woman who has witnessed the promise, beheld the wonder, glimpsed the glory, and found that there's hope for us all . . . somewhere beyond the night.

ACKNOWLEDGEMENTS

In New Testament Greek, the word for giving thanks is *eucharisteo.* It's the word we use when we say *Eucharist,* meaning "the Lord's supper" or "communion." It's a rich word that means so much more than "gee, thanks." It connotes a sense of joyfulness and sharing, along with thanksgiving. So, in the spirit of eucharisteo, I offer thanksgiving with joy for the following people:

First, to God, who gave me this story in a dream when I was in a dark, dark place in my writing career. Thank You, Lord, for showing me that there really is hope beyond the night.

Next to Bryan, my wonderful husband and first reader, who sacrifices so that I can write the books God gives me to write. Thank you for being such an unselfish and godly man, and for being a living example of the love of Christ.

To Steve Laube, my agent, who believes

in my work and is always there with wisdom and encouragement.

To my fantastic editor, Julee Schwarzburg, who caught the vision for this story and fixed the spots where I leaned toward repetition.

To Sally Tobias, who read the whole thing before I dared to send it in. Thanks for your friendship, openness, and encouragement.

To Ken Petersen . . . finally, huh?

And lastly, to Teacher Laura and Teacher Krynda, preschool instructors extraordinaire. This is what I've been doing at Starbucks while you make my girls' first school experience into something wonderful and memorable. I appreciate all you do.

NOTE FROM THE AUTHOR

Dear Reader,

On some days when I'm writing here in my office at the back of the house, I can almost glimpse eternity. It stretches outside my tall solarium window, reaching down the green valley lined with oaks, touching the distant, snow-frosted mountains. On those days, I gaze out over the tall Monterey pines and search out that special place where sky meets earth in a blaze of blue glory. And I know that God is real, that He created all this beauty, and that He shares it with me because He loves me. On those days, I have no doubts, no questions, no fear.

Today, however, is not one of those days. I can see no mountains, no valley. Even the tops of the pines are blotted from my view. Instead, fog laces through the bottom branches and swirls in thick ripples across the ground. Grayness presses against my window and forms tiny water droplets on

459

the glass. It covers the mountains, masks the oaks, camouflages the pines.

And yet, when my husband walks in and asks me, "So, how do you like your new office?" I turn and smile at him. "I love it," I say. "And the view out this window is incredible. You ought to see it. Oaks and pines, and snow-tipped mountains kissing the sky. On a clear day ... . wow, you can see forever."

I know the mountains are out there, even though I can't see them. I trust that the trees remain as green and beautiful, even when they're lost to my sight. And now, as I sit and listen to the silence tangle with the fog outside, I'm reminded of the Bible's definition of faith. Hebrews 11:1 says, "Now faith is the assurance of things being hoped for, the conviction of things not seen."

I used to live as if faith was seeing the mountains. I believed that if I only had enough faith, I would see God clearly, I would always know what He wants, I wouldn't have any doubts, any questions. There would never be any fog.

But these days, I see faith differently. Faith, I've come to believe, doesn't dispel the fog but is found within it. Faith isn't about seeing the mountains; it's about believing they are there when all my senses deny it. It's about believing in that spot of blue glory when all I see is the persistent darkness.

So when hurt and confusion press against the window of my soul, when doubts creep in and twine around my thoughts as surely as the fog twists through the trees — that's when faith flourishes. As surely as I can say I know the mountains and oaks and pines are there, even though I can't see them, so I can say, I know God loves me even though I can't see it now. I know that I am His and that He died for me. I choose to believe what I cannot see, for faith is not seeing, but believing, even in the fog. Even in the darkness.

And that's what Paul and Maddie's story is really all about. So I thank you for allowing me to share their story with you, a story of both darkness and incredible light. I hope that through their journey you have been touched with wonder, left breathless at the vision God has for you. "No eye has seen, no ear has heard, no mind has risen to understand what God has prepared for those who love him" the Bible says in 1 Corinthians 2:9. That's God's promise — a promise that the night doesn't last forever. Dawn is coming.

So it's my hope that you will live life fully,

wondrously, vividly, in the light of God's incredible love. That you will face fear, and overcome it. That you will know the peace that passes all understanding. That your faith will grow strong in the darkness, and you will be filled with light.

If you enjoyed Paul and Maddie's story in *Beyond the Night,* I hope you'll send me a note and tell me so! You can e-mail me at marlo@marloschalesky.com, or send a note to me via my publisher at:

Marlo Schalesky
c/o WaterBrook Multnomah Publishing
 Group
12265 Oracle Boulevard, Suite 200
Colorado Springs, CO 80921

And for more info on me and my books, please visit my Web site at www.marlo schalesky.com, and my "Tales of Wonder" blog at www.marloschalesky.blogspot.com. I'd love to hear from you!

READER'S GUIDE

1. In this story, what was Maddie's true enemy? Was it blindness . . . or something else?
2. In the present-day story, what do you think the water that Maddie saw represented?
3. When Maddie discovered she was going blind, she felt that God had betrayed her. How do you respond when God allows your plans for your life to go awry?
4. In chapter 6, Paul said that he once believed that if you lived right, God would spare you from pain, that a good life was one free of trouble. But Maddie taught him differently. She taught him that God was in the sorrow. God worked in the pain. How did God work through the sorrow and pain in Maddie's life? How might God work in the dark times that you experience?
5. In chapter 6, in the present scene, Mad-

die asked God to send her hope, but she didn't perceive an answer. In this scene, how had God already answered her? Who had God sent? Have there been times in your life when you've called out to God yet still felt alone? How might God already have been working in your life during those times, even if you didn't recognize it?

6. In chapter 9, Maddie felt that God was distant, out there somewhere beyond her reach. During this time, how was He actually orchestrating events to help her face her fear and grow through it?

7. At the end of chapter 9, Maddie prayed that her mom wouldn't find out about her condition. Immediately, her mom discovered the truth. Why do you think He answered "no" to Maddie? Have there been times in your life when God has answered your prayers with an emphatic "no"? What did you learn during those times?

8. Our culture often presents love as an emotion. It talks about love filled with passion, marked by desire. But in chapter 12, Paul realized that real love wasn't an emotion at all. Rather, it was a bond, a way of being, a force built from the very breath of God, built on the ordinary and com-

monplace ins and outs of daily life. How does this type of real love reflect the kind of love God has for us?

9. In chapter 13, Paul's mother assured Maddie that God would heal her blindness someday. Was Rhena right? Why or why not?

10. In chapter 14, Maddie considered that maybe God was like the sunlight off the ocean's waves, "so bright that even a glimpse through the darkness was enough to overwhelm the senses." Do you think she was right? Why or why not?

11. In chapter 23, Paul realized that God loved Maddie even more than he did. How did this help him to accept Maddie's blindness and just "do his part" instead of trying to fix her? How can accepting God's love in your own life help you to face difficult times?

12. In chapter 24, Maddie came to understand that she'd been more concerned with what she was losing rather than what she still had. She learned that God hadn't betrayed her, but fear had. How did fear make her encounter with blindness worse? Are there places in your life where fear is painting dark pictures in your mind of what "might be"? What can you focus on to erase those pictures?

13. In chapter 24, Maddie told her mother that she already had a Savior. Are there people in your life whom you are trying to "save" instead of allowing Jesus to be their Savior?

14. In chapter 25, Maddie realized that God wastes nothing, even her blindness, even her struggles. Think of your own struggles and dark times. How might God transform them for His glory?

15. Regarding chapter 27, can you think of an incident in the Bible where someone who had died appeared again on earth? (Hint: Think Transfiguration.) What does this tell us about the possibility that God could choose to send back someone who has died if there was a specific, brief purpose?

16. Consider the parable of the rich man and Lazarus in Luke 16:20–31. Why did Abraham say that Lazarus could not cross over to the rich man? Is such a crossover possible? Why did Abraham say that Lazarus would not be sent back to warn the rich man's brothers? Did Abraham say that such an act was not possible, or was there a different reason? In the context of this parable, would it be possible for God to send back Lazarus if He chose to? Were there any circumstances suggested in the

parable in which God might have chosen to send him back?

17. Ultimately we discover that fear has been keeping Maddie from responding to Paul's calls. How does she finally overcome that fear?

18. Maddie's blindness was a metaphor for the dark places in life that we all face — times when life doesn't make sense, when we can't see where we're going, and everything seems black and hopeless. How can love, specifically God's love, help you to face your own times of blindness with faith instead of fear?

19. The Bible tells us in 1 John 4:18: "But perfect love throws out the fear." How did Paul and Maddie's story demonstrate the truth of that verse?

ABOUT THE AUTHOR

Marlo Schalesky is the author of several books, including *Veil of Fire, Only the Wind Remembers, Cry Freedom,* and *Freedom's Shadow.* A graduate of Stanford University, Marlo also has a masters of theology with an emphasis in biblical studies from Fuller Theological Seminary. She lives with her husband, Bryan, and their four daughters in California.